Victoria McKay
and the
Kingdom of Creatures

by Marina Aerin Richardson

To my grandma, Eva,

who instilled in me my love of books and reading;

to Tilly, my beloved dachshund,

whose name was my first word;

to Jane, my patient and encouraging editor,

without whom this book would never exist;

and to my family,

for their love and belief.

Contents

CHAPTER ONE: The Monster in The Hospital Hallway 1

CHAPTER TWO: Take Care What You Wish For 9

CHAPTER THREE: Family Problems 17

CHAPTER FOUR: The Book that Glowed 24

CHAPTER FIVE: Summer Hols.. 32

CHAPTER SIX: Emma the Cardenere 39

CHAPTER SEVEN: Scotland is in the Air... 49

CHAPTER EIGHT: Walking Away Towards My Problems.................... 60

CHAPTER NINE: Sunlight, Sweet Sunlight 71

CHAPTER TEN: The Eyes on the Wall 84

CHAPTER ELEVEN: Turned Upside down by Magic 93

CHAPTER TWELVE: Time for a Makeover 100

CHAPTER THIRTEEN: The Fifteen Stages of Becoming Beautiful 110

CHAPTER FOURTEEN: The Girl in Red... 116

CHAPTER FIFTEEN: Going to the Chapel 122

CHAPTER SIXTEEN: Court is in Session... 132

CHAPTER SEVENTEEN: Clive.. 141

CHAPTER EIGHTEEN: The Curious Case of the Cardenere............... 147

CHAPTER NINETEEN: Just a Small Town Girl.................................. 156

CHAPTER TWENTY: Everything You Say Will DEFINITELY Be Used Against You.. 162

CHAPTER TWENTY-ONE: One Question to Rule them All 169

CHAPTER TWENTY-TWO: Inside the Mayor's Office 175

CHAPTER TWENTY-THREE: Aunt Marge Saves the Day 184

CHAPTER TWENTY-FOUR: Memorial Park at Midnight....................193

CHAPTER TWENTY-FIVE: Victoria McKay, Real Life Ghost Whisperer 203

CHAPTER TWENTY-SIX: Bloodhound's Plot for World Domination....209

CHAPTER TWENTY-SEVEN: Nothing's Ever Easy 215

CHAPTER TWENTY-EIGHT: Frightened Family Functions 223

CHAPTER TWENTY-NINE: Emma's Brave Gambit 233

CHAPTER THIRTY: One Last Sprint...242

CHAPTER THIRTY-ONE: Just when I Thought I Was Out 247

CHAPTER THIRTY-TWO: Return of the (Victoria) Mack(kay) 252

The Monster in the Hospital Hallway

Everyone knows that families can come in many shapes and sizes; but mine consisted of a slightly overbearing Mum and a slightly distracted Dad, and a completely adorable daughter…me. It might not be everyone's cup of tea, but it was perfect for me. That's why I was completely perplexed when my parents announced that Mum was pregnant.

Most people think new babies are angels – so perfect from their chubby cheeks to their cute little feet.

I think the exact opposite.

Even before she was born, my little sister was a *burden.* From the moment she entered my life, she did nothing but throw tantrums, steal my things, and get our parents to blame *me* for whatever mischief she'd most recently been up to.

She was born seven years ago during a London winter with snow piled thick on the ground. Thinking back now, as I sit here waiting for my flight, I remember it as a time of inconvenience and mystical dilemmas.

BONG, BONG, BONG!

Big Ben strikes twelve in my head as I summon that day in my memory, the brass clanging as clear and thunderous as if it were right outside my house. My father was hurrying me across the streets of London with a firm grip on my mittened hand, desperately trying to find a decent looking taxi. I trotted along behind him as fast as my little legs would go.

You see, Mum had been off visiting her sister at the zoo when her water broke, so Dad and I had to cut short our nice, relaxing shopping trip and head off to the hospital. My sister wasn't even born yet, and she was already an inconvenience. We'd just pushed through a crowd of Christmas shoppers burdened with parcels and packages when a tinkling of windchimes from somewhere near the candy shop caught my attention.

Wind chimes in the dead of winter?

Despite the cold, a warm tingle ran across my shoulders as I turned in the direction of the odd noise. There, crouching by the corner of the shop, was the oddest little creature – no bigger than a plump watermelon – I had ever seen in my life!

I could tell by its luminous shadow that it was no sort of ordinary creature marked down in a wildlife book you might collect from the library. Oh no. This was a new species *entirely.*

Soft, purple hair covered its entire body like a woolly coat. When it caught sight of me watching, it stared back with colossal indigo eyes the size of dinner plates, unblinking.

Its eyes *glowed.*

I tugged against my father's firm grip as he ploughed through the tsunami of people plaguing the street. His grasp tightened, but nevertheless I persisted. I just *had* to get closer to the strange little furball of a beast. Once I was free, I ducked through the crowd and back toward the candy shop, craning my neck this way and that.

But…where had it gone?

Before you say anything, let me assure you that even at four years old I was not the whimsical, naive kind of child to simply *imagine* an impossibly short and round creature wandering about the crowded streets of London. All my imaginary friends at that age were perfectly rational people with whom you could discuss serious things like the economy and foreign politics.

No. I was sure I had seen what I had seen. I just needed a bit more time to search around, and…

"Come on Darling, we mustn't keep Mum and your new sister waiting! I bet you're excited to meet her!" Dad caught up to me and hauled me up – the indignity! – shoving me inside the backseat of the taxi he'd finally managed to hail. Just like that, we were whisked off to the hospital and away from my new discovery.

For the record, I was *not* excited to meet my new little sister. No one had even consulted me about this inconsiderate addition to our family, and frankly, I was not one bit pleased about it. Why had my parents felt the need to ruin a perfectly good family of three with another child? Was I not enough for them? Didn't they have their hands – and more importantly – their hearts plenty full already with me?

But I said nothing, and an hour later, I was sat in the corridor of St. Thomas's Hospital on a metal armchair, waiting for my sister to be born (because Dr. Pie-Face wouldn't let anyone under the age of seven in the delivery room). My legs swung to and fro, barely scraping the floor tiles, when the tinkling of wind chimes rose from somewhere down the hallway to my left.

Wind chimes? In a hospital?

Surely not.

I turned, scanning the corridor, searching for the source of the sound. At first, all I could see were plain hospital doors, more uncomfortable chairs, and the occasional forgotten tray of medical equipment.

But then, I caught a glimpse of something *very* out of the ordinary. Goosebumps pimpled my arms as I spotted it: there, at the edge of the corridor, that same woolly, purple little creature from out on the streets!

It had tucked itself into the shadows, clearly trying to be inconspicuous, but its sparkling shadow completely ruined any chance of that. Whatever this thing was, hiding did *not* seem to be its forte.

I watched the creature, intently observing its anxious movements. Its miniature fingers wiggled incessantly, and its feet seemed to never quite touch the ground as it padded to and fro in the shadows, up and down the corridor, peering this way and that.

"Pssst!" I waved.

It jumped three feet straight up into the air, its face creasing like a piece of origami paper with such displeasure that I looked behind me, sure it was glaring at somebody else.

Only, there *was* nobody else.

The corridor was empty coming and going. I was the only person in the waiting area.

After a few moments, the bizarre little thing gathered itself together and tiptoed toward me. It held its hand poised like a shield in front of its eyes, like it couldn't bear to look at me – as if I was a hideous, warty ogre.

Moving swiftly, it leapt lightly up onto the arm of my chair. In its padded little fingers, it held a small piece of yellow, ashy parchment, folded up neatly into a square, which it handed to me cautiously before jumping back to the floor and scurrying off down the corridor the same way it had come. With a tinkling sparkle of stars in the corridor, the puffball disappeared from sight.

To this day, I swear I heard it mutter something to itself as it blinked away:

"...should do better, Clive. So terribly sorry, my dear…"

I unfolded the parchment tentatively. *What a strange little creature,* I thought. And a rude one, too, looking at me like I was the yearly winner of the Ugliest Girl award.

The paper itself stank like spoiled eggs. Pinching my nose, I held it at arm's length as my eyes scanned the words written in emerald ink by a fastidious hand. Luckily, I was a precocious four-year-old and had been reading *The Daily Mail* for months by this time.

Dear Human Child,

You may be surprised to be reading this just now. We are unknown to mankind, except for a lucky few who have been granted a wish. You are now one of those lucky people. We will not share our location or specific identities, in case you desire to give the wish back, as returns are strictly ***forbidden.*** *You can wish whatever your heart desires whenever you desire.*

The High Magical Council

P.S. A word of warning: if you use this gift selfishly or for ill purpose, there will be dire consequences. I am telling you now, be very careful in what you wish for. This wish has no expiration date. Guard it (and your tongue) wisely.

That last bit was written in plain black ink, and in different handwriting than the rest. But that was hardly what held my attention. High Magical Council? I didn't know about any High Magical Council!

More to the point, what did 'dire consequences' mean? First, the purple tennis ball grants me a wish, then it disappears, and now it was threatening me retroactively via stinky parchment?

I rolled my eyes. My parents had always told me magic only existed in fairy tales, so I knew it would be no use showing them the note. I folded it up and slipped it into my pocket right before I closed my eyes and nodded off into a nap.

In my dreams, an army of purple fuzzballs chased me down long, winding corridors, covered in what seemed like tree roots and dirt. Only, sometimes it seemed more like *I* was chasing *them*, screaming myself hoarse and furiously waving the note I'd just been given at them.

I was so caught up in the chase that I almost didn't catch *myself* when one last turn abruptly brought me teetering on the lip of an infinitely deep, looming pit. It gaped as large as a rugby pitch. I turned around to try another route only to find the same tiny creature from the hospital staring gloomily up at me.

"I'm terribly sorry, truly," he muttered in a voice pitched so low and quiet it almost seemed to be for himself rather than for me. Before I could ask what it could possibly be apologising for, it delivered one quick shove that sent me careening into the pit behind me.

I fell. And screamed.

Screamed with such gusto, in fact, that I woke myself up.

"Whoa there, Vicky," a voice said as I hollered myself back to the waking world. I looked up to see Dad standing over me. "It's only me," he said in a reassuring voice. "The way you shrieked, you'd think I was some sort of monster!"

"Of course you're not a monster, Dad," I groaned. "You're far too tall to be one."

He gave me a puzzled look before shaking his head. "Come on, darling," he said, rather too cheerfully for my mood. "Come meet your new little sister!"

I sighed a long, deep sigh of resignation and stood up. Completely oblivious to my less-than-enthusiastic body language, Dad led me to a room where a podgy-looking baby lay in Mum's arms. She stroked its head tenderly, making soft cooing noises at it while Dad gazed down at them both affectionately.

The baby was golden. It was plump and joyful. It had beautiful blonde hair, chubby cheeks and dazzling blue eyes.

At least, that's what Mum and Dad kept exclaiming.

To me, it looked...*wrong*. It was a sickly mauve colour. This *thing* – my baby sister, I mean – didn't look like Mum or Dad, and certainly not like me. To be frank, it didn't even look human.

On the taxi drive home, my parents discussed suitable baby names for their precious little bundle, who was belted in an infant seat between Mum and me in the back. Mum suggested Veronica. Dad said it didn't suit her.

"Why don't you name it Ashley?" I scoffed. I turned to stare out the window at the crescent moon instead of looking at the mewling burrito between Mum and me. There'd been a chimp born at the London Zoo last summer that the zookeepers had named Ashley.

"Why, that's a wonderful name for her," Dad nodded approvingly.

Mum liked it as well. "Like that chimp at the zoo," she said, a smile blooming on her tired face.

What? I goggled, astounded they'd taken me seriously. Staring down at the little thing in its car seat, I whispered, "Welcome to the zoo, little monkey."

Suddenly, I smelled something rotten. Pinching my nose with two fingers I stared in horror at the little thing in its car seat. She'd started to fuss, her little fingers clenched in tiny balls while she kicked her cotton-socked feet, trying to break free from the swaddling. Probably so she could eat us.

I held my breath the rest of the ride home, unwilling to inhale the foul-smelling fumes of poop overlaid with cinnamon. While Mum tenderly unclipped 'Ashley', I bolted from the taxi and stood on our stoop, waiting while she handed the Burberry-wrapped bundle out to Dad. He cradled her in his arms, cooing softly. I just rolled my eyes.

I was *not* looking forward to my new life as an older sister.

2

Take Care What You Wish For

And thus it began.

As we entered the next week, a perpetual wheel of turmoiled emotions turned through my mind, each thought even more negative than the last. For the next *month* it was nothing more than rows of sleepless nights and headaches. The following *years* weren't much better.

"Ashley!" I shouted one day, yanking her back by the collar of her shirt as she scrambled past me on the stairs. Yes, my parents *had* named her Ashley. Horrible name, I know. Sadly, she more closely resembled an elephant than the monkey I'd been thinking of when I'd sarcastically suggested it. Monkeys may be mischievous, which Ashley certainly was, but elephants are ENORMOUSLY loud and destructive, which she *also* was.

At seven, she thought she owned the entire house and everything in it, including me and my parents. She didn't follow rules, nor did she respect anyone's *privacy* or *personal space* or *boundaries*.

Ashley went *where* she wanted *when* she wanted, and if I ever tried to interfere, she'd stomp down to Mum, trumpeting tears like a fountain who'd sprouted legs to go on parade.

Mum would say, "Vicky, as an 11-year-old elder sister, I expect you to be understanding and set a good example for your little sister. Stop tormenting Ashley all the time. My poor nerves!"

What utter rubbish. Being a big sister *sucked.* I was constantly being punished for 'upsetting' Ashley.

Upsetting Ashley! What about upsetting Vicky!?

This particular memory is permanently etched in my memory, not only because of what was to follow, but because it was the first day of spring holidays, just four months ago. I remember being in a particularly happy mood as I'd received high marks on my midterms at school, and Dad had promised to take me somewhere, just him and me to celebrate. It had been literal ages since I was taken anywhere without my terror of a little sister. Before she'd been born, Dad and I had a handful of restaurants we'd visit together to escape Mum, and Mum would take me to a different handful of restaurants we'd visit to escape Dad. Either way, we'd end up talking and goofing off for hours. Now every outing has to be pre-approved to fit Ashley's preferences.

And then…

Ashley's elbow caught me in the side of my neck.

"Ouch!" I gasped, stumbling to my knees as her collar slipped from my grasp.

She giggled and scampered out of my reach. "Haha, too slow!" she taunted, reaching the top of the stairs and darting down the hallway to my room.

"I told you to stay out of there!" I shouted. "You have your own room and an entire playroom. My room is off limits!"

Mum and Dad had basically given up parenting Ashley by this point, and Nanny had quit years ago…not that I blamed her. Consequently, *I* was the only person standing between my little sister and complete chaos.

Before I could regain my footing, a loud, heart-breaking shatter exploded from the end of the hallway.

I raced toward my room to find Ashley standing on my bed, her mouth stretched wide around a shocked 'O' of guilt…an emotion she'd likely never *actually* experienced before.

Oh no. My eyes followed hers to the floor, where a lidless hydro flask spilled water across my carpet, two pillows, and the rumpled comforter Ashley had flung from the bed.

But that wasn't all.

My eyes stung with instant tears as I stared at the twisted silver picture frame beneath the water bottle. Glass shards littered my white carpet, glittering like tiny stars from the light streaming through the window blinds.

"Noooo!" I wailed, hurtling from the doorway to the scene of the crime. That photo was one of the most important belongings I possessed. It held a black and white photo of my grandfather in his officer's uniform after returning from the war.

Granddad died two years ago, and this was the only photo I had left of him. He'd been such a lovely man, so full of joy and humour and patience, and we had been particularly close. As much as I missed the perfection of my Family of Three before Ashley was born, my relationship with my Granddad had been my consolation. Without him, things had been difficult, to say the least.

Stinging tears welled up in my eyes, pouring down my cheeks in a flood of emotion as water from the hydro flask soaked the print, puddling on the surface. My grandfather's handsome features bled from his face like blood from a wound.

"I'll rescue it!" Ashley hopped down from the bed.

"NO, ASHLEY DON'T…!"

Too late.

As she fished the photo from the pool of water, it came apart in her hands.

"I hate you!" Hateful words I'd kept buried inside cascaded from my mouth like lava from an active volcano. "This family was perfectly fine until you came along! I wish you'd never been born!"

A sudden, howling wind flung my bedroom window open. Odd. The weather had been quite calm throughout the evening. But that was the least of my worries.

Ashley's lips quivered with what looked like real remorse. But she couldn't fool me. She wasn't sorry. She never apologised.

"Maybe you could be a bit nicer," she whispered. "Just a thought." Then she marched out of my room.

See? Somehow, *she* was the victim and *I* was to blame. She probably went straight downstairs weeping to Mum about how mean I was.

A sharp fragment of glass pierced deep into my skin as I knelt beside the pale pieces of drenched photo paper. The resulting trickle of blood turned the whole mess a muddy red.

"Bullocks," I cursed. Picking the piece of glass free, I didn't bother stopping the blood. I hoped it scarred. I wanted a physical reminder of the pain Ashley caused me on a daily basis. I kicked the empty hydro flask across the room, bruising my toes, then jumped face first onto my bed, burying my head into the depths of my blanket for a good cry. I figured I might as well take the time to feel sorry for myself. It was likely the only sympathy I was going to get.

***

With a tinkle of distant windchimes, the fluffy, purple creature appeared in Vicky's room. The Lawfur was an Official Representative of the Magical Community, and had been for several centuries already when he first met Vicky in the hospital corridor seven years earlier.

He was called Clive.

Wrapped in a cloak of sapphire and twinkling diamond stars, Clive stood awkwardly next to the unfortunate hydro flask in the corner of the room by Vicky's wardrobe. He peeled a stinky, hundred-year-old boiled egg – his favourite snack – and tsked sorrowfully as he squinted through the shining sparkle of innocence which surrounded the poor, heartbroken girl weeping in her bed. He knew, with a sort of knowing that came with his line of work – namely that of bestowing immensely powerful wishes on innocent human children – that things were about to get much worse for her.

And not the kind of 'worse before it gets better,' in the tradition of people who prefer to look for silver linings, either.

No. Clive knew that things were going to get much, *much worse* for Vicky, and likely continue getting *significantly worse* until it all ended in tragedy.

Try as he might to keep himself aloof from the goings-on of mortal humans – and oh, how Clive had tried – he felt something *shift* inside him at the sight of poor Vicky clutching the remains of her Grandad's photo in her hand with the blood still drying.

It had all become too much.

In fact, his depression had started when he'd given Vicky her wish seven years earlier. He'd become so distraught about bestowing such a heavy burden on such a young girl – there'd never been one younger than ten before – that he'd appealed directly to the Magical Committee for the Distribution of Wishes on Human Children (MCDWHC), recommending the discontinuation of the program entirely. His arguments were these:

1. It was a proven fact that humans, like other mortal species such as trolls, lacked the ability to grasp the concept of permanent consequences.

Furthermore,

2. It was a proven fact that humans in general stubbornly persisted in refusing to acknowledge the existence of magic.

Additionally,

3. It was a proven fact that human *children* lacked the ability to control their tempers.

Therefore,

4. It was undeniably immoral to burden human children specifically with power they were doomed to use irresponsibly.

In response, the MCDWHC issued a strongly worded reply warning that Clive's appeal sounded, "speciest at best," and, "very disagreeable at worst," and recommended that he "keep his rather up-turned nose out of issues that were above his paygrade." The response also quoted the Committee's motto word-for-word, as if Clive could ever forget:

"Every species, regardless of lifespan, magical ability,
and maturity level at birth,
deserves the opportunity to wish and to have their wishes granted.
As long as it's very far away from us."

That last part was the real sticker. The Committee might spout off about how they were enlightening a lesser species and bringing them opportunities they'd otherwise never experience, but it was all a mask. He knew why they did it. And he wasn't the only one.

With a deep sigh and toss of his woolly purple mane, Clive watched for the…well, he couldn't rightly say how many times he'd seen it…the *many-ith* time as the wish took effect. An aura of sapphire night and stars expanded to fill the room, seeming to coalesce and deepen over Vicky's sleeping form.

With a final pulse of light, the wish was sealed. As the faint tinkle of chimes once more filled the room, Clive's body became wispy and unsubstantial. If Vicky had awakened then, she might well have heard the words he uttered to cheer himself up:

"I did warn her, after all."

Family Problems

I woke up to the morning sun of late spring shining on my face and illuminating the room, which blazed with yellow speckles and shadows. Rubbing sleep from my eyes, I gripped the bedside table as I stood up and staggered over to my wardrobe.

In the bottom drawer, I fumbled around for my hairbrush before grabbing it and beginning to tear the bristles through my frizzy hair – which had poofed up overnight – when I saw something: the hydroflask I'd kicked into the corner.

In an instant, I remembered what had happened the night before: how Ashley had knocked it and Granddad's photo over while jumping on my bed. How my careless little sister had ruined my most prized possession.

Slowly, I turned, bracing myself for the devastating sight of the broken silver frame, the broken glass, the remnants of my Granddad in his uniform. Fresh tears stung my eyes as I mourned my loss all over again.

Only… My carpet was clean!

Had Mum come in during the night and cleaned it up?

Something twinkled in the corner of my eye, pulling my eyes to my nightstand.

I gasped.

My Grandad's handsome features smiled out at me from its grinning silver frame, good as new.

Did Mum have another copy she hadn't told me about? And that frame had been one of a kind… How on earth could she have found another of the exact same design?

I crept down the staircase, hugging the banister as I jumped down the last two steps at the same time. Mum had gone away for the weekend, so this would be the perfect time to get to the TV before Ashley came down.

"You overslept!" Mum said as I entered the kitchen.

I was so startled by her being there that I almost fell flat on my rear end!

"We had a whole schedule planned out today! Your Aunt Marge is expecting us to meet her at the zoo by noon, don't you remember? The new squirrel exhibit is opening then, and you know how much your auntie loves squirrels! I hope you were up there tidying your room."

"*My* room?" I was shocked. "Look at Ashley's! She's the one with the room that's an utter pigsty! My room looks like paradise compared to hers!"

"What do you mean, 'Ashley's room'? Who's Ashley?" Mum replied, giving me a confused, scrunched-up look.

"Nice try, Mum," I laughed. "*I* don't want to claim her either, but she *is* your daughter, after all!" *Wait till I tell Ashley that Mum forgot who she was!* I thought to myself.

But Mum's face had gone from confused to worried, and I doubted she'd even heard what I'd said. "Vicky, darling! What on earth have you done to your hand?" She swooped in like a mother hen, clucking sympathetically as she tenderly removed the tissue I'd wrapped around it.

"I cut it on the glass from the photo frame," I said. "Thank you for replacing Granddad's picture. I didn't know you had another."

She had the scrunched up look again and pressed the back of her hand to my forehead. "Are you feeling quite well, Vicky? What are you on about, darling? You've broken the silver frame with Granddad's photo in it? Oh sweetheart, you really must try to be less clumsy…"

"Not me," I insisted impatiently. "Ashley! Last night she was jumping on my bed and knocked it clean off the nightstand. Didn't you even wonder why I didn't come down for dinner? Didn't you wonder what she was raving on about?"

Mum retrieved the first aid kit from the medicine cabinet and gently swabbed my wound. "Well, I've always appreciated your imagination, love," she said as she worked, "but don't you think you're a little old to blame accidents on an imaginary friend? I wouldn't have scolded you for simply telling the truth. Sometimes I very much wonder where I've gone wrong with you. Lord knows I've tried my best."

My mouth gaped. Was she having a laugh? Mum had been upset with Ashley and me plenty of times, but she'd never said anything like this before. Why was she being so strange and hurtful? Had she hit her head?

Did she have amnesia? Why couldn't Mum remember her own daughter…?

I walked slowly back to my room, pondering what had just happened. Vivid memories of my obnoxious little sister swirled in my brain. Maybe Mum hadn't hit her head…maybe *I* had. Was I in a coma? Had I completely hallucinated my little sister?

Once I was back in my room, I shut my door and locked it before getting down on my hands and knees to paw under my bed for the box I kept memories in: polaroids, school art projects, notes from friends, that kind of thing. I dug through all the odds and ends, desperate to find the diary I'd started keeping in kindergarten, just after Ashley had been born.

It was a simple spiral notebook with a purple cover that I'd decorated with heaps of butterfly and unicorn and rainbow stickers. As I flipped through the notebook, though, the stench of rotten eggs assaulted my nose from seemingly nowhere. I began to sniff around to try and identify the source of this horrendous scent just as something small slipped out of the pages of the notebook and dropped onto the carpet. It was an incredibly stinky, folded-up piece of yellowed paper.

Huh? Why would a younger me have pressed something rancid into the pages of my notebook? More to the point, how could one tiny bit of parchment give off such an odour in the first place?

But then a strange dread rose in my stomach as a faded memory crept slowly to the forefront of my mind.

The creature from the hospital hallway seven years ago.

Flinching as if it were a dead cockroach, I picked up the note and unfolded it. As I read the words penned in mostly emerald ink (save for P.s. and the signature), the memory grew vivid until I recalled every detail of my encounter with the little purple creature who gave me the note I currently held in my hands. The note that entitled me to a single, irrevocable wish.

No.

No, no, no, no.

That couldn't be what happened. Could it?

"This family was perfectly fine until you came along! I wish you'd never been born!"

The angry words I'd shouted at Ashley the night before echoed in my ears.

Oh no.

This was all my fault. I'd gotten so angry at Ashley last night for destroying my photo of Granddad, that I'd wished her away.

I squirmed on the floor where I sat, surrounded by memorabilia. My forehead creased as a wave of powerful emotions flooded over me.

Astonishment hit me first. I hadn't thought about the little creature from the hospital hallway and his folded-up parchment in *years*. Until this moment, I hadn't even remembered that I'd kept the note!

But astonishment fled quickly, chased away by fear. When Mum regained her memory of Ashley and realised what I'd done, she'd go straight to Dad. They'd start with grounding me for the rest of my life, and then who knew what they'd do? Put me in the public education system? Make me do chores before tea?

But before my brain could process what that might be like, another emotion hit, a kind of gnawing around my ribs. Was that guilt?

Yes. *Heavy* guilt. It grew and grew until it drowned out everything else. I'd always had what some liked to call a "volatile temper." I'd been assigned detention for mouthing off at the headmistress and even lost friends for being snappish, but I'd never lost an entire sibling because of it before.

Hang on, though, my inner-rebel said. Why should you feel guilty? It's not like you've ever exactly enjoyed your younger sister's company over the past several agonising years. That destroyed photo wasn't nearly the first thing Ashley has ever carelessly obliterated.

My inner rebel was right. I had very few fond memories of Ashley, and most of those were from when she was a baby, napping in her crib all snuggled up with one of her hundreds of plushies. She'd certainly made my life more difficult over the years. I'd often dreamed of going back to being an only child. Maybe this wasn't the end of the world?

I tried the thought out: Oh well, guess I don't have a sister now.

THE END

…although, I *suppose* there were a few times she had been tolerable while awake. Like when we'd vacation on the beaches of Spain. She and I had run ourselves dizzy on the white sand, shrieking with laughter and chasing flocks of seabirds who flapped and wheeled into the air, only to twirl lazily in the piercing blue sky and land again a few yards away in the other direction, all while my parents laughed from their jewel-coloured beach towels and the salty ocean air tangled in our hair…

No - snap out of it. I told myself. You have nothing to be guilty for, period.

Oh, but why did I feel so terrible then?

With *one* sentence – uttered in anger, and completely on accident – I'd wished my sister away…

Except even to me, "accidentally" wishing someone away sounded a lot like "accidentally" pulling someone's hair, which was exactly what Ashley always claimed whenever she pulled *my* hair.

Complete rubbish.

Maybe it hadn't *technically* been an accident, but I certainly hadn't *meant* for her to vanish! I'd had no way of knowing that stinky piece of paper would actually let me make a real, magical wish! And it certainly wasn't fair of whoever had granted the wish to decide I'd been speaking literally. Intention matters!

This was a clear case of entrapment. It was downright sneaky cheating. I hadn't even had my solicitor present!

...come to think of it, who *had* granted my wish?

Smoothing the yellow parchment I'd been grasping tightly in my fist, I flattened it on the ground and scanned the faded words. There. At the end. It had been signed "The High Magical Council".

Well, that settled it. I would find this so-called High Magical Council, explain to them that I hadn't *actually* wished for anything, and get them to undo it and bring Ashley back. Not only that, but I was entitled to a wish that I actually meant to make. And if that meant having to continue living with Ashley, so be it.

The Book that Glowed

You know, for someone as *obviously* brilliant as I am, you'd think I'd have an easier time tracking down information about the High Magical Council. I mean, isn't the internet supposed to know everything?

No such luck.

For one thing, Mum would simply *not* leave me alone. Before I'd made my dreadful wish, she'd been desperate to get away from Ashley and me every chance she got. I still remember the countless times she stuck us with some random babysitter while she and Dad bathed in the hot sun of Portugal or Pompei. But now she was clinging onto me like wisteria to walls. Wisteria that I was frantically trying to shake off.

Meanwhile, Dad followed me around like a lost puppy, wanting to play card games and read books with me and have conversations about what I wanted to be when I grew up. His most recent idea was starting a

Father and Daughter Fish & Chips Restaurant. The only way I could shake him was to tell him I needed quiet time to come up with batter recipes. If I had my accidental wish back, I'd use it to wish he'd go back to watching water-skiing squirrel memes on YouTube. That had been his go to on weekends whenever Mum would ask him to play with Ashley and me and he'd said he couldn't because he was 'busy with quarterly reports'.

Yet another reason I needed to get Ashley back *pronto*.

Over the next few weeks, I had to be increasingly clever to get any time away from Mum and Dad. My usual excuse was that I was studying for end of year exams. If either ever found out I was researching mythical creatures and High Magical Councils instead of whatever useless nonsense we were supposed to be going over in school, they'd probably start home-schooling me so they could keep an eye on me round the clock. Shudder.

But over-attentive parental figures were the least of my worries compared to how poorly my search for information was going. I started at home with my Mum's computer, but that was a dead end. I still can't believe nothing useful came up, considering my *very* exact google searches, including 'tiny woolly cartoon creature in hospital' and 'High Magical Council of purple tennis balls' and 'underage wish granting' and 'my little sister broke my photo frame and now she's disappeared', to name a few. The only thing remotely interesting was a demented looking internet sensation: Jet the Tie-dyed Labrador. It was a purple pigmy schnauzer (despite being called a Labrador) that was rentable for children's parties from the Magical Wishes shop on High Street in Hampstead.

I had to up my game, so I started creating distractions and then slipping out the backdoor for the library when Mum and Dad's attention was on something else, just simple things like misplacing Mum's favourite stainless steel frying pan, or changing the password on Dad's laptop.

Alas, all that time was for nothing: I couldn't find anything at the library, either. Oh, there were plenty of books about magic and wishes to be found, but they were all obviously intended for children. I mean, I suppose technically I'm still a child, but I've always been serious-minded, not given to daydreams about silly little leprechauns and faeries meant to teach youth important life lessons like the value of honesty and friendship.

By the time my distractions had escalated to things like catching a rabid squirrel and trapping it in Mum's underwear drawer, I'd visited five local libraries and was becoming desperate. The librarians were no use either. They'd either direct me back to the stupid kid stories or ask with varying degrees of politeness that I stop interrupting their work with questions about "made up nonsense." It was all a hopeless, despairing mire of interminable agitation.

I must have gone through thousands of books, microfiche, and old magazine articles. I prayed for a sign – *any sign!* – of the creature or the High Magical Council, but I began to think it would never happen.

And then one day out of the blue, I found it.

I knew it was a portentous day right from the start. The sun had made a rare appearance, and Mum wanted me to go outside with her for a walk. But as soon as we got past Westminster, it started to rain.

It wasn't just regular rain. It was a *downpour*.

I don't know what it was about the rain – maybe the suddenness of it, or maybe how the dark clouds up above seemed perfectly in line with my frustrations at getting nowhere with my search – but I knew then and there that something had to give. I knew I was going to find what I was looking for, and I was going to find it within the hour.

A tinkling chorus suddenly rose around us in a gust of wind, as if every windchime in the world were hung on this particular street in

London. I covered my ears, it was so loud. I'd never heard such a ruckus before, yet at the same time, there was something oddly comforting and *familiar* in it, too. Raising my head to look for the source, I was gobsmacked to see we were standing in front of a library I hadn't been to yet.

Mum clutched my hand to yank me back the way we'd come. When she let go just long enough to pull the hood of her jacket up over her head, I made my move.

"Bye Mum," I shouted over a crack of thunder. "I'm off to the library!"

"What? Now?" Mum yelled through the rain, a strand of hair pressed against her forehead.

"I need to study for a test!"

"Well, don't just stand there," she shouted, "Run, Vicky! But be back by supper!"

I scurried across the street, skipping puddles and dodging rain-soaked pedestrians. The doors of the library opened automatically as I rushed in and shook myself off. I removed my wet jacket and hung it on a hook in the coatroom, then started toward the stairs leading to the second floor where a sign said the histories were kept. I'd had no luck whatsoever in the fantasies, or in biology, for that matter. To be honest, I didn't have much hope that history would teach me anything, but the sudden downpour, the tinkling wind chimes, and the proximity of an unsearched library were too many signs to ignore. I couldn't give up.

I'd just made it to the top of the stairs when I froze. Oh, no.

It was *him*, over by the Winston Churchill section.

Who, you may ask? Only the most horrid, boisterous boy at school: Caleb Bilchfilcher. There were many bullies at school, but they all cowered in Caleb Bilchfilcher's monolithic presence.

You see, there are many types of bullies out there in the world. Some are just plain stupid, not knowing any better than to think that punching other children is funny. Others do it for self-worth, needing to prove they're better than everyone else. Often, they're looking for attention they aren't getting at home (hah – wished I had that problem!). But for every ten or so ordinary bullies, there is one utterly rotten one; one for whom the limits of polite society exist solely to be trampled over.

Enter Caleb.

Even worse, Caleb held a spot of hate in his ugly heart specifically reserved for me. He'd hated me ever since the first grade when I told everyone that he had farted during a game of Chinese whispers. I know it wasn't kind to say something like that, but at the time, it had seemed funny, and it was definitely true.

Unfortunately, Caleb hadn't found it nearly as funny. No, the only thing Caleb probably found funny was inflicting bodily harm on the children around him.

What in Old Blighty was Caleb doing in a *library* of all places!? It certainly couldn't be for reading, could it…?

My thoughts were interrupted by a snorting sort of grunt. He'd spotted me!

Thinking quickly, I pulled a piece of taffy from my pocket and lobbed it at him before ducking behind a nearby rubbish bin. The snuffled munching of the taffy wrapper being chewed gave me the courage to peek around the edge of the bin.

Huge mistake. Caleb's big bald head swivelled toward my hiding spot, his little pig-eyes lighting up with evil glee.

I pulled my head back in, but it was too late; he was already bounding towards me like an overgrown moose. His stench (consisting of rotten eggs today, which was unusual even for him) reached me before he did, mingling with the musty odour of the old books that were organised on the shelves behind me in alphabetical order.

Faint wind chimes tinkled again from over to the left, and without any time for a plan, I made a dash toward the sound, sprinting out from behind the bin and squeezing between a pair of empty book shelves.

After a few moments of blind turns through the labyrinth of bookshelves and near collisions with library patrons, I paused to catch my breath. Hands on knees, I surveyed my surroundings. Caleb was nowhere in sight.

In fact, *no one* was in sight.

I had stumbled into a deserted corridor, completely dim and silent.

Silent…except for the clear chime of tiny bells.

Turning around, I realised I was standing in front of a huge oak door with a rope barrier that cut it off from the rest of the library. A colossal sign on the front that read:

FORBIDDEN: DO NOT ENTER

The tinkling was definitely coming from behind the door.

With a certainty I can only describe as magical, I knew there was something behind the door that *wanted* to help me save my little sister.

Wanted, you may ask? Since when do 'somethings' behind doors *want* to help with sister-saving?

But there's really no other way to describe it, so you'll just have to take my word for it.

I. KNEW.

Cautiously, I sneaked over the barrier and approached the door. It opened silently, seemingly of its own accord.

Well, it can't be THAT forbidden if it opens up for every passing child, I thought to myself as I slipped in.

It smelled as if no one had been in this room for a very long time. But that didn't matter to me in the slightest at the moment. Because the inside was *filled* with books. Hundreds and thousands of books. Colossal ones, too. Tomes several inches wide sat on shelves that groaned under their weight. Everything was covered in a thick layer of dust.

I walked along, fiddling with my still-damp skirt as I did so. That abomination Caleb was now a mere afterthought. The books seemed to whisper to each other as I inched further in, their pages rustling as if in excited conversation.

At the end of the corridor, on top of a cracked, marble pedestal, sat a book shining like a shooting star. I squinted against the glare glinting off the golden embroidered leather cover. It was so bright I almost couldn't make out the words.

Upon closer inspection, the curling calligraphy spelled out the title: *The Tome of Hidden Creatures.*

A glimmer of hope ignited in my chest. Excited, I advanced towards the book. This was it. I could feel it. This was the key to righting my wish and getting my sister back!

The book pulsed with magical energy; it bewitched me, pulling me closer as if I were in a trance. I drew ever nearer, transfixed by its power, the light radiating from the leather cover dazzled my eyes.

Spellbound, I picked it up. It was big, alright, but somehow lighter than I expected. For what it weighed, you'd almost think it would be small enough to fit in the palm of your hand! Gently, I brushed dust off the gleaming cover with my sleeve, then ran my finger over the smooth, golden lettering.

Before I even knew what I was doing, I'd stuffed the book under my jumper and was racing out the door of the secret room, back down the labyrinth of corridors and passageways to the front of the library.

It wasn't until much later that I realised the tinkling had stopped the moment I picked up the book.

5

Summer Hols

I ran until I had a stitch in my side, and even then I kept going, forgetting my jacket entirely. Thankfully, the downpour had let up, leaving only a clinging fog behind. As I ran, I occasionally sneaked peeks over my shoulder to make sure no one had followed me. Besides Caleb, I was worried that snatching the book might have set off a silent alarm. But as far as I could make out through the gloom, the coast was clear, at least for now. I ran all the way home, where I was met at the back door by a very angry-looking Mum.

She had a test score clutched in her hand and a frown turning down the corners of her mouth.

Ugh. I panted, pacing in a little circle and breathing deep, waiting for the stitch in my side to fade. Thank heavens the book hadn't weighed more. I'd run *hard.*

"Excuse me, young lady!" Mum grew impatient with my pacing and stalked up to me until she was practically standing on top of me.

I had a brief moment to wonder which test it might be – all of my teachers had threatened to mail my most recent results home – before Mum shoved the paper into my face. History. I'd been so careful about checking the mail every day for just this purpose, and the one day I forgot… But there's no use crying over spilt milk, as they say, and there I was.

"An F *minus*?" she cried, her piercing voice ringing in my ears. She ragged on and on about how irresponsible I was until at least an aeon had passed. I didn't pay much attention. I was desperate to search the pages of the book, desperate to find a way to get in contact with the High Magical Council.

When I finally managed to get a word in, I told her I was extremely sorry and that I was just as concerned as she was about my poor grade, which was the very reason I'd been spending so much time at the library. I told her I'd only come home because it had been too noisy there to finish my homework and pleaded that if she let me up to my room so I could get back to it, I would work through dinner as penance.

She wasn't expecting that, and to tell the truth, neither was I. I didn't lie often to my parents (besides the distractions I'd been laying for them lately, but that wasn't *quite* the same as lying), and I *never* gave up dinner. The simple truth was that I'd been too engrossed in my research to concentrate on my studies, and I hadn't heard a word any of my professors had said since the morning I'd woken up to find Ashley gone. In this case, the lie was much more believable than the truth.

Mum stared at me with her mouth hanging open in shock for a moment before letting me go.

My hair trailed soggily behind me as I sprinted up the stairs to my room. The springs in my bed creaked as I leapt onto my mattress.

The book's bright golden glow had dissipated to a dingy copper throb by then, and I was able to open the cover and devour the pages without any protection from my shades.

Page after page contained lush, colour illustrations and curling annotations about all the monsters I never would have guessed exist in this world. My mind whirled with images and information it couldn't possibly process all at once, but I kept going, kept turning pages one after the other until finally, on the 231st page, I found what I'd been searching for: the creature who had given me the wish that day so many years ago at the hospital!

On the left page was a picture of a watermelon-sized creature, purple and furry all over. Its face was almost completely consumed by dense fur. It was cute, but its hair looked greasy and unkempt. Behind him, there was a watercolour landscape of a peaceful forest, dense with fern and tall, slender trees. Underneath the picture was a short text. I blew off the film of dust that had settled on top of the page and began to read.

The Lawfur

"The lawfur is a tranquil creature who is timid and industrious. Lawfurs live on the outskirts of Scotland in the Black Wood of Rannoch – also known as the Forbidden Forest of the Kingdom of Hidden Creatures – with all the other monsters of the Unknown listed in this book. This creature is often trusted with carrying out various bureaucratic responsibilities within the Magical Community. Though some view their arrival as an omen of ill will, the lawfur is actually quite peaceable. This negative reputation stems solely from their tendency to be entrusted with carrying warnings, and from the dark magic they wield to do so. They are

also sometimes known as 'granters of wishes,' as wish-granting is one of their main tasks."

I put the book down.

I had to get to Scotland.

A plan was formulating in my mind, one I wished I didn't have to think about. Summer holidays were coming up. Could I convince Mum and Dad to spend them in Scotland?

Drat. My insides felt all stabby and weird, like I'd just swallowed a fistful of rocks. I couldn't tell if it was because I was afraid my parents would absolutely refuse Scotland based on principle, or that they'd give in and I'd actually have to go to the dreary place.

***

"Victoria!" Mum called from downstairs. "Suppertime!"

I groaned, having just spent another evening reading through the *Tome*. Quickly, I heaved the heavy book off my bed and stowed it in my memorabilia box under my bed.

As I descended to the kitchen, my mind raced. I'd been putting it off, but I didn't have much longer to figure out the next step in my plans: how would I convince my parents to go to *Scotland* of all places?

"So, how has school been going?" Mum asked. "I expect History is the *only* f-minus you have?" *All according to plan.* Little did she know, I had been anticipating that very question. Mum is terribly predictable in that way. It's as if she has a nagging quota she has to reach every night, and pestering me about school is one of her go-to's to fulfil it.

"It's great!" I mustered all the fake enthusiasm I could manage. "Loads of people are going on holiday. Vivy is going to Wales, and a few people are going to America, but the two twins in my class, Archey and Livy, are going to Scotland for the holiday!" I lied, trying to sound as dull as possible until the end.

Mum arched her eyebrows. "Scotland?" she asked, taking the bait.

"Oh yes, it's *beautiful,"* I lied. "In fact, I was meaning to suggest we go there. It's so gorgeous and… sunny… and you should see all the…umm…nature! Oh, it's brilliant, and there are romantic restaurants and castles and beautiful lakes! Doesn't that sound perfect?" I tried to sound as energetic as possible.

"But you hate nature!" Mum stared at me like I'd sprouted a second head.

Drat, I knew I'd get stumped on something. She was right of course. Nature and I have never meshed well – it's far too uncivilised. Did you know there are no bathrooms in nature? You just have to go on the *ground.*

"Ummm," I stalled for time to think. "Well, I went on a trip to Hyde park to do some investigating for a science project, and now I really love nature! It's so…*natural*!" I tried smiling at her awkwardly. Dad, of course, had only been nodding along and hadn't said anything this whole time.

"I don't know, Vicky." Mum forked a lump of meatloaf into her mouth and spoke through her chewing. "Scotland isn't exactly the most exotic of vacation spots, and it's not exactly *travel* to only go a couple hours north…"

"But-"

"That's enough dear," Mum put a stopper on the conversation *and* my plans.

I had figured it wouldn't be easy, but it was still disheartening to have my first attempt ruined so unceremoniously.

We ate in silence for the next several minutes. I tried my hardest to subtly, but noticeably sulk. The only sounds filling up the dining room were Mum and Dad's chewing and the musical tinkle of windchimes…

Just then, the T.V. we kept in front of the living room couch sprung to life seemingly on its own.

"Honey, the T.V. is acting up again," Mum said.

Dad only grunted in response. I wasn't too surprised; they'd had that T.V. since before I was born.

"...and situated right by the scenic Black Woods of Rannoch," an announcer droned on, "it truly is the perfect getaway spot for your next holiday. And if you call now, your first two nights are completely free!"

A miracle! "Mum, look!" I shouted. But she was already watching. Her whole body perked up like a dog who'd just seen a squirrel.

"Huh," Dad grunted once more, still gnawing on some meatloaf. "What a coincidence. Did you see this ad earlier, Vicky?"

"Erm…yes! I guess I just forgot."

"Well why didn't you mention the part about the free nights first?" Mum rose from the table and bolted for her phone.

Brilliant. I guess I wouldn't have to do much convincing after all.

6 Emma the Gardenere

The summer holiday homework was packing in, which meant I had the perfect excuse to lock myself in my room every day when I came home from school. To be on the safe side, I'd taken the initiative and changed our address with the school. Officially, Abercorn Prep now had on record that the McKay family resides in the East Indies. No more surprise school reports for me to worry about, then.

At school, all anyone could talk about was summer holidays. Especially Gloria. Anyone who made eye-contact with her had to endure her speech about how she was going to "bathe in the lifted rays of the African sun as it shone down upon her from cobalt skies, while wild animals passed her, screeching their songs as she lounged in the back of the jeep on a Safari in Serengeti."

Normally, I'd be sick with envy, but this year, the only thing I was sick about was having wished away my little sister. How could I have been so idiotic to have wasted a magical wish on something so colossally stupid? Though, to be fair to me:

a. I had been four years old at the time my bothersome little sister had been born,
b. I hadn't entirely believed wishes were real,
c. It had been seven years, and what with being constantly overstimulated by said little sister, I'd completely forgotten about the wish.

Focus, Victoria, I told myself. You need Ashley back. Remember when Mum rescued that parrot from the animal shelter and then basically bored it to death with her incessant chatter?

To all of my readers who indulge in daydreams about being an only child, I pray you learn from my mistake. There was no way I'd make it to adulthood if I didn't get my sister back.

Opening my closet, I hauled out my suitcase from the back. The suitcase itself was purple with squirrels, monkeys, and hippos in party hats on. It was an unwanted birthday present from my zoo-animal obsessed Aunt Marge.

Scrabbling under my bed for my bin of memorabilia, I grabbed two packages of batteries I'd hidden there and zipped them into a side compartment of my zoo case. Next in went a large flashlight, a Swiss knife I stole from my friend Audrey's house, a lighter with the words 'I Love Apple Pie' on it, a large two litre hydroflask, and The *Tome of Hidden Creatures*.

Then I shoved in some clothing essentials almost as an afterthought: underthings, t-shirt's, jeans, a bathing suit, a rain poncho, a couple jumpers, two nightgowns, and some ski boots. According to The Tome, the Kingdom of Creatures has rather unpredictable weather. It could be gale force wind one minute and raining toads the next. The book explained that it had something to do with the "immense inner chamber being fed by comparatively small ventilation shafts," and "unpredictable pressure gradients caused by interactions with topside weather," and "ancient toad-based alchemy."

I didn't understand any of that, but it sounded reasonably scientific.

Finally, I figured I'd want to document my discoveries. I grabbed a blue journal from a pile of unused school supplies laying in my closet. I flipped through the pages to be sure I hadn't accidentally used it for something stupid like notetaking in class. All the pages were blank except the second. An arrow drawn in pencil pointed to the first page, followed by: Pleese disregard, this is a **seryus** notebook for **seryus** note taking, scribbled in my handwriting from years ago.

Realisation struck me. I received this journal a few days before starting Year 4. Ashley found it on my nightstand doodled all over the first page before I'd ever even used it. It was a poorly composed scene featuring Ashley and me holding hands in a flowery park, in pink marker. At the time, all I could think was that she'd made a mess.

Now the page was blank. I guessed the wish erased that, too.

I stuffed the journal in with the rest of my luggage. It only seemed fitting that I take this with me.

After struggling to close the now bulging suitcase for well over five minutes, I sat on my bed, panting but proud. As long as Mum didn't check my packing sometime before we left, I'd be the most prepared girl in the world.

***

Finally, departure day dawned. The vacation started off messy well before we'd boarded the flight. Mum fretted that my passport was out of date all the way to the airport, and Dad claimed Mum's persistent squawking made him nauseous. As we got onto the flight, a sickening feeling fell over me, too. What if I got lost in the Black Wood and died of starvation? Though I *was* brilliant at survival in the fashion jungle that was London's upper east side, I'd never done actual *camping* before.

Too late for second thoughts now, Vicky! I scolded myself. You're on your way to dreary Scotland to put things right. Think of Ashley! Think of Freedom from being an only child!

I began my slow, cramped crawl to the back of the plane. Of course, the one time I wouldn't have minded being in my parent's company they decided they could only afford first-class tickets for the two of them and not for me.

"Chirp!"

That certainly pulled me out of my ruminations. Whatever could be making that sound on a plane? Had someone smuggled their pet chicken aboard?

And then, distinctly, the tinkle of wind chimes. I almost didn't bother noticing them anymore, they'd started chiming randomly as far as I could tell.

"Chirp!"

I stopped – much to the chagrin of the man trying to get to his seat behind me – and began scanning the nearby seats for the source of the noise. I took a mental inventory of all I saw:

- An obese man and his thin wife – both already taking a nap.
- A single mother with several rowdy children – the youngest secured on a leash.
- A small, brown, nubbly creature with quills around its head who was hidden in an overhead luggage compartment.
- A flight attendant trying to help someone sort out their seating arrangement.
- Wait…
- A *what* in the luggage compartment?

There it was! A small, nubbly creature with quills around its head tucked up between some knock-off Gucci luggage, peeking out at me with yellow, cat-like eyes. It was somehow familiar, even though I knew for a fact I'd never laid eyes on it before in my life. How could that be possible…?

The Tome! I'd seen this creature before in The *Tome of Hidden Creatures*!

It was a cardenere. I remember it being described as heavy as a ton of bricks, although it didn't look so. This creature was long and thin, like one of those low-to-the-ground wiener schnitzel dogs, except this one was standing on two legs, clutching the handle of the faux Gucci overnight bag it was hiding behind with tiny, clawed hands. Its skin was a nubbly brown with short, buckskin fur, except for the face, abdomen, palms of its hands. A scattering of hedgehog quills protruded from its head, falling down its back like hair that just reached its knees.

Just then, a flight attendant passing behind me reached up and pulled the overhead compartment door closed with a sharp click.

After buckling myself into my economy cabin seat, I fumbled in my rucksack for The Tome and flipped through the pages until I found the right entry:

The Cardenere

"The Cardenere is a peculiar creature covered in short, soft hair in varying shades of thrilling beige They have semi-retractable quills in various areas of their bodies. This creature is well-known for being reasonably friendly, but incredibly timid. A Cardenere will run at the first sign of danger, real or imaginary. Perhaps this is in part because they are the only creatures from the Kingdom of Hidden Creatures in existence who possess no magical powers."

"How strange that creature is flying coach from London to Scotland," I murmured to myself. But I guess if it didn't have any magic, it would be stuck using conventional methods of travel. The appearance of a non-magical magical creature must be a sign I was headed in the right direction.

I gripped my armrest as the turbulence of take-off tossed and rattled the plane about like a rag doll. Sitting in Economy with my rucksack at my feet, I mumbled curses at my parents for not spending a bit more money so I could travel Business class with them.

Once the plane had settled, I scanned the overhead compartments. The cardenere had stowed itself in the compartment above a heavy-set man who had just retrieved his giant body pillow, re-closed the compartment, and promptly fallen asleep.

Holding completely still, I watched the compartment slowly open. I wished Mum or Dad, or even Mr. Higgenbottom, the maths professor, could see how patiently I waited. It was Mr. Higgenbottom who had rudely suggested to my parents that whatever it was that possessed me, it certainly *wasn't* an attitude of patience. *Insufferable man.* But the longer I sat still in my uncomfortable seat, the more I wondered if he might have been right when he insisted that "patience wasn't lethal," and that despite my certainty to the contrary, waiting my turn wouldn't kill me. I was doing it. For possibly the first time in my entire 11 years, I was holding still, and what's more, I felt robust as ever!

Finally, one of the cardenere's large, golden cat-eyes peaked round the imitation Gucci bag. As soon as it saw me watching, it gave another *"chirp!"* and dove for cover.

Quietly, so as not to disturb the sleeping girl next to me, I unfastened my seatbelt and gracefully climbed over her. My eyes scanned the interior of the plane from front to back, scrutinising each row. No one was paying the slightest attention to me, and for once, I was grateful. Carefully, I crept over to the creature's hiding spot.

"Don't be scared," I whispered to the bags it was hiding behind. "I won't hurt you. My name's Victoria. What's yours?"

"*...chirp...*" I heard from a suitcase.

"Listen," I carried on, "you'll be perfectly safe with me, I promise. In fact, I'm trying to get to the Black Wood of Rannoch. That's where you come from, right?

"*...chirp*?"

"Alright. Well, if you're going back, I could really use a guide. Would you mind helping me? I'd be *ever* so grateful."

For a long, painful minute, there were no further *chirps*. But eventually there was rustling from amidst the luggage. Then, spry as a flying squirrel, the Cardenere leaped out from the compartment and onto my shoulders.

Whoa! It really was heavier than it looked! If I hadn't been so strong from my bi-monthly yoga practice, I would have fallen flat on my rear end! Instead, I straightened my spine, engaging my toned core muscles, and quickly escorted it back to my seat.

"Psst!" it whispered, poking me in the neck. Then, it spoke in a meek voice straight out of the Irish countryside. "I'll guide you if you'll keep me secret and safe on our journey. I'd rather my family didn't know I'm returning, it's…it's kind of a…surprise."

The way it said 'surprise' didn't necessarily sound like a good thing. But who was I to judge?

"Families, am I right?" I asked. Then I whispered, "Mine doesn't know I'm going to the Kingdom of Creatures, either. I guess it's kind of a surprise, too."

"Twins!" it said.

I liked the thought of that. Twins in purpose. Smiling, I retrieved my rucksack, zipped open the main compartment, and offered my hand to the creature. "You can hide in here for now."

The little creature eagerly jumped into my palm, and I lowered it into my bag. It scurried inside, easily making itself comfortable.

"Thank you," it squeaked at me.

I grinned. Whispering, I addressed its big round eyes peering up at me from the backpack. "I'm Vicky. What's your name?" I asked.

It grinned and stuck its hand out to shake mine, "I'm Emma, pleased to meet yah!"

I was a bit taken aback by Emma's sudden boisterousness, since the book had made such a point of cardeneres' shy natures. But then again, I am quite charming, if I do say so myself. I couldn't blame her for feeling especially at ease in my presence.

"Well, Emma," I smiled back, "it's very nice to have met you. Now, if you don't mind, I think I'm going to get some reading in and then nod off for a bit. It's been a stressful few weeks."

She nodded up at me as if she knew exactly what I meant and curled up into a little ball that very much resembled one of Ashley's old stuffies.

An odd...*missing*...pinched at my heart when I thought of my sister, but I brushed it away. I was just tired, that's all. No one could even *imagine* my problems, let alone manage them with the quiet grace I was exhibiting. But then, I never complained.

Shifting about in my seat proved a waste of time. There was no comfortable position to find in economy class. Finally, I shoved *The Tome* and my diary in the seat pocket in front of me, pulled down my flimsy tray table, and bent over, resting my head atop my arms, praying the flight attendants wouldn't bother me when it was time for tea service.

I certainly needed plenty of rest for the adventure that was ahead of me, but at the very least, I'd just solved one of my problems without even trying all that hard: Now, I had a guide.

Scotland is in the Air

"Wake up! Wake up!"

A violent shake brought me to my senses. I must have successfully dozed off while reading from The Tome, because Mum was staring down at me. Behind her, people piled down the corridor. I sat up and opened the shade to peer out the tiny plane window.

Scotland was…dreary.

Incessantly dreary.

My goodness, was there even a country out there somewhere in the fog?

Mum grabbed my rucksack from the ground while I unbuckled my seatbelt.

My rucksack…

Emma!

I snatched the pack from her grip, praying she hadn't peeked inside. But then I reasoned that since she wasn't currently screaming and jibbering as to why I'd smuggled a tiny monster on the plane with me, she hadn't. I carefully felt along the material of the sack so as to confirm her presence without having to open it.

"*Chirp!*" I heard as my hand passed over a very conspicuous lump.

I barely restrained myself from shushing my luggage.

"All right then, carry it yourself," Mum sighed. "I was just trying to be helpful."

"Sorry, Mum," I said. "It's got my snacks in it."

"No one wants your snacks, Vicky," she sniffed, heading off down the aisle.

I leaned down to the rucksack. "Try to stay quiet," I whispered. "I'll let you out as soon as I can." There was a slight rustle, but no chirp. Emma seemed a smart little cardenere.

I trooped out of the plane, across the narrow plank, and down the stairs, which were wet and slippery. The air was heavy and humid, and my wool jumper pressed against my skin as we waited by the square box marked on the cracked concrete for the shuttle bus stop. People were prickly and fidgety as they chatted about how ridiculously long the shuttle was taking. They rumoured amongst themselves that the airport had forgotten there were even any planes arriving today.

I didn't mind. It gave me a moment to think. Before I'd fallen asleep, I'd read more from the *Tome of Hidden Creatures*. I wanted to learn as much as I could about this fantastical place I was going to in the short time I had before I actually *got* there.

Alas, studying was never my strong suit, even if it was studying about magic. I had learned *some* things of course. I'd read that most creatures- like the lawfur I'd seen and the new cardenere I'd just met- lived in the Kingdom of Hidden Creatures, but that was a no brainer. I'd also learned that creatures who could talk and walk (or move in some similar fashion) were generally called 'faeries', but that was a very broad category. There were species I'd heard of before, of course, like elves and goblins. But for each name I'd read in a fantasy book before, there was another I'd never dreamed of.

Take tropper-hoppers, for example. They were apparently a whole race of creatures who looked like sugar gliders who were incredibly intelligent, save for the fact that they firmly believed that all ground was lava and therefore studiously avoided it. There was no basis to their belief, no magical curse that burned their feet when they walked on the ground, but nothing could convince them that doing so was safe.

I could go on for pages about all the strange things I'd read, but for all I knew, that would put me in magical copyright violation. And, like I said, I am quite bad at studying, and I would probably misremember a lot. So, you'll just have to learn about things in the order I stumbled across them.

But, after I had absorbed enough moisture through my clothes and skin to scientifically be classified a cantaloupe, a bus did finally arrive. It was a short, grey vehicle that seemed about as dreary as everything else in Scotland, if first impressions were anything to go by. By the smell, there were several sheep toward the back, though I didn't actually see any.

The scant crowd of passengers jammed itself onto the bus one by one. I was too busy making sure I didn't bang my rucksack and my hidden passenger into any bodies to worry too much about being polite, earning me a scowl from Mum. I took my seat and tried to put my surroundings firmly out of my mind. Once we got to our destination, it was planning time. This little ride on the bus might be my last chance for who knows how long to just sit and relax.

***

It was exactly 5:00 a.m. by the time we got to the hotel.

Oh, sorry, I of course meant The Atholl *Castle* Hotel, because apparently every important building in Scotland is a castle. I genuinely wondered if Scots are aware which millennia we were in.

“Well, isn’t this just incredible,” Mum gaped, nudging me on the arm as I came awake and stared through the bus window.

I suppose it was very authentic, all in all. Spectacular turrets pierced the air, and the Scottish flag billowed in the wind, proudly standing against the endlessly cloudy sky. The grounds themselves were green and luscious, with orange morning sunlight filtering through the clouds and tree branches to highlight the stone gargoyles keeping watch from up above. The moat surrounding the castle was alive and thriving, the murky depths bubbling and broiling like a witch's cauldron brewing up a potion.

Dad seemed…less than impressed. He made a face that reminded me of the ‘meh’ emoji. Mum gave him her signature raised-eyebrow look and tapped him on the foot, prompting him to immediately perk up. With a strained smile on his face, he led us off the bus and towards the hotel entrance. He muttered to himself as he tried to avoid the thorns from the shrubbery lining the walk that occasionally snagged his jeans. A poor bellhop offered to take our luggage, and Dad grumbled something unintelligible at him.

Moss covered most of the circumference of the cobbles, and it could be *quite* slippery. Who thought it was a good idea to let so much green and untamed nature grow rampant in a place where civilised people were supposed to be lodging?

Behind the hotel, the immense Black Wood of Rannoch loomed, just a stone's throw away, menacing at me. I gulped my first gulp of the day. *That's where I need to go if I want my wish back. That's where I need to go to find Ashley.*

The strange loneliness pinched at my heart again as I thought about my sister. Where *had* Ashley gone to? What had actually happened to her when I used my wish? Because – curse my fantastic memory – I remembered only too clearly that I hadn't simply wished my sister away. I'd wished *she'd never been born…*

The toe of my boot caught on an uneven cobblestone as an image rose in my mind: Ashley huddled in her white nightdress, barefoot and frightened in some dark, possibly monster-filled forest with no Mum, no Dad, no *me* to comfort her. What if it was raining where she was? She was terrified of thunderstorms and had always come running to my bed when one woke her up in the night.

…or worse? What if she wasn't anywhere at all? What if she'd never been born…?

"Watch yourself, Vicky!" Mum reached out and caught my arm right before I face planted on the wet stone path. "You'll break your neck, darling! Are you daydreaming again?"

'Thanks," I mumbled. "Just sleepy, I guess." Stupid wish, I muttered to myself. Stupid mythical creatures, making me feel all…complicated.

"I hope you aren't thinking of running off in there," a young man's voice startled me to my left. The bellhop stood beside me, staring down at me and stacking our luggage on his cart.

"Uh…" I sputtered. Did he know what I was planning?

The lanky man bent down and frowned melodramatically. "They say those woods are *cursed*, you know. Haven't you heard the story of young Bob?"

I shook my head incredulously. The bellhop's eyes narrowed menacingly.

"Back when this place was an actual castle, you see, Bob was the son of one of the servants here. He was also the last little kid to take an interest in those woods. Legends say he walked in one day and, poof! He was never seen again." He cupped his hands around his mouth, looked side to side, then whispered, "His body was never found. Some say he was taken by… ***A GHOST!"*** He leaned back and gasped at his own story.

I rolled my eyes. Did he seriously expect me to believe that no one had walked in those woods since mediaeval times? What did he take me for? I'm 11 whole years old and *far* beyond being frightened by dumb stories. Everyone knows ghosts aren't real! I'm going into that forest to seek a *Magical Council*, not something as childish and fake as a *ghost.*

Life had been so simple before that idiotic, accidental wish. I couldn't wait to get my hands on the "High Magical Council" and force it to make things go back to normal.

Speaking of things that weren't normal, we were standing at the base of the moat. The wooden bridge was lowered, giving passage over to the other side, and a set of colossal, black metal chains held the whole thing together. I was so captured by the sheer beauty of *all* of it, I didn't notice the cardenere struggling to climb out of my rucksack until it was almost too late.

“Where are you going?" I hissed, pulling my rucksack off my shoulder.

“Whadayah mean?” she squealed, her hands tightening. “The Black Wood is right there! We made it!”

“Keep up, darling” Mum shouted over her shoulder, her heels clicking against the wood of the drawbridge.

“One second!” I called back. “Just tying my shoes!” I knelt down, discreetly placing my rucksack next to me and zipping it open. I looked back to check for the bellhop, but he had mercifully moved into the building.

“Listen, Emma,” I whispered, “we can’t just run off in broad daylight –F well, *foglight,* at least – while my parents are watching, okay?” Mum was staring at me, but it was more of an impatient stare than an oh-good-God-what-is-that-thing-in-your-bag stare, so I figured I was safe for the moment.

“Well, when *are* we going, then?” Emma squeaked, finally settling down.

“We can plan tonight,” I responded, “after my parents go to bed.” Dad is a pretty heavy sleeper, and his snoring usually forces Mum to take sleeping pills and put in earplugs, so we’d be safe then.

Just then, I nearly jumped out of my skin as I felt a hand clamp down on my shoulder. I looked up to find Mum staring at me in concern.

Oh no, I’m caught! I thought. I can explain my way out of a bad grade, but how am I going to get out of this?

“Are you alright?” she asked, staring down her nostrils at me and gently placing her hand on my shoulder “Ever since you mentioned that

Ashley girl, you've been acting strange. Is there anything you want to tell me?"

I breathed a silent sigh of relief. "I'm fine," I said, shrugging her hand off. "Just excited to finally be here in dreamy old Scotland with you!"

***

Our suite overlooked a shimmering lake and was blessedly split into two adjoining rooms. I had the smaller one all to myself; my secret planning session with Emma that night would be able to go off without a hitch.

Mum and Dad started unpacking in their room while I trampled my bed. A series of windows climbed the wall, one above the other. The topmost window promised a gorgeous view of the town and surrounding forest.

"Hey, Emma," I said, bending down and opening my bag, "do you think you'd be able to get up to that window?" I pointed. "Maybe we could get a lay of the land, figure out which path to take once we're out of the hotel."

"*Chirp!* Of course I can! Cardeneres are world class climbers!" she replied a little too loudly for my liking.

"Ok, perfect. Later tonight, then –" I tried to continue, but I was cut off by a streak of brown darting out of my bag and towards my bed. Emma scrambled up the curtains draped around the four-poster bed in a blur of motion. She kicked and climbed the folds of the thick fabric, making startlingly good progress.

"No, Emma!" I half-shouted, almost losing control of my volume. "I didn't mean right now. You're making too much noise!"

"Vicky," Mum called from the other room, as if on cue, "what on Earth are you doing in there?"

"Just unpacking!" I called back before making a grab for Emma. Curse the nimble little monster – she slipped right through my fingers like it was the easiest thing in the world.

"You humans are too slow," Emma said in the midst of her expert upholstery-climbing. "We need to get going now, now, now!"

She leaped towards the tall Cheshire drawer next to the bed but missed by a hair. Instead of landing on top, she clung like a spider monkey to the knob of one of the drawers before pulling it open by pushing off the bottom one and sliding it out a fraction. I would have been impressed if I weren't growing more and more infuriated by the second. I marched over to the drawer and tried to grab her, but she ducked inside and nestled in the back, hiding behind a pad of paper.

I groaned in frustration and closed the drawer. What was I supposed to do? It was just my luck that the guide I'd been so fortunate to find would go rogue on me. I huffed and puffed for a good minute or so, trying to resist the urge to just tip the chest of drawers over.

But the more I huffed, the more I felt…sorry for Emma?

Oh goodness gracious, was this what introspecting was like? My school counsellor had always talked about it as a way to assess our feelings. I'd never been good at it, and I hoped it didn't become too much of a habit. But the thoughts were here now, and I couldn't quite make them just go away. Might as well *examine* the feeling I was having.

So what was this feeling? Well, I suppose I could understand why she was so eager to get going right this second. I still didn't know all the details about why she was here with me and not back in the woods with her family, but I couldn't imagine she enjoyed being separated from them. Just like Ashley was separated from us because of me…

Oh fine! I suppose I could take a more understanding approach to this situation. I walked over and yanked the drawer open (though I was still a *bit* upset, so it may have been a little more forceful than it strictly needed to be) and began to work my magical persuasion skills.

"Emma," I started, "I'm sorry I got mad at you, and I'm sorry we can't get going right this second, but we *need* to be careful. If my parents see me just running off into the woods, they'll probably call the rozzers on us or something. How are we supposed to get to your family if we're locked up in our rooms after they make us come back? You understand, don't you?"

"Oh drat," I heard from somewhere up above me. "I suppose you have a point."

Oh dear. I slowly tilted my head upward, and sure enough, there was Emma, hanging precariously from what looked to be a portrait of King Henry the Eighth!

"Wha…! How…! You were in the… How did you get up there?"

Emma just shrugged her shoulders. "I did say we're world class climbers. But you *are* right, I suppose," she continued. "I guess the forest will still be there once night falls."

I sighed in relief. In fact, I almost wanted to *cry* in relief. I guess using your words *was* sometimes the right way to go. I owed several of my Abercorn teachers an apology.

"Um, one small problem," Emma said. "I'm…sort of…*stuck* up here. Could you help me get down?"

Right after the "world-class climber" comment?

But there was no use getting angry. I rolled down my socks and started scanning the wall and furniture. I hadn't done much serious climbing since I'd gotten myself excused from PE lessons at school by way of forged doctor's note, but I was three times taller than Emma. Certainly I could rescue one smallish cardenere?

I used a ladder-back chair to climb on top of the dresser, and from the dresser to the top of one of the bed's four posts. On tiptoe, I could *almost* reach Emma. "Come on," I urged, "you can reach my hand with your foot."

After a moment of hesitation, Emma did start to reach out, placing one furry foot in my outstretched palm. Oh goodness me, how could she weigh so much for something so small?

My bicep shook beneath her weight, and she was still clutching Henry's gilt frame! She eased down little by little. Sweat beaded on my brow, but I gave a triumphant squeak as she was about to let go…

Did the painting just shift? And was the bedpost I was perched on starting to wobble?

No, the painting wasn't hanging. It was *falling*.

And so was I!

I heard two things right before my head hit the floor. One was the painting crashing to the floor with a horrendous thump.

The other was a single scream from the adjacent room: "VICKY!"

Walking Away Towards My Problems

My eyes fluttered open woozily. I lay sprawled on the plush bed comforter, the back of my head throbbing. Someone had placed a cool, damp washcloth across my brow. Probably Dad. He fancied himself quite the Florence Nightingale when it came to home remedies. In the adjoining room, Mum argued loudly with the hotel manager.

"How many pounds?" she screamed. "For that piece of junk?"

The manager was taken aback. "But madam, that portrait of King Henry is an original from the eighteen hundreds. It was painted by the King's personal artist Hans Holbein. It is priceless!"

"Don't be ridiculous!" my mother quipped back. "It's signed 'Hank Holbert'. You can buy them at Tesco."

"Actually, original Holberts fetch nearly £500 pounds," the manager sniffed.

Footsteps warned me of Mum's approach. I closed my eyes and played possum, peeking through the barest slit beneath my lowered eyelids as Mum entered the bedroom slowly with her fists clenched. She reached in the safe and took out a fat wad of cash.

"Here," she whispered, handing the money to the manager, who waited in the doorway. He snatched it and stalked out, his blunt pug-nose in the air. I heard the door to the hallway slam shut behind him.

"Come on now, darling," Mum tried to sound caring through gritted teeth. "We know you're awake."

"How?" I was genuinely curious, and slightly offended that they didn't better appreciate my acting skills.

"Because you're not snoring like a steam engine, for one," Dad smiled. He at least didn't sound like he wished I'd never been born. Meanwhile, I hoped no magical creatures were thinking of giving Mum a wish any time soon.

"That was our money for the rest of the holiday," Mum sighed. "We didn't budget for the recreational destruction of second-rate hotel art."

"Well, it's a good thing I love working around the clock!" Dad said cheerily. He sat down next to me on the bed. "To be honest, I was looking for an excuse to postpone my retirement indefinitely, anyway..."

"Do be quiet, Harold," Mum exclaimed. She turned back to me. "Vicky, have a rest and then pack your suitcase. And for the love of all that is good and holy, do *not* touch anything else! We leave for home first thing in the morning."

***

I spent most of the rest of the day sulking in my room and pretending to pack. I should have expected that this wouldn't be an easy outing, but I hadn't thought things would get so disastrous before I'd even left the hotel.

Fortunately, Mum and Dad went to bed early that night. I guess losing £500 had worn them out quite a bit.

Once they were soundly asleep, I crept out of bed, the deep carpet cushioning my feet. Dad snored noisily in the adjoining room – he was one to talk about steam engines! – and Mum was muttering grumpily in her sleep.

Sliding the wardrobe door open, I retrieved my rucksack. Emma the cardenere slept soundly, snuggly sandwiched in the big, back-zippered pocket of my rucksack between all of my balled-up socks. She looked so peaceful, curled up in a nubbly little amber ball with her quills tucked around her like a blanket, I almost didn't want to wake her up. But I had to. We had plans to make.

It only took a few gentle nudges to get her stirring, and with a stretch and a tiny yawn, she was up and ready to go.

"Are you ok?" she chittered. "That looked like a real nasty fall."

"I'm fine," I assured her. I really was, too. My head had throbbed a bit earlier in the day, but now I felt as healthy as a spring chicken. You could probably make some very tasty chicken nuggets out of me at that moment with how healthy I felt.

"I'm terribly sorry," Emma squeaked, her big golden eyes downcast. "You never would have fallen if I hadn't gotten stuck up there.

"It's quite alright, I promise." I patted her tiny head. I meant it, too, at least for the most part. It hadn't *entirely* been her fault. If I'd stuck to using my words in the first place and not slammed the drawer shut with her in it, she might not have ever tried to climb up there.

I was immediately glad I hadn't gotten angry. She beamed up at me in response to my reassurances and then leaped up onto my shoulder. "So," she chirped, "what's the plan for getting to the forest? Were we going to use the tunnels?"

"Well, I was thinking we… Wait," I paused. "What tunnels?"

She tilted her head, her eyes still fixed on mine. "The tunnels under the castle, of course." She gazed at me like a doctor trying to assess if I had a concussion: *What year is it, Vicky? Who's the Ruler of England right now? Don't you know about the secret tunnels under a castle you've never been to?*

"Ummmm…" I stuttered, "maybe you could remind me?"

I didn't think Emma's head could tilt any further, but she was currently proving me very wrong. "You know, the tunnels that connect all the nearby castles to the Black Wood," the cardenere explained. "Didn't they teach you about this in school? Did you not have a good "Black Forest Mysteries" teacher in the first form?"

"I don't think human children get those kinds of classes…" I started to explain, but I stopped myself. The most important thing right now was that there were apparently tunnels that could take us to the forest, and Emma seemed to know all about them. "Well," I picked back up, "I guess I didn't pay attention. Would you mind showing me the way?"

"Heeheehee," Emma giggled. "You humans are so forgetful. I'll give you directions if you carry me in here," she slapped the outside of the rucksack. "I've got fallen arches, so my feet get tired."

"Deal," I grinned at her before scooping up all my supplies. Gathering my phone and the gratis water bottle from the bedside table, I arranged everything carefully in the big front pocket where the textbook and iPad had been. I stepped up to the door and stopped. This journey deserved to be documented. I turned and tip-toed to my suitcase and produced the blue journal Ashley had doodled in. Just like when I packed it the first time, it only felt right for me to bring this along.

Breathing deeply to calm my nerves, I opened the door between the two adjoining rooms and quickly crept across the floor to the bathroom to retrieve some more items. The pull-out couch bed creaked as Mum sighed and turned over, swatting Dad in the face.

I froze. My heart hammered in my chest, but Dad just kept on snoring, so I tiptoed onward. In the bathroom, I grabbed one roll of toilet paper and a packet of milled soap, just in case they didn't have any in the Kingdom of Creatures.

Next stop was the mini-kitchen and fridge, where I stocked up on essentials: a six pack of mini Sprites, a rotisserie chicken Mum had picked up from the airport shop, and a family-sized packet of crisps. My rucksack bulged at the seams, or I would have brought the tub of baked beans, too. Regardless, what I had managed should keep me going for at least a few hours until I could forage for something in the Kingdom of Creatures. Or who knew? Maybe they had shops?

I ran my eyes over the night-dark room, looking for anything else I might need, but nothing caught my eye. My feet were silent as I tiptoed across the room's deep-pile carpet, turned the doorknob, and slipped out into the hall.

Once the door had closed with the barest click behind me, I leaned against the wall to slow my breathing.

That's when it hit me: I hadn't even left a note! What would my parents do when they woke up in the morning to find me gone? Would

Mum cry inconsolably while Dad rang Scotland Yard and begged them to find me and bring me back no matter the cost? Or would they both just shrug and move on with their lives, like they'd done the morning they woke up and Ashley had disappeared?

No. That wasn't fair, and I knew it. My wish had somehow altered reality in the most terrible way possible: my baby sister Ashley – who looked up to me and just wanted me to try being nice once in a while – had ceased to exist in everyone's memory except *mine*.

It wasn't Mum and Dad's fault they couldn't remember Ashley; it was mine and mine alone. I didn't know how long I'd be gone, and leaving a note that I was headed off to the Kingdom of Creatures to rescue the daughter they didn't know existed didn't seem helpful at the moment. But I *did* whisper a sorrowful good-bye before I left. "I love you, Dad. I love you, Mum. I'll be back with Ashley as soon as I can."

I stood out in the hallway, geared up for my expedition. I had dressed out of pyjamas into sweatpants and a white shirt with rainbows all over it. I had also packed three jeans, four shirts, my bathing suit, two jumpers, and a raincoat.

Emma cleared her throat and poked her head out of my bag, which I'd made sure to leave slightly unzipped. "First things first," she said, "we need to get to the nearest elevator and use its emergency exit. Come on," she urged, cracking an invisible horse whip at me to get me going. "Yee haw!"

"An emergency exit in an elevator?" I mused. "Are you sure this will be safe?"

"Who said anything about safe? Now like I said, YEE HAW!" She mime-whipped me with even more urgency. I started trudging in the direction of the elevator I remembered using when we first arrived at the hotel.

Pressing the call button, I was relieved when the elevator doors slid open to reveal an empty interior. Once the doors had closed behind me, Emma instructed me to hit the button labelled "G."

The elevator moved slowly, creaking with effort as it descended. I hopped from foot to foot, anxiety swimming in my head as I watched the numbers of the floors laboriously tick down. Emma, on the other hand, seemed perfectly content. I took some small comfort in that. At least one of us seemed sure we weren't doing anything dangerous. Even if she was the reason my head currently throbbed the way it did.

Once the unassuming 'G' to the left of the number '1' lit up on the overhead panel, Emma turned her attention to a square divot that sat in the centre of the wall panel beneath the array of buttons – the emergency exit, I presumed. Emma leapt from her place in my rucksack and scurried down my arm. Her nimble fingers wiggled into the crevasse around the panel's edge and dislodged it. Behind it was a tiny metal door.

It took a bit of wriggling on my part, but the emergency exit wasn't *too* hard to get through. The elevator shaft on the other side was dark and dingy, made entirely of concrete. At its base, only inches from the exterior of the cab, was an opening just large enough for me to crawl through. And wouldn't you know it, it did let out into a tunnel!

Emma handed me the flashlight from my bag and began feeding me directions. My beam lit up the dirt-covered corridor that seemed to wind on endlessly into the distance. Gnarled brown roots poked through the ceiling, and there was an echoing dripping sound from somewhere in the distance.

As we walked, Emma educated me about the history of the castle. It was ever so slightly condescending, but I suppose I appreciated having something to listen to in the pitch-black darkness.

It turns out that the tunnel was used in the 1700s to protect kings and queens in times of need. It led right underneath the town and onto a hilltop by the woods, which was only a mile away. The emergency exit we'd used was the only door that led to the tunnels.

Despite the anxiety building in my stomach, I felt quite daring. Here I was, a tween girl about to go off on an adventure to find a High Magical Council to make them restore my sister after I'd unintentionally got rid of her due to *their* improper mishandling of a dangerous wish. A few weeks ago, I would have laughed in someone's face and called them crazy if they told me that!

I crept down a flight of stairs after several turns in the winding tunnel. Whoever maintained this system of tunnels must have never heard of lightbulbs, because it was vantablack dark, despite my torch. I crawled through the inkiness, inching along the wall, sensing more than seeing the damply cold earthen ceiling arching above my head. I tried not to think about how far underground we were, or how much weight pressed down upon the top of the tunnel from above.

My footsteps echoed around me as I continued to feel my way along the pitted wall. Then, the snap of a twig cracked from somewhere behind us. Only, I couldn't remember stepping on any twigs. What *was* that noise?

Whatever it was, it was nowhere near as unnerving as what followed it. I could only describe it as…chittering, maybe? Like something small – scratch that, *several* somethings small – clawing and the ground behind us.

It's nothing, I told myself, *no one could possibly be following us.* But prickles of unease needled the skin between my shoulder blades, and my breath became slow and laboured as if I didn't have enough air. *You're being ridiculous, Vicky!* I scolded myself. *You're not claustrophobic!*

"Emma," I tentatively broke the silence of the tunnel. "I thought I heard some…*things* behind us. It's probably nothing, right Emma? Right?"

"You should run," her tiny voice urged me.

"Right, I figured nothing was down he – what?"

"Run!"

I finally processed what she said and broke into a sprint. My rucksack shook and bounced uncomfortably against my back. Muffled cries rose as Emma shrieked in alarm.

"Hold on tight!" I yelled, but I didn't slow down.

I ran and ran for what seemed like miles until my feet stumbled and I lurched to my knees, inhaling huge gulps of air that smelled like a fusion of damp moss and soil. I only began to relax in the slightest once I was sure I no longer heard the sound of our mysterious pursuers behind us.

"Let. Me. OUT!" Emma screamed from inside my rucksack, which had fallen to the dirt beside me. The entire pack shook in the light of the torch that lay against the tunnel wall.

"Oh no, Emma!" I cried, quickly unzipping the largest pouch.

It was a mess inside the bag. My phone lay at the top of the pile, having been thrown out of its little pocket. The Ziplock bag was closed, but the soap inside it was broken into quarters, sweating bubbles. My hydro flask was chipped, and underneath it were two skinny, furry legs. The cardenere lay squished between the two hydro flasks, her little hands in fists, punching the air.

"Oh, you poor thing," I began to coo. "Here, let me help you get ou…"

THWUMP

Several bits of my survival gear went hurling past me, narrowly missing my head as Emma burst free of the pile she'd been 'trapped' under. Goodness me, how could something so small be so strong?

My arms ached like they'd been detached from my shoulder sockets. "Long live the King," I groaned, keeling over sideways.

"Vicky!" Emma squealed. "Are you okay?"

"Well, you did just throw my boots at me," I groaned. "And not for nothing, you must weigh two stone! How much further is it?"

"I may be scrawny, but I'm three stones at least!" she huffed. "Anyways, buck up! If we keep on at the same pace, we'll be out by morning."

"By morning!?" I stared. "I'm not going to make it any further tonight," I said shamefully. I hated admitting any weakness, but my entire body ached.

"We can camp here tonight," Emma chirped. "Seems like they've lost our trail, so we've got nothing to worry about at the moment."

"Slow down, Emma," I panted. "Who're they?"

Emma barely looked up to acknowledge my question as she began picking up all the discarded bits of rations she'd sent flying all over the place. "Best you let me worry about it. There are plenty of creatures set to patrolling the outskirts of the Forest – could've been any one of them, I suppose."

She chattered on, but I didn't have the energy to pry more information out of her. I was too busy contending with a bleak despair that was seeping in through my pores with the cold, cutting me off from the rest of the world. I retrieved a jumper and my raincoat from my pack and pulled them on, then rolled onto my side and hugged my knees to my chest, shivering.

My head was resting in a crevice between something hard and something harder. I was dimly aware that Emma was bustling around on her little legs – making a camp, I assumed. At one point, I felt her cover me with the aluminium emergency blanket I'd packed.

I closed my eyes. I thought about all those nights when I was little when Mum told me stories. She'd sit cross-legged on the edge of the bed while our little collie, Cooper, curled up beside my pillow as I listened. Then I thought about how Dad had always greeted me with a warm hug and a cherry lollipop in hand when I came home after nursery school let out. Then, the memory of those magical Friday evenings when we would all curl up on the couch together, covered in blankets, and I could feel the weight of Mom's chin on my head and Dad's on top of hers and Ashley snuggled up next to me.

I wondered if Ashley was thinking about those moments, too, somewhere. I hoped she was. I hoped she believed that someone was coming to rescue her so she could make even more of those memories with me and our parents.

That thought hurt worse than my strained arm sockets and cuts and bruises. I closed my eyes, wanting to forget the terrible mess I'd made by wishing Ashley away, letting the cold envelop me and pull me down to a numb, deep sleep.

9

Sunlight, Sweet Sunlight

I woke up some time later. Emma was sleeping with her arms pinned to her sides and her head stuck out of the tissue box she'd turned over. It was warm now, with scant rays of sunlight drifting down from small holes in the tunnel ceiling and evaporating into the soil. The aluminium blanket crinkled like a pile of Autumn leaves as I pulled it off, withdrew my legs from under my jumper, and took my hood off my head, raking my fingers through impossibly tangled hair. A lovely, soft breeze from down the corridor grazed my skin.

Maybe we were closer to the end of these blasted tunnels than Emma had realised? I didn't want to spend a moment more than I had to down here.

Thankfully, she stirred not a moment later, languidly stretching her tiny arms as she yawned herself to full wakefulness. She stared open-mouthed at my hair for a moment, but wisely didn't say a word.

I handed her a packet of crisps from my rucksack and opened my own, nibbling feebly. Not that I had any appetite. My body ached from sleeping on the hard ground, and my heart was heavy and homesick.

Emma set her packet of crisps on her tissue box/sleeping bag and scurried about gathering twigs and sticks from along the corners of the tunnel. Once she had a fistful, she arranged them into a small pyramid and placed rocks around the whole thing.

"What's this," I asked, curious. "Some kind of ritual for finding the entrance to the Kingdom?"

"Are you daft?" She gazed up at me with what appeared to be genuine concern. "I'm making a fire. For tea." She pulled a lighter from what must be a hidden pocket in her…*hide?*...and before I could blink, she had a merry little blaze going.

I nearly choked on my crisps. "Tea!?" I cried. "Where on earth did you get tea?"

"I nicked some from the flight attendant's trolley during tea service," she answered, matter-of-factly. "And a teapot, too!"

She whipped out a gleaming silver teapot and service for two from her…*hidden kangaroo pouch?*

Obviously, the authors of The Tome of Hidden Creatures had done a rubbish job of describing cardeneres.

Emma handed me a cuppa. I took a tentative sip.

All the good cheer of a genuine English breakfast blend spread through my body, instantly warming me.

"Oh, Emma!" I whispered, tears of gratitude in my eyes. "Thank you!"

"Course!" she smiled happily.

"Is that… Is that something all Cardeneres can do?" I asked, unsure if I was being rude, referring to her enormous secret pockets.

"What, make tea?" Confusion wrinkled her nubbly brow. "Even trolls can make tea," she said, sounding mildly offended.

"No," I corrected hastily. "I meant the teapot and cups…"

"Oh, that!" Her grin was a mix of sheepish and proud. "Nah, that's my own *talent*, I guess you'd call it. My mum says I have sticky fingers. I've gotten a bruised bottom for it more than once," she said, ruefully.

"I…" I took a deep breath and tried again. "No, I meant, do all Cardeneres have giant pockets in their, erm…you know…bodies?"

"Don't you?" Emma asked, eyes wide and startled.

I slowly shook my head, sipping my tea. I felt a bit like Alice on her adventure to Wonderland. Things were becoming curiouser and curiouser by the minute, and we hadn't even reached the Kingdom yet.

When we were done with our breakfast of tea and crisps, Emma packed the service back inside her…*pockets*…jumped into the rucksack, and we were off.

Before long, we'd reached the opening of the cave, which led out to a patch of meadow.

Wildflowers sprung up from the earth, presenting their colourful petals with graceful movements. Wisps of grey and white flitted by across the vast, currently orangish purple, surprisingly clear sky. I guess the weather in Scotland could be pleasant on occasion. Who knew?

I watched for a moment, lost in my own little world, leaning against the smooth rock face that jutted out of the cliff's edge. Maybe the rest of this adventure wouldn't be so bad after all.

I let the wind ruffle my matted hair playfully, taunting the strands to climb higher towards the sunrise. The clouds, which were set alight in a blaze of oranges, blacks, and reds, tunnelled their way towards the horizon. An everlasting ball of light shimmered bright, painting the atmosphere beyond pink. I watched as the sunrise was slowly washed over by a baby-blue sky. Everything was peaceful and colourful, a patterned ombre that reached all of earth's corners.

There, with the sunlight beaming on my face, I knew I could do this! No matter how hard it was! I would get my sister back!

And, I had to acknowledge, it was all because of Emma. I'd have never made it through those dark twists and turns without my new friend. In fact, had I been on my own, I probably would have tried to sneak out the front entrance of the hotel and would have been caught by a janitor or something. I'd have been returned to my room promptly, and my parents would probably be installing the 27th padlock on my door as we speak. But I wasn't, and they weren't, all because I had a proper guide with me.

"Emma," I started, cautiously feeling my way toward the new experience of expressing gratitude, "now that we've made it through the tunnels, I wanted to say…erm…*thank you*. We're very close to the forest, and…"

…and she was off. By the King's grey hair, I don't think I'd ever seen a living being go from half-awake to zooming off into the distance so quickly. She'd jumped out of the rucksack and was almost three-quarters of the way out of the cave mouth and to the forest line before she stopped and called back to me, saving me the trouble of having to project my voice over that distance.

"Come ON, slowpoke!" She hopped from foot to foot for a moment before continuing on. "We're here, we're here!" Then she was off towards the woods again, only this time she was lumbering at a slow crawl, stopping frequently to glance back to see if I was catching up.

Great. She was clearly mocking me. Maybe this 'using-my-words' thing wasn't *always* the best approach, but I could worry about that later. For now, I had a brown, leathery hooligan to catch up to.

And, just like that, we made our way into the Black Wood of Rannoch, Emma careening ahead and me trying to keep pace. My only saving grace was her tendency to frequently stop as she gorged on brown speckled mushrooms that grew along the path. When her moustache was bespeckled with dirt and bits of fungus, she would stick her tongue out as far as it would go and roll her head to lick off the remains on her upper lip before once again tumbling further on.

At one point she offered a particularly large specimen to me, her mouth full of crumbs. The bulbous mushroom was blue with yellow and orange spots and little bits of smaller fungi around the edges. I eyed her with distaste as she egged me on with huge, emotional cat eyes.

On the one hand, the mushroom looked absolutely disgusting. On the other hand, I was hungry, and she probably wouldn't be offering it to me if it weren't safe to eat, right?

Wrong.

I took the tiniest nibble and was immediately assaulted with an absolutely *abhorrent* taste and texture. I spent the rest of our foray into the forest clutching at my stomach. It felt like a battalion of knights was duking it out in my intestines.

Our surroundings were doing very little to help my mounting distress. We weren't too far in, and I certainly hadn't seen any signs of the otherworldly, but the forest was swallowing us whole.

Enormous, ancient trees loomed over us at every turn, all gnarled and preening like they *knew* something we didn't. Many trunks were dead and black, evidence of a recent fire. Leaves clung to the dry branches, brown and crisp.

Who knows how many secrets – how many animals and how many lives – had passed through this wood? Moss covered everything like huge cushions of spongy green carpet as we neared a river edge. The air smelt like ash and rotten fish; mud constantly squelched under my shoes.

"Is the Black Wood usually this dank and mouldy…?" I began to ask, but Emma cut me off, scrambling up my body like I was a jungle gym and jumping onto my shoulder, from where she hurled directions at me.

"Turn right at that gnarly Sycamore tree and then a left at Big Ed," Emma called out, as if I knew all the trees here by name. "No, not that one, you mushroom head, the other one. Not that one either! That one right in front of ya!" she shouted.

Mushroom head? Maybe it was a term of endearment? She certainly seemed to enjoy eating them enough.

Eventually, we reached a particularly muddy river. It rippled with murky brown water and large twigs.

Fantastic, I thought. I'm going to spoil my first set of clothes before noontime.

Emma had, of course, already jumped off my shoulder to the riverbank. She'd sunk up to her waist in muck, which wasn't saying much, considering she only comes up to my knee.

From the corner of my eye, I spied a set of very small footprints in the mud. I was useless at identifying tracks – aside from those left by stray cats, maybe – so I had no idea what could have left those tiny prints. But they looked fresh.

Just then, a flash of light drew my attention to the opposite bank of the river. I stared. While our side of the riverbank was brown and murky and stank like garbage, the other was crystal clear and teeming with fish of all kinds and colours. The trees were different, too. Not scorched to a crisp and gnarled like the ones we'd just tramped through. On the opposite bank, their limbs were slender and green.

It was as if the forest was divided.

Could this be the boundary between realms? Could the other side of the river mark the entrance to the Kingdom of Creatures?

"Emma," I called, "why on earth are we mucking through this disgusting slop when we could find a crossing to the other side and walk on dry ground?"

"You don't like the mud?" Emma's voice was bewildered.

I stopped mid-step. Was she laughing at me? Turning to give her my full attention, I gaped in surprise. She'd completely covered herself in foul-smelling sludge!

"Emma," I cried. "You've soiled your fur!"

"And it's about time," she sighed, happily. "You humans could do with more mud."

Shaking my head, I hopped about, struggling to remove my shoes and socks. I was *not* going to get wet socks just to save my sister! Next, I rolled up my pant legs and waded into the water…

…and slipped almost immediately. The current was *very* aggressive, pulling me underway and down the river. I fought to regain my balance all while being pummelled by branches and who knows what else. I only barely managed to regain my footing before being completely swept away.

Meanwhile, Emma waded gracefully down into the water. Dodging the large sticks with ease, she made it to the other side without stumbling once.

I took much, much longer to stagger to the other bank, gasping for breath the whole time. The force from the murky side compared to this side was so strong that when it ceased, my forward momentum sent me pitching over onto my face in the clear water.

The gentle current tumbled merrily over me. The water was the perfect temperature. I savoured the warmth for a moment as I opened my eyes, which had been clenched shut until that moment.

My hair galloped around me in all directions as little fish wove in between the fingers of my splayed hands. Their green scales shimmered in the wavering sunlight; their fins splattered with fuchsia pink.

Emma stood a few meters away in the forest. She smiled at me, hands on her hips as I resurfaced.

I paddled over to her, walking up onto the shore. The grass glistened with water, cushioning my bare feet as I stepped toward her through an opening in the trees. My shoes and socks, of course, had been lost when I'd fallen in the water.

My breath caught in my chest at the sheer beauty of my surroundings. All through the forest, fireflies flitted between thick branches; the bark of the slender trees was so smooth, I thought somebody must have painted it on. Wildflowers bloomed on every possible surface with petals the texture of silk on large green stalks, their fragrance perfuming the light breeze.

"This is beautiful, isn't it Emma?" I asked, almost ready to caper amongst the falling leaves (which was *very* uncharacteristic of me, let me assure you).

Emma didn't answer. She'd taken off at a gallop on all fours, something that gave me pause, since I'd only ever seen her walking on her hind legs like all civilised creatures. A thought struck me: could I run on all fours like that? Perhaps I ought to try? She made it look so easy. bent over double, my hands in front, and mimicked her gait.

Definitely not as easy as it looked! I giggled to myself, imagining what Ashley would say if she could see me behaving in this absurd manner, lost my footing – er, *handing* – and tumbled face first into the grass. I came up spluttering and chortling at my own stupidity, my hair full of twigs and leaves, scanning the terrain for Emma.

She was nowhere in sight.

"Emma!" I shouted. "Wait! You can't just leave me! I don't know where I'm going!"

Almost instantly I was flat on my back again as the prickly bowling ball that is Emma slammed into my stomach, pinning me to the earth.

"Gerr off!" I gasped, "you weigh ten tons!"

But she didn't get off. "Shhh!" she hissed, pressing her paws to my lips. "Keep your voice down! Haven't you ever been through an Enchanted Forest?? You'll wake them!"

"Wake who?" I mumbled around her fingers, trying to push her off as she was sitting directly atop my bladder, and I certainly wasn't about to pee my pants if I could help it.

Then I froze.

What was that? I pricked my ears, listening hard. Faint sounds – a rumble from the ground, a whisper on the breeze – rose around us. But where was it coming from? We both sat up. I turned and turned like a human Ferris wheel, trying to locate the source of the sound.

"Now you've done it," Emma sighed.

The sound grew louder and louder, a kind of chittering mixed with occasional thumps. My wet skin prickled as illustration after illustration from The Tome flashed one after the other in my mind and certain dread rose in my chest. Some kind of creature was about to descend on us.

A throng of squirrels appeared out of nowhere.

All at once, the previously still trees shook and rattled, as hundreds of furry legs clambered across their branches.

Wait, squirrels? We'd stumbled into a magical forest where faeries supposedly lived, and the first creatures we encountered were *squirrels?*

Aunt Marge would have fainted with joy.

They stood up on their hind legs with their paws raised and their little pink noses twitching in unison. Each one wore a tiny breastplate made from pristine steel and a beret not unlike what a girl scout might wear. They had us completely surrounded. One of them started to click, and the rest of them began stamping on the tree branches where they stood and clapped their paws together, making a drumming sound.

I didn't know squirrels could clap, and it struck me as an ominous skill for them to have. When the noise reached maximum level, they suddenly froze, peering down at us from the tree's smooth, slender branches.

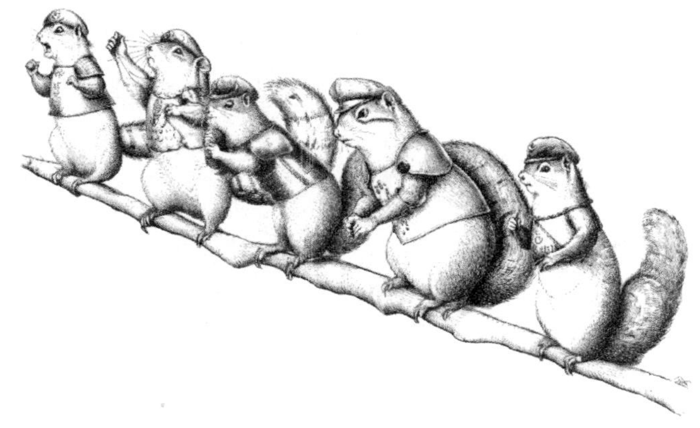

The biggest squirrel, dressed in a smart uniform with a series of decorative gold buttons and boasting an acorn hat, jumped from its perch onto the leaf-carpeted floor.

"Stay still and let me do the talking." Emma spoke under her breath, directing the words at me from the corner of her mouth without turning her head. She kept her eyes locked on the leader, who put its snout to the ground and buried its face into the leaves. It then raised its head, a leaf now balanced on its nose, and sniffed the air (partially sucking the leaf into its nostril), before wrinkling its nose and sneezing.

"God bless you!" I said, out of habit.

"Shhh!" Emma hissed. "What part of 'let me do the talking' didn't you understand?"

"*Who* are these people…er…I mean squirrels? What do they want with us?"

"They're Officers of the High Court," Emma whimpered, clearly terrified.

"The High Court?" I asked, a jolt of hopefulness racing through my veins. "Do they have any connection to the High Magical Coun…" My words tapered off to a squeak as the leader put its nose to the ground again, walked over to my feet, sniffed them, and then padded right up my leg with its pointy little claws, springing to my shoulder and sniffing at my ear.

"Pee-ewwww!" It muttered, pinching its nose.

"Excuse me," I sputtered, "how rude! I don't always smell like this, I'll have you know. I lost my footing and slipped in the riv…"

"Quiet!" it yelled and sprang back down to the ground. It raised a forepaw into the air and squealed. The other squirrels all shifted their weight, their tails frolicking about wildly in the air.

Then, they pounced.

Their paws stretched out in front of them, their steely eyes fixed on us like lasers. All at once, the small army of furry animals slammed into me. It was like being singled out in a game of dodgeball, except if all the balls were squirrels for some reason. And angry.

Emma scrambled up one of my pant legs, clutching onto my knee like it was the only thing that stood between her and oblivion. She shuddered. The squirrels' razor-like claws clung to my clothes, clawing at the fabric, ripping it to shreds.

I let loose a long, blood-curdling scream as the squirrels toppled me onto the ground and pried Emma out from my pants. I heard her thrashing, trying to get away. More squirrels pinned me down. My head spun dizzily.

Out of the corner of my eye, I saw a needle and an IV tube containing a sickly, acid-yellow goo.

As my mind raced, overwhelmed by the dozens of squirrel toes padding across my body, I managed a single, strained thought: *This makes zero sense – where on Earth would a bunch of squirrels get medical equipment from? Am I hallucinating?*

A sharp prick lanced the inside crease of my elbow, and my thoughts became sluggish. Heavy drowsiness pressed down against my limbs, tugging at my eyelids.

Confusion filled my brain like a wad of cotton balls.

Then, darkness.

The Eyes on the Wall

I was groggy. And disoriented. Some impossibly annoying sensation was pulling me pre-emptively from a deep sleep.

Thin, pointy spikes pushed through the fabric of my shirt, pricking my back. Ugh, I thought. Why did Mum and Dad buy me such a spikey mattress? Ashley's mattress isn't spikey. It isn't fair!

I wiggled around a bit, trying to find a more comfortable position, but no matter which way I turned, the pain of a thousand tiny needles punctured my skin. So much for having a lie down. Groaning, I tried to roll over, but found that my body wouldn't obey.

Then, it all came back in a rush. My captors – *had they really been squirrels?* – must have put something immobilising in the I.V.

Dizzy, I blinked to open my eyes, but crusty sleep-dust stuck to my lashes, making it impossible to separate my top and bottom lids. I couldn't see *anything*. When I tried to lift my hands to rub my eyes, they wouldn't budge either.

"Emma?" I whispered. The last thing I remembered with any clarity was the squirrels prying her grip from around my knee. They must have dosed her, too.

"Emma!" I hissed this time. I needed her to help me come up with a plan to escape. After all, I had to assume that we were in her world at this point, as squirrels don't attack in squads in Britain. She would know more about this place than I did, which was nothing at all.

No answer.

Once again, I tried to move my arms. Why did my hands feel so heavy, almost like they were being held down? Why couldn't I turn over? I fought to open my eyes, straining with all my might. Finally, the sticky crust cementing my lashes shut gave way. My eyes sprang open.

I was in a small, square room. Alone.

"Oh no," I moaned softly. "What have they done with Emma?"

Faded pink and yellow floral wallpaper hung on the walls. I craned my neck to the side to see what I was laying on that was causing me such pain.

Grass? The entire floor was covered in grass: long, wild, and overflowing with neon-yellow mushrooms speckled with purple dots and wildflowers all the colours of the rainbow.

Emma would love it here, I thought. When I get free, I'll pick some of these mushrooms for her!

My body had been arranged in a perfect starfish-shape and shackled down. From the corner of my eye, I could see that my head was resting on a pillow woven from long flower stems, twined with blossoms.

Colossal chains linked to the cuffs around my wrists and ankles snaked across the grassy ground, one each to the four corners of the room. I was all chained up like a younger, more stylish, more modern Gulliver.

But my captors couldn't fool me into relaxing my guard, if that's what they were trying to do by putting me in a room with floral wallpaper and a fancy, mushroom-strewn lawn for a floor. As the brilliant, astute, and observant girl I knew I was, I was able to look past the decor and recognise the chains for what they were: a sinister portent of doom. No matter the pleasantness of my pillow, there was nothing comforting about being chained up.

"Someone had better explain what's going on – and *why* – pretty darn quick, or I am going to become *fully* put out!" I yelled. "I know you're officers of some High Court or other, but I haven't done anything wrong, and I demand to be freed immediately!"

BLINK

Hold on, let me explain.

You're probably wondering why I wrote *BLINK* like that, as if it were a sound I heard in that moment. *'Silly British girl,'* you might even be telling yourself, *'blinks don't make noises. Now get back to telling us the story about Hidden Creatures and squirrel law enforcement.'*

Well, I don't know what else to tell you. The sticky *thwapping* sound I'd just heard behind me could be nothing other than a rather pronounced *BLINK.*

I craned my neck to stare at the wall behind me…and blanched. The pink and yellow papering was covered in hundreds – no, *thousands* – of clocks.

And each of the clocks had *eyes.*

Their irises were every colour of the rainbow, some of which were *very out of place.* One eye was droopy and sleepy, while another blazed hot pink, and a third darted everywhere at once.

A scream erupted from my throat, shrill enough to curdle milk, and kept straight on erupting. My shrieks ricocheted around the room, bouncing off the walls, becoming louder and louder. I screamed, and screamed, and screamed.

No one came into the room.

I was all alone.

All alone except for the eyes. And my screams.

After what seemed like hours, my vocal chords gave up, quitting out of sheer exhaustion..

The eyes goggled at me – well, some of them, at least. Some in pairs, others quite singular. Their movements seemed to be random; sometimes they'd roll around so incessantly I thought they were trying to make themselves – or me – dizzy. Other times they would stare at a spot on the floor or ceiling for minutes on end.

But always, there was *blinking.*

Then, I noticed that even though the eyes didn't have mouths, I could hear them…*whispering?*…to each other.

Maybe I wasn't as alone as I'd thought.

Straining, I tried with all my might to make out what those ominous voices were saying, but the thudding of my heartbeat in my ears drowned out anything distinct.

Helpless, I could only lie there and listen to my own words race around and around my mind: *Who are these creatures, and what do they want with me?*

Suddenly, the door in the corner started to shake, the knob throttling from side to side. A grunt of annoyance came from behind the door, along with, oddly enough, the sourceless sound of a brass gong. It tickled my memory slightly, almost like the windchimes I'd heard occasionally oh so long ago, only much dryer sounding, as if whatever was making the sound was only doing so to check it off of a to-do list.

Too soon, a click of the knob told me the lock had opened. Whatever was on the other side of the clock-wall was coming through.

A small, squat, familiar looking creature stomped into view and stood over me, glaring down. There was no mistaking that he was a lawfur; he had the same purple, fuzzy fur and rounded shape as the one I'd seen in the hospital so many years ago. But, beyond that, the similarities ended. This one was wearing a bow tie and a suit that fit somewhat poorly over his pot belly. His ears were more pointed, and one sported a headset, the sort you might see on someone working in retail.

Tufts of blonde hair sprouted from the creature's upper lip, spreading out from his face into a sort of stretched-out, snot-brake moustache. It was the kind of caricature moustache villains from old-timey melodramas always wore.

"What have you done with my friend, the cardenere?" I screamed at him – somewhat hoarsely, given all the *previous* screaming I'd done. "I need her! Where is she? I must see her!" I thrashed and kicked, much to the lawfur's concern.

"Typical delinquent behaviour," the lawfur grimaced, "barging into somewhere you don't belong and making demands right off the bat!" He walked over to me and stared down at my immobilised form. "Why are you here, human? How did you stumble your way into a place no mortals should know about, let alone be able to find? And in the company of a suspected conspirator?"

I gritted my teeth. "I wouldn't know about this stupid place to begin with if one of you lawfurs hadn't interfered with my life and granted me a wish," I spat back at him. "Which, by the way, clearly broke some sort of terms and conditions or something, because the wish I actually got was certainly *not* one I intended to make!"

For a moment, the lawfur just kept staring down at me. Then…did he just roll his eyes at me?

"*Harumph.* Another one of your types, I see," he chortled. I began to wonder if forcing me to deal with this terribly rude creature was intended as some sort of torture. Were creatures from the Kingdom bound by the Geneva conventions? I'd have to check – if I ever got out of here.

"Well," the insufferable lawfur continued, "the Council will indeed hear from you. But we have other business to attend to first."

Really? Just like that?

I tried to restrain myself from showing any signs of outward joy, as I didn't want to give this high-and-mighty lawfur the satisfaction. But hope surged in me. This morning, I didn't even know if or when I'd ever find the way into the Kingdom, let alone how to procure an audience with the High Magical Council. And here I was, being told I'd get to see them after all!

"Whatever the council decides though," the lawfur picked right back up, "you'll need to be seen by a professional first. I mean, just look at you! Humans are rarely presentable, but you're *particularly* unseemly."

A professional? A professional *what?*

Also, *I* was unseemly, was I? I tried to maintain my calm demeanour, but this time, I guess it was too much to keep a lid on.

"Now you listen here, you mattress-salesperson-looking twit," I began. "I'm currently *unseemly* because I was just attacked by a group of sentient squirrels in the forest after sleeping all night in a subterranean tunnel and falling into a muddy river! Do you think I roll around in the muck and ruin my own clothing for fun? I know that maybe you uncivilised creatures enjoy that sort of thing, but we humans are *far* more sensible. Also, how on earth did a group of woodland creatures get their grimy little hands on an I.V.? Do faeries not have health standards? Have you not invented the concept of sterilisation? I don't know what's going on, but some tiny faerie doctor somewhere needs to lose their licence. And another thing…"

But there was no other thing. The squat creature turned on his heel in the middle of my tirade, stomping back out of the room and shouting something unintelligible at someone I couldn't see.

Immediately, all the eyes in the clocks snapped shut. Silence stretched out for an eternity, during which I contemplated gnawing my arms and legs off in order to escape. But before I'd so much as broken the skin, the lawfur returned.

He brandished a long, wooden branch at me that had a sort of rod stuck onto the end of it. With a click of metal, the shackles around my ankles and wrists snapped open.

Oh. Well. Score one for Angry Vicky, I guess?

I sat up and hugged my legs to my chest. My still river-damp clothes clung uncomfortably to my skin, musty and itchy. Perhaps I'd slightly overestimated the length of time I'd been unconscious and chained, since my clothes hadn't even dried yet. Maybe it hadn't been an actual eternity, even if it felt like aeons had most *definitely* passed.

Rubbing my sore wrists, I watched through narrowed eyes as the creature stalked by me to the far eye-wall. He tugged at one of the eyelids, and it swung open. The eye inside rocked to and fro from the motion, blinking rapidly but staying open. Next, the lawfur placed his palm right on the fleshy, goopy eyeball with a firm, wet sounding slap. I winced as if someone had just slapped *my* eye.

The eye didn't seem to mind, though. Nor did it apparently care when the lawfur pushed his hand across its surface like he was trying to spin a globe. And spin it did, completely turning around to reveal a backside that looked impossibly metallic compared to the front. The lawfur punched some numbers into a newly revealed keypad, taking care to block his input from my view with his fuzzball of a body, then stepped away as a series of whirs and clicks flowed out of the wall where he'd been standing.

The metallic panel clinked and clanked momentarily before it slid open like a hatch. Behind it was a spherical compartment not unlike an iron hamster ball and, troublingly, a plain metal chair. The fuzzball stared at me expectantly and motioned at it.

"Excuse me, but I am *not* getting into an *eyeball*, of all things." I crossed my arms from my seated position.

He snorted. "You very much are. Unless, that is, you *don't* want to talk to the High Magical Council about the wish you used."

He had me there. Plus, though I had stopped complaining about it a while ago, the pointy grass was prickling my bottom.

So, without saying a word to acknowledge the lawfur's request, I promptly sprung to my feet and began nervously walking towards the now-open eye-capsule. I had to bend down to fit myself in, but not too much.

"See you underground," the lawfur chirped before unceremoniously slamming the hatch shut behind me.

Underground?

I suddenly felt it might be wise to be sitting for whatever happened next. I rushed over to the chair and plopped into it.

"What? Where was this thing going to take *MEEEEEEEEEEE...*"

Turned Upside down by Magic

"...EEEEEEEEEEE!!!"

My heart went in my throat and my organs were rearranged as the strange compartment dropped me and the chair through a brightly coloured tunnel. It was like rushing through a timelapse of bright purple, dark blue, and seafoam white. Deafening, whipping wind lapped around outside as I hurled at unimaginable speeds past who-knows-what. My stomach clenched and dropped and rolled and then grabbed onto my bladder and squeezed like I was on a rollercoaster.

Before I could assess what was happening, the compartment braked suddenly, slowing to a fraction of the speed it had been travelling before. I launched out of my chair and into the glass panel in front of me. My cheeks squished up against the glass like a toddler trying to get a view of an orangutan at a zoo. But I didn't care. Like a toddler at a zoo, I was *completely* fascinated by what I saw.

Sprawled out before me inside an enormous, underground cavern was a bustling townscape the likes of which I'd never seen. The compartment continued forward, hundreds of feet from the ground, but what I could see was so fantastical, I began to wonder if I was still dreaming after being put to sleep by the squirrels.

Buildings large and small either jutted into the air or clung to the ground as if they were trying to sink into it. Some were built from mildly odd metals painted in eye-dazzling colours, while others looked to be made of mushroom or tree bark. Many of the structures boasted open roofs with gardens, work spaces, and open-air bedrooms and living spaces. Everything was illuminated by light spilling out of an enormous hole in the roof of the cavern. Looking directly at it almost hurt as much as looking at the Sun.

I couldn't make out any individuals clearly, but countless tiny specks flowed through the Kingdom along its twisty-turny streets and in the air.

My compartment suddenly plunged downward, and I hung above my seat for a second of weightlessness. The bizarre town below me raced up at me until I was seconds away from smashing into the ground. At the last moment, the compartment swooped up and levelled out. I breathed a shaky sigh of relief.

Now I was flitting just above the rooftops. A few dozen feet below me, countless magical creatures traipsed along the streets. A pair of pink and purple panthers held leashes in their mouths that lead to the neck of a huge, barely clothed troll, who was busy sniffing a dinner-plate sized flower in front of a toadstool-shaped house. A gaggle of taller, pointy-eared individuals cackled and slapped their thighs about who-knew-what. A colourful creature barely a foot tall floated by on a levitating armchair, studiously surveying all it passed.

And those were just the land-bound faeries. Countless other creatures whizzed past me on either side, carried by vibrant wings of every colour. One particularly ornery fellow almost got squashed on my 'windshield' and was sent bouncing and bobbing into the sky off to the side, waving his feathered fist at me and spewing what I presumed to be curses. He didn't seem *too* perturbed at having nearly been splattered on a *flying eyeball*, so I guess it wasn't that uncommon of an occurrence down here. In fact, looking past him, I saw a handful of orb-shaped objects zipping around in the air all about the town.

Dominating the underground-city-skyline a few miles away was a gargantuan oak tree. It nearly scraped against the roof of the dome, and its trunk was wide enough to fit an entire city-block in its interior. Wide, twisting branches cast shadows on the section of town beneath it. The area looked to be the fanciest, perhaps their equivalent of a town hall.

In fact, everything looked relatively fancy. The only part that looked out of place was a patch of desaturated grass dotted with stones. It reminded me of a cemetery, but it was too far off to tell for sure. A grey obelisk towered ominously above the other stones in the centre. If this was a burial ground, I wondered who was buried there? The thought of such a morbid place in an otherwise fantastical city made me shiver for some reason.

My head spun. Everything playing out in front of me was almost too much to take in. I know I'd already made a magical wish, travelled to Scotland of all places, run away from my parents (without leaving a note!), befriended a non-magical creature, and been captured by talking squirrels, but *this* was different. *This* was an entire *city* the size of Paris nestled who knows how far underground beneath the Black Wood of Rannoch. In the past handful of seconds, I'd seen more things that most rational people would tell me don't exist than I had fingers to count. If this wasn't the final straw that pushed me over the edge of sanity, I couldn't imagine what would.

Finally, my ride began to slow and dip closer to the ground. Glancing around and below myself, I ascertained that we must be in an urban district of some sort; these buildings were taller and more packed together, dotted with long wooden structures that resembled warehouses.

I'd just started to think about how it reminded me of North London when I heard a *plop*.

Before I had time to properly judge how wet and slimy that sound had struck my ears, the floor of my compartment dropped from under me. I plummeted into the open air below.

Good Heavens. What now?

I'm sure I was screaming at that point, but I wasn't paying enough attention to myself to care. My mind was simply waiting for the inevitable impact. I had no idea what kind of landing it would be, but logically, I couldn't stay airborne forever.

SPLASH!

Water, wet and cold, enveloped me, a frigid chill invading my ears and nose as I plunged beneath the surface. I scrambled and kicked, flailing around for a foothold until my upper thigh brushed against something hard. Only then did I stop thrashing so I could feel around with my foot before forcing myself to open my eyes.

I was submerged in thick, colourful liquid, my cheeks bulging with my last gulp of oxygen. With nothing left to lose, I reoriented myself and launched upward. Thankfully, my head broke the surface of the water before my breath ran out.

Blinking my bloodshot eyes, I surveyed my surroundings.

The water lapping around me was part of a massive, marble fountain in the centre of what seemed to be a village square. The fountain rose meters high, tier after tier of crumbling stone carved with life-sized gargoyles. Each one held a marble bowl from which beautiful, glowing blue water overflowed, shot through with streams of dazzling colour.

The gargantuan dome of dirt and rock that encapsulated the kingdom rose above the city a few kilometres away in each direction. Craning my neck, I followed it as it curved up into that bright hole I'd noticed earlier.

Then, turning to the rest of the square, I also saw that I wasn't alone.

A gaggle of houses surrounded the square, each looking like it had come from a different city – maybe even a different culture or time altogether. The first one I spied looked like a somewhat miniaturised castle straight from above-ground Scotland, complete with its very own moat. Something scaley floated beneath the surface of the dank, green water, but it submerged as soon as I focused my eyes on it. Its neighbouring house looked more like something out of the seventies, all glass windows and shining disco-balls glimmering from within. I could just barely hear the *thump-thump*ing of a bass beat accompanied by what could only be yowling cats floating out onto the street.

In the square itself, a shoddily constructed wooden platform occupied the space opposite me, facing me in a semicircle large enough to fit at least twenty small creatures. At the moment, though, it was only half occupied by several human-girl-sized individuals, all dressed in red robes and a variety of ridiculous hats. They all also held small, open books in their hands, and my brain quickly fit the pieces together: they struck the perfect image of a bewilderingly costumed choir! Not an actively performing one, of course, for they were all occupied at the moment.

Occupied with staring at me, mouths wide with shock.

"So terribly sorry," I said politely. "Do carry on. I'm sure that whatever you were singing was perfectly-"

"AHHHHHHHHHH!"

Terrified screams filled the square as the choir faeries scattered. Books flew, robed figures tripped, and even a few horrified shrieks harmonised despite the confusion.

"-lovely…" My sentence trailed off as the last of the frightened singers ducked into a nearby alley or random store front.

"Can't rightly blame them, can you?" The familiar, annoyed voice from the clock-eye room floated down from above, preceded shortly by that same *gong* sound from earlier. "You're likely the first human any of them have ever seen." Gazing up, I watched another eyeball-sphere as it descended. The lawfur's voice was being projected out over some sort of speaker system.

A hatch on the bottom hung open to release its passenger. Except the lawfur wasn't falling. *He* was obviously too good for that. Instead, he kicked his legs as if walking down an invisible set of stairs. His fuzzy, melon-shaped form floated down to me as he straightened his ill-fitting suit.

He touched down after a moment and began assessing me in my soaked, sorry state. "Not to mention a human who can't follow proper disembarking procedures concerning transport in a Securi-Car." He sniffed. I stared back defiantly.

"Do you see wings on my back?" I asked, loading up generously on sarcasm.

"Do you see any on mine?"

"Maybe if you'd told me 'proper disembarking procedure'…" I began.

"Maybe you'd have heard me if you'd stopped screaming long enough," he retorted.

Fair. I wrung some water out of my sweatpants and jumper and waited patiently for him to explain what was going on, taking care not to scream.

The lawfur pulled out a pocket-watch, gave it a glance, and snapped it shut. "Come along," he said. "We're running late for your appointment."

"What appointment?" I demanded. My shoes squelched as I stepped out from the pond. Exasperation mounted in my chest. "Where even are we?"

"Oh yes." He'd stalked off towards a nearby building but stopped at my words to mockingly sweep his arms around himself. "Welcome to the Magical Community of the Kingdom of Hidden Creatures. So sorry we don't have time for a tour."

What a warm welcome.

12

Time for a Makeover

The lawfur stood in front of a large, peach-coloured brick building. The archway of the door was curled into lettering at the top, and it was adorned with splotches of bright red and mint green. It read, "Miss Pettigrew's Makeovers for the Ugly."

The door was periwinkle and featured a large gold knocker in the shape of two lion-headed monkeys chasing each other. But I didn't pay too much attention to that. Instead, my eyes were drawn to a woman who was standing at the door, hands crossed at her waist, and a half-smile-half-scowl on her face. She was almost up to my shoulder and sported a head of scarlet hair.

She was a stern-looking creature, with light, lilac skin and a beauty mark drawn on her left cheek. Her eyebrows arched exquisitely up into a steep slope at the end, and her false eyelashes glittered like diamonds. An orange, satin, form-fitting dress clung to her angular body from her calves all the way up to her chin, fastened with one long row of turtle-clasps. Lime green patent leather military boots with three-inch thick rubber soles completed her outfit.

Everything about her was *extra.*

I quickly presumed she was a pixie because she was a perfect match for the description I'd read in the book:

The Pixie

"The pixie is a flighty, mercurial creature more prone to whimsy and fanciful craft than all other creatures in the Kingdom (and, this author notes, that's quite the bar to clear). Standing anywhere from two to four feet tall, the pixie labours most days away pursuing their most recent obsession, be it a great architectural work or a simple Springtime outfit. Pixie skin comes in all colours of the rainbow. Once upon a time, a pixie's skin colour had a tendency to shift colours when they felt strong emotion. Unfortunately for everyone, they learned to control their chameleon-like qualities and now use them primarily to mess with other creatures."

There was more, of course, but I hadn't memorised it all. Reflexively, I reached to my shoulder for my rucksack so I could confirm my presumption with The Tome. My fingers grasped at air.

Oh. No. MY RUCKSACK WAS GONE.

"What have you done with it?" I cried. And before anyone could answer I shouted: "I demand it back AT ONCE!"

"Do calm down, little human," the red-headed pixie spoke. Her tone was posh and no-nonsense, and her words arched up slightly at the ends, like her eyebrows. "Let's not make a scene."

Had this pixie just told me to calm down!? 'Let's not make a scene'?!

I was quite certain she had never seen the kind of 'scene' I was about to make.

"HELP!" I hollered at the tops of my lungs. "HELP! I'VE BEEN ROBBED! STOP, THIEF! THEY'VE TAKEN MY PACK!! THEY'VE KIDNAPPED MY FRIEND! THEY'VE DRUGGED ME AND TAKEN ME AGAINST MY WILL! HELP! I'M BEING TRAFFICKED!

The pixie woman sniffed once, turned around elegantly, and glided back inside her shop. The lawfur rolled his eyes at me and followed her, slamming the door shut in my face.

On the street, passers-by – including the mushroom shaped ones - had begun picking mushrooms from where they grew in abundance off the ground and stuffing them in their ears.

That's nice, isn't it? There was a helpless child on the street in a foreign town screaming her head off, and everyone was just ignoring her!

Ugh. I did the only thing I could under the circumstances: I went up to the door under the "Miss Pettigrew's Makeovers for the Ugly" sign and pounded on it.

Which is when I saw the smaller sign taped to the door that read, "The uglier you are, the louder you knock."

Terrific.

A spattering of snickers and snorts rose from the other side of the door, but only the barest hint of amusement played on the pixie's lips when she opened up.

"Yes?" she asked, as if she'd never seen me before in her life.

Two could play at that game. "My name is Victoria McKay. I'm here for my appointment."

She consulted the clipboard in her hand and made a tick with a…glow worm?...she held in the other hand. "Come along quickly, or you'll be late," she chirped, "and we have our work cut out for us to find a contour that matches those…*interesting*…cheek bones of yours. Good heavens, she's as pale as a ghost and as tall as a giant. Gerttous, what have you brought me?"

"It's just *'Gertt'* Madam."

"Well, don't dawdle either, Just Gertt." Her voice was stern. "We have miracles to perform and very little time."

Miracles? And was this pixie woman just going to ignore my demand for my missing items? She was very like a headmistress I'd had in the first form, and I briefly considered running, but decided against it rather quickly. I had no idea where in this strange city I was and didn't have anywhere to run to. Hopefully my belongings would pop up at some point. I took a nervous step forward. I certainly disagreed with the 'for the ugly' part of the sign. but as to the rest of it, how bad could a makeover be?

Right?

The pixie woman ushered me up the stairs and into a hallway, keeping one brightly polished fingernail pressed against my back.

The hallway was *colossal.* The floor was composed of countless gnarled, intertwining twigs and branches laden with leaves. The cement walls were intermittently plastered with green and golden piped-fabric squares, each one proudly displaying the same image: a red fox slinking across a paved path smeared with autumn foliage with a single green leaf hung in the air above its head. I paused in front of one, trying to figure out what was happening in the scene. Was that a bandage wrapped around the fox's left foreleg?

"Enough gawking, Tori," the pixie said. "Haven't you ever seen a family crest before? The 'Red Fox Limping Betwixt Indeterminate Seasons' is known throughout the land as a symbol of my family's loyalty to the Magical Community. Now do give over dragging your feet."

She waltzed off through the forested corridors, dragging me along by the arm as I tried to determine how I felt about being called 'Tori.'

I decided to try a tactic I usually reserved for particularly hard cases when dealing with adults: obscene politeness.

"Excuse me, Madam," I began. "I'm ever so delighted to be here. What a lovely…erm…woodsy hallway you have here. It must be the talk of the Kingdom! Pray, what *precisely* is my appointment for today?"

"Oh, do be quiet, Tori," the pixie said.

"It's *Victoria,"* I said, unable to keep the sullenness from my voice. "Vicky for short."

"She's a Tori if I've ever seen one," Gertt the lawfur said, practically jogging to keep up.

"Which you haven't," the pixie said. "Now be quiet, both of you."

I stuck my tongue out at her back.

At the end of the hall, we came to a stairwell that, perplexingly, lacked any stairs. Where the steps ought to have been, a collection of plush pillows floated in the air. The pixie woman seemed angry at this.

"*Abner*!" she yelled.

A timid, green face flushed with red peered around a corner on the floor below. "Ma'am?" Abner asked, meekly.

"WHAT DID YOU DO?" she demanded. "Where has the carpet gone? Can't you see I have guests?"

Abner – a youngish looking creature I couldn't readily identify – stepped out from behind the pillar. He wore a red, white, and blue baseball cap, like you'd see in cartoons with a pinwheel on top. Holes had been cut out to fit his abnormally large ears, which poked through and ended in sharp points. His pink and yellow cropped t-shirt had a few rips in it, and his skirt – or kilt, maybe? – billowed around his ankles, covered in 3-D pink and green polka dots stitched across the thighs.

My eyeballs burned from overstimulation. Good gracious! I certainly hoped Abner wasn't an example of a makeover!

"I'm sorry, Ms. Pettigrew," the hooligan-looking pixie whispered. "I was just practising my magic for the exams."

"Put it back, now!" Ms. Pettigrew ordered.

Abner waved a thin, silver wand and yelled gibberish in the direction of the floating cushions.

Suddenly, there was a *pop!* And the staircase was a set of stairs again. The cushions drifted to rest on top of the chandelier; one teetering off the edge.

"Aybek, get over here *now*!" Ms. Pettigrew demanded as she descended the stairs to the bottom with Gertt and I following after her.

Another creature – this one with lumpy green skin, a black sweatshirt, and baggy jeans that bunched up around his ankles – galloped over to us. He held his shoulders shrugged back while eyeing me with obvious interest.

"Now, I want you to sort *this*," Ms. Pettigrew gestured to the four pillows that had started ramming at each other for best position on the chandelier, and the five others that were struggling to extricate themselves from between the wedges of tree branches they'd become stuck in.

Aybek nodded. With a snap, he summoned a long, metal rod into his hand and used it to coax the pillows towards him.

Gertt tutted and checked his very ornate pocket watch. "The other one should have made it through processing by now," he said, "so as much as I'd *love* to stick around for this, I'll be taking my leave now."

And so, he was off before I could ask what 'other one' he was talking about. "I'll see you later darling!" Mariposa called to his back before ushering me along once more.

We passed through the room and into another hallway, which seemed to be a gallery, as it was lined with paintings of different Hidden Creatures. Halfway down, my breath caught in my throat. I abruptly stopped walking and stared.

There, hanging on the wall in front of me was a painting of a cardenere!

The portrait was of an important-looking fellow, whose quills were golden and stuck out around his head like a halo. He held a pocket watch in one hand, a black wooden cane in the other, and had a large handlebar moustache that seemed weightier than the rest of him all put together.

Poor little Emma, I thought to myself, *where are you?* I stopped myself asking again about what they'd done with her, as neither Gertt nor Ms. Pettigrew seemed particularly interested in being helpful.

I knew in my heart that wherever Emma was, she would be fine. She was small, but she was scrappy and fierce. I knew *she* wouldn't be scared, but *I* definitely was without her. I missed her.

Ms. Pettigrew collided with my back and almost sent me sprawling onto the branchy floor.

"Well, I never," she chided from behind me. "Clumsy *and* rude. Silly little child. It's no small surprise we don't usually let your kind down here. Now come along, Tori, we have an appointment to get to. We have so much work to do, and…"

I slowly turned to face her, fists on my hips. "No." I stared her down, not moving an inch.

"Excuse me, dear, what did you just say?" The pixie's face flamed as red as her hair.

"No," I repeated. "I may be just a silly little human, but I'm no toddler. I'm fully *11* years old, and I have. Had. ENOUGH! You're going to tell me what's in store for me, and you're going to do it *now*." My chest heaved and my cheeks were warm with anger. I stared at Ms. Pettigrew, praying my tantrum didn't make things worse.

Her face softened. To my surprise, she actually looked *sympathetic*.

"Oh darling, I am terribly sorry for this twisty-turny afternoon we've had," she tutted. "I hadn't stopped to think how confusing it must be for a simple, lowly human to have to take in the pure majesty of the Kingdom of Hidden Creatures and the Magical Community that inhabits it. Why, you probably thought you'd died and gone to heaven with how amazing things are down here compared to the ugly drabness of the mortal world."

I awarded myself a perfect ten out of ten points for how well I kept myself from laughing. I certainly hoped Heaven would be less confusing than…*this*…but I wasn't going to interrupt the manic pixie while she was feeling sorry for me.

"I suppose you could use with some explanations, but we are on *such* a time crunch, and you look so *particularly* unfashionable at the moment. Seriously, darling, what are those clothes you've got on? And who even wears anything comfortable anymore? *So* last season." She stopped herself as if to spare my feelings before continuing. "Look, if you'll cooperate, I'll answer as many of your questions as I can, but my dear, we really *must* get going."

I sighed. *Finally*, I might be getting some answers. Whatever Ms. Pettigrew had in store for me, I could endure it for an explanation of my situation. Maybe she even knew about Ashley? Or Emma? I didn't want to seem too eager, so I simply nodded.

She hopped a foot in the air, clapped her hands, and grinned from ear to ear. "Excellent, darling! Now come right along – we'll get you all fixed up in no time."

Before I followed her, I needed to test the sincerity of her offer. "Not so fast, Ms. Pettigrew," I addressed the back of her head. "I've got my first question: where on Earth are we about to go, and why?"

Rather than appearing annoyed, her grin stretched even wider. "Why, darling, we're going to where I've cultivated my life's work. We're going to put you through the Fifteen Stages of Becoming Beautiful!"

The Fifteen Stages of Becoming Beautiful

Ms. Pettigrew seemed ready to literally pop from excitement as she led me down a final hall to where a grand oak door loomed before me. Letters etched in an ominous yellow read:

THE FIFTEEN STAGES: ABANDON HOPE, ALL UGLIES WHO ENTER HERE

I didn't have time to consider the troubling implications of the message before Mariposa shoved the doors open and led me inside. The chamber was enormous – probably larger than my entire house. Neon colours adorned the walls and ceiling, and speckled sunlight shone through a skylight above me which appeared to take the shape of Mariposa's face…

…wait, not sunlight, surely? Could the tower extend above ground? Who knew, and it wasn't exactly at the top of my priority list to find out. The rest of the room was vacant aside from a single beauty station, complete with a mirror stand and a comfortable looking chair. The levers and buttons protruding out of the side of the mirror were a tad bit concerning, but I was sure they weren't there for any nefarious purposes.

Reasonably sure, at least.

Grabbing hold beneath my armpits, Ms. Pettigrew hauled me up, plonked me on the chair, and strapped me in with a seatbelt, of all things!

As an author's note: she was considerably stronger than she appeared, and her grip was so agonisingly painful that my armpits still throb as I write this. When I am lauded in the future as the bravest author who ever lived, they will display my diary, and nobody will be able to read it, for my hand is shaking so terribly at the memory. The shaking is so intense that my handwriting has transformed into a secret code that you would use with your friends to gossip about your terrible chemistry teacher. I guess it's for the better; I don't want the magical paparazzi chasing me down.

"My name is Mariposa Pettigrew," the pixie announced as she frowned at my reflection in the floor length mirror positioned neatly in front of me, as if realising for the first time how horrific my hair looked. "You may call me Mariposa."

"Only if you'll agree to call me, Vicky," I said.

She inclined her head in acknowledgement. "As I said earlier, I'll answer as many of your questions as I can, but do please cooperate while I get you ready, Tor…erm, that is…Vicky. We have almost *too* much to do."

Experimentally, she tried running a brush through my hair, which was currently a sea of tangled knots, stray strands, and the occasional clod of dirt. She pulled it back and let go, pushing her hands deeper into my scalp.

I strained to hold my head still and asked, "Where *are* we, exactly? I mean, I know that we're in the Kingdom of Hidden Creatures, and Gertt – the lawfur from earlier – kept saying something about a Magical Community, but what does that mean? Is it the same thing?"

Mariposa chuckled in response. "Darling, I hadn't realised you'd be asking such *easy* questions," she responded as she released her grip on my scalp, reaching over to some buttons on the mirror. "You are in *both* right now, but one is technically not the other. Everything on this side of the Mundane Stream makes up the Kingdom of Hidden Creatures. I'm sure you noticed the difference as you were crossing it. All manner of beasts and beings live within the Kingdom's confines, but not all are…civilised, shall we say? Those who are make up the Magical Community. We tend to stay down here, out of the way of you humans on the surface."

Satisfied with her own answer, she then began muttering to herself. "*No, that's still not right. No, she needs to be upside down to vertical, not horizontal face down,*" she mused as she pressed some buttons. Suddenly, my chair had flipped itself over and around, leaving me dangling almost completely upside down.

Blood rushed to my face, and I barely managed to keep my squawking to reasonable levels while Mariposa lowered my head onto the head rest at the base of the wash basin, where she flicked my hair into the bowl and began applying something sudsy.

Bright orange bubbles floated up from the basin as she scrubbed at my scalp, accented by bright pink.

"Why was I ambushed by squirrels up in the forest?" I asked in what I like to think was a conversational tone. "Was I trespassing? I hope you know that I certainly didn't mean to if I was. I was just trying to find a way to talk to the Magical Council."

"Tsk, tsk," she tsked. "Terribly unfortunate, that. They can be a tad overzealous in seeing to their duties."

Without warning, my chair flipped back upright to its original position. A pair of white-gloved mechanical hands carefully tied my hair back away from my face and scrubbed my skin until it was raw.

"Squirrels serve as Officers of the Courts in the Kingdom," Mariposa continued. "Is that not how things work in human courts?"

I shook my head from side to side, unwilling to open my mouth to speak and risk having my tongue scrubbed out.

"Either way," Mariposa said, "you technically *were* trespassing, but I'm sure it won't be held against you. It's not like you *knew* you were doing anything wrong."

My chair whirled back to an upright position to face the mirror, and I gasped.

Not a pleased gasp.

My hair, which used to shine golden in the puckered rays of light from Mariposa's large face-shaped skylight, was now as black as a moonless night.

Before I could protest, my chair jerked around at a 90-degree angle, and Mariposa shoved a device that looked like a miniaturised jet-engine in my face. A ripping rush of crisp wind blew the skin on my face backwards, sending my hair billowing out behind me like a veil.

When the blast stopped and the chair had turned back to the mirror, I saw that my hair had settled in a huge, fluffy cloud atop my head. It was now a chalky violet, no longer black. My eyes were locked as wide as dinner plates in my reflection. It was utterly…*magical!*

I'd always begged my parents to let me dye my hair, but Mum had always said no.

Oh, Mum. The corners of my mouth involuntarily tugged down into a frown, and a fat lump formed in my throat. I wondered what she would think of me looking like this. Sure, I was starting to *look* pretty, but I didn't *feel* that way for some reason. I *felt* like a selfish, ungrateful wretch who had mistakenly sent her sister into possible oblivion and then run away in the middle of the night, probably leaving her doting parents sick with worry. For all I knew, every minute here could age my parents by months.

I was a monster for wishing away my wonderful sister. My sister, who would ask me to read stories to her, and who would spend time with me on holidays while Mum and Dad were off being boring adults. As much as she annoyed me, and as much as Mum put *far* too much responsibility on me as an older sister, Ashley had probably been the only thing that had stopped me from going insane.

A single tear slid down my cheek.

"Oh darling," Mariposa clucked, "Do try not to cry about how beautiful you're becoming. If you think this is an improvement, wait until we've run you through the rest of the stages!" She pulled some levers and pressed some buttons.

The whole room shifted. My chair rose, and the section of floor beneath me flipped over to reveal…train tracks? That couldn't be right.

But it was! The wall on the far side of the room had opened up into a tunnel. I could barely make out the tracks arching downward into darkness from where I sat.

Before I could steady myself, my chair slowly lurched in that direction, click-click-clicking along the newly revealed tracks on the floor until I was right at the opening of the tunnel. Mariposa walked alongside me. I gulped.

"Alright, darling," Mariposa patted me on the back, "I won't be able to chit-chat while you're down there, so are there any other questions you have before I see you on the other side?"

I gulped again. I swear, my gulping muscles were going to be honed to an Olympic level by the time this makeover was through. I had to make this next question count.

"Why are you going through all of this trouble to make me 'beautiful'?" I asked. "Is it all just to make me more presentable for the Council?"

"Well, *sort of*, darling," Mariposa answered. "Specifically, we've got to get you ready for your appearance in court. You know, for the trial."

"What?" I squeaked as Mariposa pushed one final button. "What trial? I thought you said I hadn't done anything wr*OOOOOOOOOOOONG*..."

The Girl in Red

I'll spare you *most* of the details of what followed my screaming descent into what turned out to be a vast, sprawling, and *totally* nonsensical complex solely devoted to Mariposa's twisted sense of beauty. I certainly don't remember every bit, anyhow. In fact, I don't even know exactly how long I *was* subjected to the "beautification." It's quite possible I missed my twelfth birthday somewhere around the fifth step. Or maybe I was only gone a few hours – who's to tell?

The first step turned out to be a shower, which seemed strange after she'd gone to the trouble of drying my hair. Nevertheless, I was stripped down and subjected to a fully automated scrubbing-up process that reminded me of a car wash, only with animated hygiene products. A tiny brigade of leaping bars of soap, dancing globs of shampoo, and rhyming sugar-scrubs sang as they cleaned me from head to toe. It was choreographed to a frightening degree, and I was left wondering how this could have possibly been more effective than bathing with non-sentient shampoo.

The next several steps were all a blur, but similarly nonsensical. There were mechanical hands and sewing needles, steam vents, and even wild animals at some point. I lost track of all the inexplicable contraptions I was shoved through. To be honest, I'm not even sure if there *were* exactly fifteen steps. Mariposa might have just named it that on a whim.

But it *was* eventually over, and I was spat out of a trap door back into the room this madness had all started in. Mariposa, who was stood by the beauty station, clapped her cheeks and gasped at me in wonder. Silver, crystal-like tears formed at the edges of her eyes, and a filed-tooth smile shone from her face.

"You're breath-taking," she managed through a quivering lip, her hand shooting up to press against her mouth. I craned my neck to see my reflection in her mirror, but she turned my chair around before I could catch a glance.

"Not yet," she tutted. "You'll have to wait for the *big reveal!"*

I could only imagine how I looked. My muscles ached and my skin stung from the strain of so much beauty.

"I've really outdone myself this time," Mariposa gushed. "Who would have thought such an *ugly* little human could ever clean up so well?"

She began nudging me towards a set of velvet curtains to the side of the salon, but I wasn't having any of it.

"Mariposa," I said, locking my knees and digging in my heels so that we skidded to a stop. "What did you mean when you said you were getting me ready for court? I thought I hadn't done anything wro…"

"Oh, not now, dear," she cut me off. "I'll answer all your questions in a moment, but you *must* come see the finished result." Then, she pinched the ticklish part of my side just above my left hip. My knees unlocked immediately as I doubled over with laughter, and she pushed me unceremoniously behind a velvet curtain.

Behind the curtain was a room lined with mirrors framed in wood, metal, and plastic of all different colours.

I stood in the centre, exhausted, and stared ahead.

All of the glass reflected the same thing: a girl with beautiful, purple hair that fell in waves past her shoulder, clad in a shimmering, red party dress piped with gold. Puffed sleeves consisting of several layers of frill somehow perfectly complemented silver lace sandals and nails that were cut, shaped, and painted red, with gold flowers decorating the thumbs.

The girl's skin glistened with the perfect amount of highlight. Her nose hairs had been plucked and her nostrils washed out. She was, admittedly, the image of perfection.

She was me. *I* was the image of perfection.

"Oh," Mariposa exclaimed, clapping her green, manicured claws together. "We must show this to Gerttous! Except, wait, there's something missing."

She pulled two rubber ears out of her pocket and fixed them onto both *my* ears. They were the same as my human ears, except these ones had pointed tips and an ear piercing at the top. "Now come along, dear, we just *must* show you off!"

"Now hold on just a second." It was my turn to do the interrupting, and I planted myself as solid as a rock in place before she could start throwing around those pointy elbows again, even making sure to cover my ticklish sides from any further squeezings. "You promised me more answers, and it's time you pay up. WHY AM I GOING ON TRIAL?"

"There's no need to shout," Mariposa sulked. "Though I can see how that might have been a little confusing for you. You must forgive me. I've just been so distracted by how gorgeous you've become."

She reached out to pinch my cheeks, but I dodged with lighting speed I didn't know I had in me.

"Very well," Mariposa said. "I said we needed to make you presentable for court, not that you were the one on trial. No, no, no, dear, you've been called as a witness."

I stared back at her, eyes raised. "A witness for what?"

"Dear, I *did* tell you that no one would be mad at you for breaking a rule you knew nothing about," she said, "BUT, it *is* someone's fault, and that's what the trial is meant to get to the bottom of."

"Someone else's fault? Wait, you don't mean… not Emma the cardenere! Where is she? Is she safe? Oh, those nasty squirrels better not have done anything to her! Where have they taken her? She didn't do anything wrong! She was just trying to help me. Why, I swear, if you do anything to her just for trying to help me get my sister back, I'll…"

"Vicky, darling!" Mariposa cried out, grabbing my flailing arms and forcing them down to my sides. "Calm down. You're going to ruin all my hard work making you beautiful."

That did get me to calm down, but only out of fear of being fed back through the Fifteen Stages of Driving Small Girls Insane.

"Now," Mariposa continued, smoothing loose strands of my hair, "if you'll just follow me, I think I can put all your worries to rest."

She yanked me *hard* (I'd forgotten how strong she was for her size) towards another door and back down some more flights of stairs. Big signs with lopsided letters all along the way read, *Congratulations Mariposa! You are a beautiful goddess with the power to do anything!*

More signs bearing similar messages continued until we were halfway down the stairs. I had heard of the wonders of self-affirmation before, but this was excessive.

We edged down a red carpet piped with gold twine covering another knotted wood floor. I realised that the carpet's pattern was a close-up carpet rendition of Mariposa's powdered face. The details were so amazing that I could even see the pock-marked skin and overdone beauty mark!

Then, after a long moment of staring, I tilted my head upward to get a sense of the room we were in.

Wait a minute. The concrete walls, the tapestry hanging off of it, the large entrance-style door standing in front of me across the room. We were back at the entrance of the building!

"Did you not expect me to roll out the red carpet for such a stunning piece of art?" Mariposa answered my unvoiced question.

"Hmph," I heard from off to my left, accompanied by yet another *gong*-ing sound that made it quite clear who had just harumphed. I turned to see none other than Gertt standing there, eyeing me from head to toe. He did not appear impressed; he only halted his looking me up and down to tug on my arm and scrape fake tan off onto his pristine, white gloves before wiping the mess on his pantsuit in disgust. He took a handkerchief from his pocket, embroidered with the initials G.T.U.P.S.D.F.B.V.F.D.N.T.

He must have seen me gawking at it, because he drew himself up and announced, "These initials stand for 'Gerttous Toto Unerous Preditation Sagh Devolve Frog-like Brainiac Verdane from Dianea Nest

Thumberg,' which is, of course, my name. Gertt, for short, but you may *not* call me that." He prodded me in the chest with his stubby index finger to drive the point home.

I silently resolved to address him as 'you' going forward. If I couldn't memorise my multiplication tables beyond five, there was no way I'd remember *that* mouthful.

"Hmph," the odious little melon grunted again. "I suppose she'll do, Mariposa. Adequate work, as always."

"Oh, you silly little lawfur, you," Mariposa chortled, this time reaching out to pinch *his* cheek. He grimaced but didn't say anything. "Anyway, now that I have this one ready, where's the other witness?"

"Oh, right," Gerttous grumbled and flipped open a pocket watch. "The cardenere should be here in three, two, one..."

"Cardenere?" I couldn't help from interrupting. "Does that mean..."

A surreptitious hole opened up in the ceiling, and out dropped one of the most garish looking, makeup-laden, overdressed little nubbly creatures I'd ever seen.

Going to the Chapel

Emma sat down right where she landed on the floor, the huge grin plastered across her face at least indicated she was having a good time. She wore a green dress woven of tumbleweeds and wide platform shoes with bluebells stuck all over them. A furry scarf was draped across her shoulders; it looked like the mink coat Aunt Marge had worn when I was a baby. It had been so ugly that one time while I was eating, I flung baby food at it, leaving a stain. But she *still* insisted on wearing it. And now, here was something just as ugly, wrapped around poor little Emma's neck.

Nevertheless, her appearance was not enough to put me off scooping her up in my arms and squeezing her tight against my chest.

"Oh, Emma! Are you okay? I was so worried about you! The nasty squirrels *better* not have done anything to you, or I swear I'll…"

"Let go, let go, let go! You're crushing me!" Emma chirped, desperately scrambling to get out of my constricting grasp. Reluctantly, I eased up, and she fell to the floor.

Hmph. It's not *my* fault she's my only friend down here.

I contented myself to squat down and help her smooth out her new outfit. "Really, though, are you okay?" I asked again.

"Oh, I'm as fine as I can be after being subjected to Mariposa's contraptions," she answered, trying to set her new wig straight. "I'd always heard the horror stories," she waggled a finger at the beauty-maker herself, "and they are well deserved. *Well* deserved, indeed. And," she continued, turning to me, "I suppose I *did* miss you, too. You did help me get back to the Kingdom, after all."

I smiled at her and had to stop myself from ruffling her wig. "By the way," I said, "why *did* you need help coming down here? And will someone *finally* tell me why on earth we were accosted by bailiff squirrels for having the audacity to walk through a forest?"

Emma gave a long sigh before speaking. "I suppose I can explain some of that. You remember when I said that I was coming back to surprise my family?" She waited to continue until I gave a brief nod. "Well, the reason me being back is going to be a surprise is because they maybe, technically, kind of, well…kicked me out."

I gasped. "Kicked out? What kind of awful family would want to kick out someone as kind and helpful as you?" Anger bubbled up in my chest. I was *not* thrilled to hear about a family who had gotten rid of a member *on purpose* (as opposed to accidentally, as I had).

"I'm sure more details will come out in the trial," Emma continued, "but let's just say I didn't fit the typical model of what's expected of a young cardenere." She looked down for a minute, but not quickly enough to stop me from seeing tears gathering in her eyes. "I…I didn't *want* to leave, and I had so many more things to say to my parents before I left."

Emma sniffled and wiped her eyes, but then she looked back up at me, a grin spreading across her face.

"That's why I was so happy when I was told where you were going! Coming back and facing my family seemed much less intimidating if I was coming along with someone else." She stood up and jumped from foot to foot in excitement. "It was perfect really. And to think, it wouldn't have happened if I hadn't been told which flight you'd be on by that nice la…"

Wait. Someone had told her I was going to the Kingdom? Who? No one other than I knew!

"What lady told you I was going to…?"

"*Ehem!*" Gerttous interrupted. That same *gong* sound that usually accompanied his actions sprung up again, somehow managing to sound annoyed this time.

I stopped mid-sentence. Gong notwithstanding, Gertt had cleared his throat with such authority that Emma and I both turned to stare at him.

"It's already *highly* unusual to let two witnesses converse before a court appearance," he said in an officiating tone, "but I *certainly* will not permit you two to discuss the actual matter of the trial at hand."

So, I simply nodded my head and pantomimed zipping my lips shut and throwing away the key. I wasn't going to deny myself *all* forms of melodrama.

Aren't you so proud of me, reader?

Gerttous looked us both up and down before giving an indignant sniff and turning away, apparently satisfied that there wouldn't be any further witness tampering or whatever he was worried about. He gave his pocket watch another glance before turning to Mariposa.

"Well," he said, "we certainly don't have any more time for lollygagging after *that* display. Mariposa, do you have your ridiculous vehicle ready?"

Mariposa beamed with glee. "Oh, Just Gertt," she said, "do you think I'd miss an opportunity to show it off? Especially with my two newest exemplars of beauty in the passenger seats?"

Before I could get a word in edgewise, the pixie and lawfur ushered us out the door towards the street, where the strangest car I'd ever seen purred next to the curb.

My mouth dropped open. I may not know much about cars, but I know enough to recognize that this…*thing*…was more travesty than vehicle. The body of the car vaguely resembled something from the 1940's, only if the designer had sneezed halfway through the initial sketches. Colourful, painted flowers adorned every inch of metal, and all its sides and angles looked like they'd been planned right at first, then adjusted a few degrees off-right at the end as a matter of principle.

My heeled sandals click-clacked along the pavement as I approached the oddly designed hunk of metal. Reaching the door, I took hold of the handle that jutted out of a sinkhole in the side of the car and swung it open. Inside were two bean bags, a wheel, and a large space behind it with cardboard separating it from the bean bag. I sat down on a beanbag in the back, and Gertt climbed into the beanbag in front of the steering wheel. Emma hopped into the bean bag beside me, nervous excitement etched on her face.

"Hang on to…well…just hang on in general!" Emma's voice was giddy. "Lawfurs are great at a lot of things, but driving is *not* one of them. Why is Mariposa even letting you drive her car, Mr. Lawfur, sir?"

"*That* is a very harmful stereotype," Gertt scolded as he checked his rear-view mirror – composed of multiple smaller compact mirrors, of course. "And it's just 'Gerttous Toto Unerous Preditation Sagh Devolve Frog-like Brainiac – oh, never mind. Mariposa has to get herself ready for court, of course. Who else would drive? Not either of you, I presume!"

I swallowed and tried to distract myself from whatever was about to happen by taking in the scenery out the front…erm…Well, I at least looked out the space where a window *would* have been if this car *had* windows. The space where glass *should* go was an empty frame, which at least allowed me to lean out quite easily.

"Strap in – things might get a bit bumpy," Gertt announced as he pushed down a creaking gear lever. I searched around myself for a seatbelt, but all I could find was a piece of leather taped onto the door and an accompanying piece of string on the opposite side of my seat. I tied the two flimsy pieces together and gave a silent prayer that they were much sturdier than they looked.

I then tried to make peace with the fact that we were about to go hurtling down the completely confusing streets I had seen from above on my first entry into the Kingdom. *Steady yourself, Vicky,* I told myself. *You've been through a lot today; you can definitely handle a bit of bad driving. Besides, maybe Emma* is *just being prejudiced!*

My stomach lurched, but not at the thought of inter-creature racism. It was because we weren't moving forward after all. We were moving *up*. Gertt stopped fiddling with the gear stick and grabbed the wheel as we lurched into the air and then began zooming forward at speeds only slightly slower than breakneck. The engine rocked back and forth, loudly humming along with the wind whipping through the open windows, slapping unmercifully at my face.

Well then. On the one hand, I didn't have to worry about him weaving in and out of whatever sort of traffic the Magical Community has to contend with. On the other hand oh-my-goodness-this-was-terrifying!

What had my life become?

Gertt grabbed a hot-pink helmet from the passenger beanbag and tried to shove it on me. I slapped his hand away.

"Hands on the wheel, please!" I shrieked. "I'd like to live through the day at least!"

Outside of the cut-out rectangle, a flock of birds with purple, white, and green feathers flapped alongside the car. Tendrils of red-hot fire snaked down their tails. I remembered reading about these in my book. Their heads always faced East, so they flew backwards when migrating West for the summer.

I didn't have long to remember what else I had read about them, though. Wind and time morphed together to create a tunnel around the car that blurred out our surroundings. I could make out streaks of blue and shapes of white, but nothing else; the force of acceleration and Gertt's erratic driving kept me pushed back against my beanbag seat the whole time.

I can't say exactly how long I spent being blasted by G-forces (or whatever they're called) until I was squashed flatter than a bean in my bean bag, but I *can* say that it was *too* long. It came to an end eventually, though, and we finally slowed enough that I could once again make out our surroundings.

A massive tree lumbered outside the window. So massive, in fact, that I had to crane my neck to see the whole thing.

The top of the tree brushed the ceiling of the cave encapsulating the underground city. Its trunk must've been *kilometres* wide. And the many branches were as thick as entire regular trees and so spaced out that Mariposa could have opened several shops between them. Creepers criss-crossed each other as they wound up the steep bark, and each leaf was as big as a car – if not larger. They all remained eerily motionless in the still air, drooping down onto each other, and creating a sort of ladder that led up to a platform that jutted out beneath a gilt pair of double doors.

"This is the Chapel of Great Sinful Acts," Gertt said as the car gently descended toward the base of the massive tree. "The trial will begin there,"

I gulped. It had been at least an hour since my last good gulp, so I gulped for England, this time because I had looked up to see that Gertt was pointing up to the top of the ladder. At that point, I had to decide if I would be more horrified at the thought of driving up the ladder of leaves, or climbing up them.

Resolving my dilemma for me, Gert jerked a gear lever and sent the car speeding straight up the side of the tree, nearly sending my insides down and out of the car behind us. The ascent was mercifully short this time, though I had to wonder why he couldn't have driven us to the top in the first place.

I had more than that to worry about at the moment though. 'The Chapel of Great Sinful Acts' didn't *sound* very promising. But, then again, I wasn't the one on trial. I *probably* didn't have anything to worry about, right?

Suddenly, a loud honk sounded behind us, prompting Gertt to let out an undignified squeal. I turned and watched a truly garish vehicle pop into existence out of the air and nearly rear end us. Apparently, some people preferred to travel via wormhole and 'crash-land' instead of driving 'up tree' as I later learned it was called.

The new arrival swerved to avoid us at the last second, giving me a perfect view of its decomposing-food-brown paint job and passenger-van-style body as it wobbled to a stop in front of the leaf ladder.

Clad in a beautiful silver gown with a leg slit down the side, Mariposa stepped out through the van's sliding door with grace that perfectly juxtaposed with her driver's landing skills. She wore a pair of Balenciaga boots – leaf style – and a mini crown encrusted with diamonds on top of her scarlet hair, which was amassed in a nest of ringlets.

"Now *that* was uncalled for," Gertt muttered to himself as climbed out of his seat and waddled 'round to open the door for Emma and me.

"Wheeeeee! Can we have another go?" Emma cried as she hopped out of the car and onto the foliage-covered platform.

I stepped out behind her, wobbling on my sandals. It was quite crowded here. All manner of creatures were bustling about, either arriving in their own nonsense vehicles or hoisting themselves up using the leaf-ladder system. In a stroke of panic, I grabbed Emma and pulled her so we were both standing behind Mariposa, just in case another car worm-holed out of the air on top of us. The last thing I needed that day was to be squashed by a time-and-space traversing vehicle.

Gertt cleared his throat aggressively, narrowing his eyes at me as if he could plainly read my plan to use Mariposa as a pixie-shield. Wielding grunts like a cattle prod, he directed Emma and me out from behind Mariposa and herded us in front of him. We weaved through the crowd of creatures as politely as we could, which turned out to be surprisingly easy. The moment they noticed it was a human trying to squeeze by, they recoiled and let me pass.

Eventually, we reached a set of magnificent gilt doors that occupied the end of the platform, seemingly carved directly from the tree itself and flanked by two uniformed guards.

Their uniforms were interesting: navy blue and formal, like something a military officer might wear. Golden buttons secured their coats closed, and conical white hats stood vigilant atop their heads. The creatures *wearing* the uniforms were much more interesting, though. They were actually *taller* than me. Covered in white fur, they squatted on powerful-looking curved legs and sported a pair of enormous floppy ears.

I recalled the section of the book describing these creatures:

The Jackanops

"The Jackanops is a pleasant yet serious creature. Resembling jack rabbits and towering over most other denizens of the kingdom at five-foot-three on average, they are typically employed as peacekeepers. While they appreciate a good laugh like anyone else, they tend to frown upon the thoughtless pranks pulled by some other monsters. They can jump three times their height into the air, and their eyes rarely miss anything happening nearby."

"Young Victoria McKay!" the taller guard announced in a no-nonsense voice that matched perfectly with The Tome's description. "Material witness called by both the prosecution AND defence!

Court is in Session

I didn't have much time to question what the Jackanops meant by naming me a witness for both the prosecution and defence, nor to wonder why the windchimes had decided to start up again after having been silent for so long. I was too busy staring out at the scene before me. The chamber I'd entered was stuffed with rows and rows of pixies, monsters, elves, and who knows how many other creatures sitting in wooden pews that reminded me of the church Aunt Marge had taken me on the rare Sunday the zoo was closed. Thick roots and branches composed the organic walls and ceilings, and ivy jutted through rows and rows of quite uncomfortable looking benches. They were all arranged to face a large platform at the far end of the room, upon which stood an oak stand engraved with the crest of a weighing scale. Behind and above it were three imperial chairs and a black curtain, but nothing else.

I towered above most of the inhabitants, whose eyes seemed to follow my every move. Perhaps sensing my nervousness, Emma squeezed my hand, glancing up at me with an expression of commiseration and support. Bewildered by all the attention I was receiving, I focused on my friend's smile, noticing for the first time that each of her head quills had been adorned with seed pearls in a variety of patterns and colours.

"Emma, you are truly beautiful," I exclaimed, a bit embarrassed that I'd been so caught up in my own appearance and problems that I hadn't even noticed such an obvious detail before. "And look! You've got mushroom earrings in! They're adorable!'

Emma blushed happily and gave a little skip. "They're real mushrooms," she confided. "Mariposa says if I get snacky during the trial, I just have to dig around in my ear, and voila! Problem solved! And I've got more if I need them," she said, happily wagging her clutch at me, which seemed to be entirely composed of different types of curling fungi.

Behind us, Mariposa's dress swished lavishly as she entered the room and posed. Cameras flashed and creatures oohed and ahhed as her heels clicked along the aisle and turned into a pew near the front.

In contrast, Gertt curtly led Emma and me to the front row. "Now, listen here," he said to me specifically, "you may not be the one on trial, but it behoves you to wait silently until you are called. Answer all questions as honestly as you can, and make *no* outbursts when others are speaking. Do you think you can manage that?"

I nodded, offended that he would call my composure into question. I mean, I suppose I *had* subjected him and Mariposa to *some* outbursts earlier in the day, but I was still learning!

"Good," Gertt sighed, clearly relieved. "Keep a calm, collected head about you, and we just might get the Council to hear your petition on… What did you say it was you were here for again?"

I was just about to answer when, suddenly, a pixie-looking woman I hadn't seen before with four badges and a yellow and red tie in an army-green uniform grabbed me by my puffed sleeve and dragged me away to a long, wooden bench near the front of the room.

Once we were in front of the bench, the pixie shoved me down onto it gently yet firmly. Astonishingly, several branches sprung up from somewhere under the floorboards to secure me, strapping me in by the waist like a safety harness. I couldn't help but wonder why in the world they'd put such flimsy seatbelts in their cars if they had access to this kind of technology.

A different elf marched Emma up and sat her on the aisle opposite me, much too far away for my liking. It struck me that she had fast become my entire emotional support system. I wondered if she felt supported by me.

I didn't get to wonder for long, though. A yell of surprise rose amongst the crowd as another set of huge double doors crashed open at the front of the room. A procession of three female and one male jackanops entered, heaving and grunting beneath the weight of a huge throne on which sat...*nothing*.

"Is the judge a…chair?" I asked, only to be answered by the sound of a loud *smack* against the arm of my branch bench.

"The witnesses will NOT speak until they are called upon by the court!" the pixie woman cried out.

Instinctively, I covered my mouth with my hands and watched as the jackanops set the chair down behind the crested stand. *Come on, Vicky,*

I thought. *You've done so well today. Just keep it together until this stupid trial is over, and then...*

My train of thought was interrupted as some*thing* bustled in from a side door.

Flashes of a white coat and tall pointed ears lead me to believe that a giant rabbit had just entered the room. Another jackanops, perhaps?

Not just a jackanops, as it turned out, but a particularly *large* one, and seated atop a stallion, to boot.

The horse itself was purple, because of course it was, with a white moon and stars branded on the side of his fur. A colourful sash hung from the saddle on which the words "The Mayor's Mare" was printed" The rider, on the other hand, was furry and brown, and wore a pair of round spectacles. He struck me as a classically handsome gentleman rabbit of late middle years. His whiskers were neatly trimmed, and his soft caramel eyes surveyed the courtroom with genteel astuteness. He reminded me of someone...but who? Someone dear to me...

He dismounted from the purple stallion, and removed his snow-white cloak, which he handed to one of the jackanops who'd brought in the chair. The jackanops took it, clicked his booted feet together, and saluted. The regal brown rabbit returned the salute with utmost dignity.

My breath caught in my throat. This human-sized rabbit reminded me of my grandfather.

Beneath his discarded cloak, the rabbit wore deep red robes. On the back of the cloak in scrawling calligraphy were two words: "The Mayor".

Oooohs and aaaaahs arose from the crowded pews as the mayor took his place on the stand across from mine and Emma's branch-boxes. To his right and left were three empty seats, each labelled with titles I couldn't quite read from where I was.

"Order," the mayor said, clearing his throat. His voice was firm, yet gentle and kind, and it sent a wave of nostalgia washing right over me. He really *did* remind me of my dear grandfather. It was like he had stepped right out of my cherished photograph. And turned into a rabbit, of course. As he spoke, he waved what looked like a jewel encrusted mix between a gavel and wand. "May we please have order!"

It seemed like a rather unrealistic request in the Kingdom, but to my surprise,

the murmuring in the foyer shrank to whispers, and then to complete silence.

Seemingly satisfied, the mayor swept his eyes across all who were assembled. When his eyes fell on me, I could have sworn they twinkled with sympathy, and maybe even a touch of kindness…

Before I could ponder this further, the mayor gave another light bang with his gavel/wand.

"Squirrel officers!" he called out. To my surprise and somewhat disgust (as I was *not* over my treatment in the forest), two dozen squirrels reared their previously unseen heads up from various places around the courtroom. How had I missed those little vermin? They certainly were proficient at sneaking. And drugging 11-year-olds.

"Bring in the council!" the mayor continued, and the squirrels hopped into action in unison, dashing to doors on the left and right side of the court and forming lines as if they expected attackers to rush them from the pews.

The doors swung open, and in marched the oddest collection of neatly dressed individuals I'd ever seen in my life – and that was counting everything I'd already seen today. They were all wearing fine black robes, and each had a pin in the shape of a balanced scale displayed proudly on their left breast, but there the similarities ended.

The first was an elf woman. As the book had put it:

The Elf

"The elf is the haughtiest creature in the entire kingdom. Tasked with high minded affairs such as managing treasuries or bossing around underlings, she is keen of mind and snooty of character. She is known to spend hours a day perfecting a stare meant to let others know just how insignificant they are in comparison to herself."

This one had purple hair done up to look like a frozen fire. Her mauve skin was flawless, and her black eyes gleamed with displeasure. "Famarilda Scorn, present," she said with a self-important bow as she arrived at the first seat.

Next had to be a goblin.

The Goblin

"The goblin is a large, toad-like creature that dwells in the swampier areas of the mushroom forest adjacent to the Magical Community proper. When he isn't eating flies or burping at small children, he is usually gathering up a posse of his kin to impose their will on someone nearby. While not exactly rambunctious, he is certainly devious enough to make up for it."

Toad-like was an apt description. He didn't *quite* hop as he made his way to the second seat, but his green-yellow skin looked moist enough to have just come out of a pond, and I almost expected his bulbous form to let out gas like a whoopie cushion as he sat down.

"Mag Kraspus, here an' accounted for," he smugly croaked. His voice was guttural, deep, and wet, as if his throat was constantly filled with phlegm.

The last one took me a minute to identify, but fortunately for me, I had all the time in the world to make my assessment. He was *slow*. Scratch that. He was the *embodiment* of slow. Larger than even Kraspus, he moved his spherical body along in a way closer to rolling than walking, seeming to ponder breaking for a nap with every other inch of progress he made. Maybe it was an overabundance of caution that informed his slowness, as his vein-riddled blue skin looked like it might rupture if he so much as brushed up against something solid.

Got it. Lethargic, rotund, and varicose. He was a boulder troll.

The Boulder Troll

"The boulder troll is a rare and frustrating creature. He would much rather gently calcify in the breeze whilst taking a nap than do anything actually productive. Be wary, though. All that napping gives him plenty of time to hone his mental skills. Many a creature has lost in a battle of wits against a boulder troll, having sorely underestimated their opponent...when he doesn't fall asleep halfway through the encounter, that is."

"Mmmmmmmianderous Momph, here." I'd have almost believed he was sleep-talking as he announced his presence, leaning *very* far back in the third chair.

"And Mayor Nop-hops, here as well. Are we all ready?" the mayor inquired as he glanced to his left and his right. Once each member had nodded (some more slowly than others), he banged his gavel-wand on the stand.

"Very well," he said. "We can begin. Commencing now is the trial of The Magical Community versus Clive the Lawfur. Bring in the defendant!"

Clive

Clive the Lawfur!?

Clive was the name the first lawfur I'd seen had mumbled all those years ago in the hospital while I waited for Ashley to be born! The memory of his voice came back to me clear as day. It was just after he'd handed me the folded piece of smelly parchment and then scurried off down the corridor and disappeared. He'd been muttering, "...should do better, Clive. So terribly sorry, my dear…"

Sudden understanding washed over me as several revelations clicked into place:

#1: The wind chimes. The first time I'd heard them tinkling was when I'd spotted Clive in the crowd of Christmas shoppers while on my way with Dad to the hospital. And later the same day, I'd heard them twice: once when he appeared and then again when he disappeared!

As I whipped my head around to stare at Emma, the words she'd spoken in the Mariposa's shop came rushing back. She'd said that someone had told her I was going to the Kingdom of Creatures. I'd wondered who she could mean, as I hadn't told another living soul, and I'd thought she'd been about to say a nice "lady" had told her, but she hadn't.

#2: Emma had been about to say a nice LAWFUR had told her!! Which was, of course, why I'd heard windchimes when I'd boarded my flight!

#3: Clive the Lawfur had seemingly appointed himself as my magical guardian angel.

And now he was on trial for helping get to the Kingdom of Creatures.

Dear Reader. I. Was. SHOOK.

A door opened behind me, and in marched another troop of those stupid squirrels in double file. In between them, his hands and legs cuffed together, was that poor little ball of fuzz I'd seen all those years ago in the hospital: Clive.

He did not look too pleased with his situation. Besides having his arm and leg shackles, he'd been dressed in a black and white striped jumpsuit – the kind you see prisoners wearing in cartoons. He wore a pronounced frown and stalked defiantly to the front of the court with his eyes cast down squarely at the floor. He only looked up once, right as he passed me by, briefly making eye contact with me.

In the short second his eyes locked with mine, he stopped looking frustrated and just looked…sad, I guess. Then a squirrel prodded him in the back, and his eyes were right back down to the floor as he was marched forward.

This had to be all my fault, I was certain. Somehow, in wishing my sister away, I'd also ruined this lawfur's life. In that moment of realisation, I resolved myself to be the best witness possible for Clive. I still didn't fully understand what this trial was all about, but I'd do everything I could to get this little fuzzball off the hook.

Or at least not make things *worse* for him.

Clive came to a stop just in front of Mayor Nop-hops' stand, his head still bowed down.

"Clive the lawfur," the mayor read out from a sheet of paper in front of him, "you stand accused of endangering the Magical Community via improper exposure to the human world and mismanagement of a human child post wish-granting. How do you plead?"

"He pleads not guilty, most honourable mayor."

To my surprise, the words didn't come from Clive, but from Gertt, who walked up beside Clive in front of the court.

"And you are…?" the mayor asked, leaning forward to get a better look at him.

"Gerttous Toto Unerous Preditation Sagh Devolve Frog-like Brainiac Verdane from Dianea Nest Thumberg," Gertt said with a prideful voice, "or just Gertt for short, if it pleases the court. I've been appointed to serve as the defence's solicitor, your honour."

It was strange, seeing the two lawfurs standing side by side in front of Mayor Nop-hops. Was this ornery, purple cotton ball thing really the one in charge of defending Clive? He'd been nothing but rude to me and Emma all day, and now Clive's fate – and perhaps mine – was supposed to be in his hands?

I swallowed the lump that had formed in my throat, too distressed to gulp.

"Very well," Mayor Nop-Hops intoned. "That brings us to opening statements, then. First, the Council."

At this, Scorn stood up, producing a legal pad, and began speaking. "As all the Magical Community knows, our secrecy from humans is of the *utmost* importance, as is the distribution of wishes to human children. While lawfurs have been entrusted to see to the latter and ensure the former, *this* individual has flagrantly violated multiple laws and codes of conduct in overseeing his most recent wish-dispersal. As this court will see…"

Honestly, I was so appalled by Scorn's opening statement, I couldn't follow the rest of what she said. If the council members were the ones who would be deciding Clive's verdict, why was she talking about presenting evidence about his guilt? Where was the presumption of innocence? Had the Magical Community no grasp on the concept of conflicting interest!?

Just as I was about to leap to my feet to shout, "I OBJECT!" Gertt caught my eye and shook his head with a look that clearly said 'NO.' Concurrently, the branches in my bench tightened themselves around me, constricting my movements until I could barely itch my own bottom, let alone leap to my feet. I fumed at the grumpy little lawfur. He may be able to keep me seated, but we'd just see if he could make me keep quiet. I opened my mouth…

…and Mariposa appeared, sitting down in the empty spot next to me on the bench.

"Do try to hold your tongue, dear," she whispered, reaching over and smoothing a lock of hair that had fallen forward onto my face. "I understand you're upset, but Gerttous is very good at his job, and Mayor Nop-hops runs a tight ship. Interrupting is frowned upon, to say the least.

If we whisper, you and I may speak, however. I still owe you answers to some questions."

The tension in my shoulders relaxed a bit. I *definitely* had some questions that needed answering.

"Why is one of the council members reading out the opening statements for the Magical Kingdom?" I asked first. "Shouldn't there be a separate lawyer doing that?"

"Oh, is that how things work on the surface?" Mariposa asked, genuinely surprised. "Well, not to worry, darling. We have magic to smooth things out here."

She pointed to Scorn. "See that pin on her chest?" she continued. "Those aren't just fancy symbols of office. They're magically binding. Any verdict they render *has* to be in strict accordance with the laws of the Kingdom. So, darling, you have nothing to worry about as far as them being biased goes."

I looked to Scorn, who gestured emphatically from her chair as she spoke.

"...and this ugly little cretin made an absolute *mockery* of those standards, not to mention how *hideous* he is…"

"Absolutely nothing to worry about," Mariposa waved a dismissive hand. "Anything else, darling?"

"Yes, one more *big* thing," I whispered. "What did Clive do, exactly? I know he gave me a wish, and I used it very poorly, but they can't blame him for that, can they? I certainly don't! I came here to speak to the High Magical Council who signed the wish and make them undo it. But that's got nothing to do with Clive, right? Isn't he just the messenger?"

"Oh, that," Mariposa said. "Yes, darling, you see, Clive is one of many lawfurs entrusted with handing out wishes to human children. The problem is that Clive bestowed a wish on *you*, and *you* found your way down *here*. It's not your fault, you understand, but it also wasn't supposed to happen. The Kingdom of Creatures, and the Magical Community more specifically, is supposed to remain hidden from the human world. Clive stands accused of revealing our existence to a human."

Oh. Well. If all the revelations that had just dawned on me were correct, Clive might actually be guilty of what he stood accused of. I wonder why he would risk…well, I didn't know what he might face if he were found guilty…but I wonder why he would risk anything for me?

"There, there darling," Mariposa patted my shoulder. "No need to look so glum. As I said, Gertt is really rather good at his job. He will surely convince the Council that execution is *far* too extreme a verdict in this case, and…"

"Execution?!?"

"Quiet in the gallery!" Kraspus, the second council member, boomed, "or I'll be sendin' the squirrels after ye!" The toady mass gave a sadistic, belly-shaking chuckle before leaning back in his seat and gesturing to Scorn to proceed. I swear I saw one of the squirrels wink at me.

She harrumphed and continued. "Yes, well, I think I've made my point quite clearly. What Clive did was atrocious, and for the crime of endangering the Magical Community, the only fitting response is the endangerment of his life. I call for execution!" She took her seat, a smug smile spreading across their lips.

I gulped harder than I'd gulped all day. Despite Mariposa's reassurances, it seemed to me that things were a lot more dire than I was expecting.

And the trial was just barely starting.

The Curious Case of the Cardenere

"That seems a bit drastic," Mayor Nop-Hops glanced reproachfully at Scorn. "We will see."

I crossed my fingers behind my back. At least it seemed that *one* of the creatures overseeing this court was reasonable.

"Do you have any opening statements to make Mr. Garflous, was it?" the mayor directed his question at Gertt, who for once didn't throw a tantrum about someone getting his name wrong.

"Gerttous, most honourable Mayor," Gertt bowed his head.

I almost snorted. Imagine if I'd called him Mr. Garflous!

"I'll keep things brief," Gertt said, producing two separate monocles from his breast pocket and putting both on. "My client, Mr. Clive, has served the Magical Community faithfully for many decades, during which time he has acquired an intimate knowledge of humans and their workings. All Clive sought to do was oversee the correct use of the wish he granted. Any of Clive's actions that may – or may not – have led to accidental discovery of the Kingdom were purely matters of happenstance or coincidence. I intend to show this court that while Clive may have erred in some of his actions, his only crime was a soft heart, and that his only punishment should be removal from the Committee to Grant Wishes."

I silently cheered Gertt on, something I hadn't pictured myself doing up until now. He actually seemed to know what he was doing. And he definitely wasn't intimidated by these big, ugly bullies calling themselves 'council members.'

Mayor Nop-Hops gave Gertt a polite nod and smile before speaking again. "According to my ledger here, the first witness we'll be speaking to is one Emma… Hmmm, that's peculiar. It just says Emma." He looked up, adjusting his spectacles above his whiskers. "Does this witness have a last name?"

"Not anymore, your honour," Emma piped up all-too cheerfully.

"I see. Step forward, young lady," Mayor Nop-Hops motioned, and Emma's magical branch-vine restraints loosened in response. She half-stumbled, half-waltzed off her bench up to where Gertt was standing before dropping into a curtsy.

"Well met, Anna," the mayor glanced down his twitchy pink nose at her, adjusting his spectacles once more and smiling faintly. I guess it wasn't just complicated names he struggled with. "Well, I believe we can get on with questioning, then. Mr. Gertrude, if you'd like to–"

"Pardon me, if ye please, Mr. Mayor," Kraspus interrupted. "Due to the…*severity*…of the charges, I've taken the liberty of requestin' some Truth Juice for all witnesses."

That didn't sound pleasant.

Gertt didn't think so either. "Excuse me, your honour," he cut in, "but is that really necessary? I have no doubt in my mind that my client and these witnesses intend to be honest and forthcoming in their testimonies *without* any undue prodding from the court."

"It does seem a tad harsh, don't you think?" Mayor Nop-Hops agreed, turning to the two sneering council members to his right.

"Mr. Mayor," Scorn replied, taking over for Kraspus, "I understand your hesitancy. However, in accordance with the Laws of Judgement, 'Any potential breach of secrecy in regard to the Magical Community, no matter how small, must be treated as High Grade Treason for the purposes of court proceedings and witness handling.' I'm afraid our hands are regrettably tied."

Her sneer didn't *seem* all that regretful. Silently, I ground my teeth. Scorn and Kraspus, at the very least, were pure evil. Momph looked on the verge of slumber, so it was hard to get a read on him, but I didn't have high hopes there either.

Mayor Nop-Hops sighed deeply. "Sorry, Mr. Garpous, but that is the law. I suppose we'll have to have someone sent to fetch…"

"No need, Mr. Mayor," Kraspus chuckled darkly. "I already have it at the ready. Squirrels!"

These toady freaks were completely steamrolling the poor mayor! I fumed as one of those horrid forest rodents practically came skipping into the room, precariously balancing a comically oversized syringe on its back. The tiny squirrel, who I swear looked excited, was dwarfed by the long, thick needle.

To her credit, Emma handled the news like a champ. She stood firm as the sorry excuse for a nut-hoarding squirrel approached with its sickening grin. (I know most squirrels can't grin, but these ones *definitely* could and did.) Emma barely flinched as the monolithic needle entered her shoulder.

"Happy now?" the mayor asked, frustration edging into his voice. If Kraspus noticed the shift in tone, he didn't acknowledge it. He simply nodded.

"Very well then. I grant the defence the privilege of first questioning, *as is my right by law*," the mayor almost yelled, cutting off what looked to be yet another interruption from Scorn.

"Thank you, your honour," Gertt bowed his head and turned to Emma. "Ms. Emma, just moments ago, you mentioned you no longer had a last name. Would you care to explain to the court why that is?"

Emma wobbled but remained standing tall. "Right. That. You see…" she glanced around the room for a long moment before continuing, "A few years ago, I was, technically, maybe, well…banished."

Murmurs rose up from the gallery.

"I am sorry to hear that," Gertt remained neutral in tone and paced before the councillors. "What, exactly, led to this banishment, as you called it?"

Emma glanced down for a moment before answering. "You see, cardeneres like me are a timid lot by nature and by decree," she explained. "We don't have much in the way of magic, but we are good at hiding and sneaking and quiet things like that. Every cardenere that I knew growing up was taught by their parents to lay low and keep out of the way when possible. My parents tried much the same with me."

If she'd seemed nervous before, that faded away as she spoke; if anything, she stood even taller as she continued with her story.

"But I could never rightly see the point in it all. I wanted to explore and experience the Kingdom. I wanted adventure! I wasn't about all this crawling and hiding and making yourself small business."

I beamed with pride for my nubbly little friend.

"My parents were none too pleased, of course," she went on. "They tried everything they could think of, from running me through sneaking obstacle courses to putting muzzles on my mouth when I wouldn't be quiet. They even tried throwing me into a nasty troll's house one time, telling me I wouldn't survive the night if I couldn't make myself scarce until they came back to fetch me."

Emma grinned for the first time since being jammed full of Truth Juice. "Imagine their surprise when they rolled around in the morning to find me sharing tea and crumpets with the big fellah!"

That got some laughs from the crowd, though Scorn and Kraspus looked thoroughly unamused.

Emma lost her smile after a moment and lightly kicked the ground with her foot. "About two years gone, I guess they gave up trying. My pah dragged me up to our side of the Mundane Stream and gave me the boot. Kicked me clean across the river. He said, 'We've got no place for cardeneres who think they're goats and don't like being sheep. Endangers the rest of us, is what it does!'" Emma broke off, sniffling ever so slightly. "That's the last I ever heard of him or my mam."

I gripped the edge of my box. What kind of awful place was it down here where you could be forced out of your family just because you didn't act the way your parents thought you should?

Sort of like how I wished Ashley away because she'd changed my perfect Family of Three…

I completely deflated. Wish or no wish, I never should have wanted Ashley gone. I almost started sniffling myself, but just then, a green claw gently grasped my wrist.

Mariposa didn't say anything. She just gave a small, sympathetic nod.

Could she read my mind? Probably not. She probably just thought I was especially moved by Emma's testimony, which wasn't all that wrong of an assumption.

But maybe I'd been wrong about her, too. Maybe she wasn't just a self-interested socialite wannabe with questionable taste in hair care products? Maybe I wasn't as good a judge of character as I thought I was.

Ugh. Self-discovery can be depressing.

"Mr. Mayor," Gertt piped up after a solemn moment, "might I ask the court to produce any documents pertaining to this banishment? Assuming one was officially filed, that is."

Mayor Nop-Hops didn't immediately answer. Instead, he motioned for one of the jackanops guards to approach his stand. After a moment of whispering, he looked back to Gertt.

"Well, Mr. Gerthuth," he said, "it seems there are *not* any records of an official banishment. The cardeneres keep their own councils from time to time, but I can say with certainty that this court has never issued an official writ of banishment or exile against Ms. Edna the Cardenere."

Gertt gave a satisfied nod. "Thank you, your honour."

"Oh, look at him go, darling," Mariposa tightened her grip on my wrist. "Like I said, we've absolutely *nothing* to worry about."

"Esteemed members of the court," Gertt barrelled on, "I see no reason why Ms. Emma's return to the Magical Kingdom should have any bearing on this proceeding. No laws were broken by her return, so surely no laws *could* have been broken by assisting with such. *If* that's even what happened. The defence rests its questioning and requests that this young cardenere be released from further harassment."

Gertt gave a snappy gesture to a nearby jackanops guard, who promptly dragged up a chair for Gertt to sit in.

"Excellent," Mayor Nop-Hops clapped his fuzzy paws. "I certainly have no objections. Council members?" He glanced to his left and right, looking none too thrilled to be turning questioning over to them.

I expected Kraspus to speak up, but he remained mostly inert, save for pulling a cricket out of his pocket and giving it a loud, crunchy bite. Instead, Momph stirred to life.

"Mmmmm, Ms. Emma?" he started slowly. "I, mmmmm, *graciously* welcome you back to the Magical Kingdom. Might I, mmmmm, ask, though, *how* you made your return?"

"Well," she started, addressing Momph, "I tucked myself away on a plane bound from London to Scotland. I'd been eking out a living scrounging for crumbs and such around Big Ben at the time, y'see. But as much as I wasn't thrilled with my parents for kicking me out and all, I *did* miss them. And I missed the Magical Kingdom dearly. Things just aren't the same up on the surface, and…"

"Mmmmmmmmmmmmmmmm," Momph interrupted with a long, sleepy groan. "That is all well and good, Ms. Emma, but mmmmmm, *how* did you end up on that plane?"

Emma looked nervously down at her feet, and my heart lurched in my chest. Obviously, the Council knew that Clive had told her which flight I had been on. Was it possible Clive hadn't told Gertt?

"I may have…ummmm…received some assistance."

"Mmmmmmmm, indeed," Sleepyhead nodded. "Could you, mmmmmmmmm, identify the person who helped you. Are they, mmmmmmm, in this courtroom, perhaps?"

Emma's head sank. At first, she remained completely silent. But then her arms started to twitch ever so slightly. The twitching spread to her shoulders, then her torso, and then finally her face, until I began to worry she might be having a seizure.

"Is she okay?" I urgently whispered to Mariposa.

"That'll be the Truth Juice kicking in," the pixie muttered grimly. "It won't harm her, but she won't be able to stay silent for long."

Sure enough, after another short moment, all the words came tumbling out of Emma's mouth at once. "YESOKAYALRIGHT-yes, yes… it was Clive, it was Clive," she said and pointed at the sad fuzzball. "I met him in London, and he informed me which plane to hop on to get to Scotland."

She took a deep breath, regaining some of her composure. "But!" She raised her pointer finger in the air. "Like Mr. Gertt said, it wasn't *illegal* or anything for me to come back here, since I was never officially banished, so that shouldn't matter!"

"*MmmmmmmmmmmmmmM*iss Emma," Momph stopped her, "I appreciate your candour, but we will, mmmmmmmm, decide what does and doesn't matter." The horrible creature leaned forward at a glacial pace. "Did Clive, mmmmmmmm, say anything *else* about why you should get on that plane?"

I was smart enough to sense a trap when I saw one. Or heard one, I suppose. The nervous glance Gertt shot Emma confirmed my suspicions.

Emma tried to keep silent again, but it was only about five seconds before the words came rushing out: "Yes! Okay! Clive told me that I would meet a human girl on the plane and that she needed to get to the Magical Kingdom too and that we could help each other!"

Drat. Sometimes I hate it when I'm right.

Just a Small Town Girl

Angry shouts and jeers burst out of the gallery, and both Clive's and Emma's heads sank low as the onlookers hurled verbal abuse at them.

"Order, order!" Mayor Nop-Hops intoned, banging his gavel-wand with a bit more force than before. It took a few moments, but the yelling and insulting did eventually fade to mere nasty murmuring.

Kraspus and Scorn were grinning so hard I half expected their faces to just become giant, sneering mouths. Momph, on the other hand, didn't seem moved one way or the other. He merely stared at Emma for another moment before leaning back in his seat. "No more questions, mmmmmm, from me," he said. I swore his eyes started to half-close for a mid-trial nap.

Gertt shot up from his chair. "Honourable Mayor, may I have a moment to redirect?"

Mariposa leaned in to whisper to me. “That just means he has a chance for further questions now that the prosecution has had their go,” she explained. “I’m sure he’ll have something up his sleeves to deal with…that little outburst.” Her words were reassuring, but she seemed slightly less confident than before.

Before Mayor Nop-Hops could respond, Scorn reared her ugly head. “Really now, do we need to hear anything further from this witness? I don’t see how anything this lowly ‘public defender’ could have to ask would matter in the slightest after what we just heard.”

“I’ll be the judge of what we hear and don’t hear.” The mayor shot her a withering look. “Whatever you may think, Mr. Garry here has every right to ask further questions. *By law*.”

Scorn looked like she was about to respond, but just as she opened her mouth, the lapel on her robe glowed a bright blue. That seemed to shut her up, and she reclined in her seat with no more than a pronounced *harumph*.

“Thank you, your honour,” Gertt bowed. “I’ll be brief.”

He turned to Emma once more. “Emma, for how long have you been planning to return to the Magical Kingdom?”

Emma’s grin came back, if somewhat diminished. “I’ve been planning my return for abouts…six months now? Give or take.”

Gertt flashed his own restrained smile now. “And was there any way for you to do so other than by plane?”

“Not practically speaking, if you catch my drift. Walking would have taken *far* too long, not to mention it putting me at further risk of exposing myself to other humans.”

Gertt nodded, then turned back to the mayor. “No further questions, your honour.”

Okay, that was decent, I thought, though I wasn't exactly thrilled with how things were going. None of what Gertt said changed the fact that Clive specifically told Emma about me, and as far as I could tell, that was what this whole farce of a trial would boil down to.

"Ms. Emma," Mayor Nop-Hops said, "I'm afraid the court cannot ignore what you've just told us. By your own admission, you travelled to the Kingdom with a human, violating our laws concerning secrecy from mankind. We will have to make a ruling on your punishment; however, it will need to wait until after the trial at hand. For now, it's time for the next witness." He shuffled some papers for a moment. "Victoria McKay! Please step forward."

A sick, light-headed dizziness settled over me, and my heart stopped momentarily.

"Come on, darling, you've got this!" Mariposa whispered encouragement to me, gripping my arm. I was quite thankful for that, and otherwise might have tripped and fallen on my face as the tree branches released me and I tried to stand, what with how wobbly my legs were. With her support, I stepped out as gracefully as I could and walked forward.

To my surprise, Mariposa grabbed me in a quick embrace, walking with me right up to Mayor Nop-Hops' stand. "You'll do brilliantly, darling," she said before letting me go. If I hadn't been so nervous, I might have cried. I swore to myself right then that I'd never judge a person for being irritating again. Even if they did subject me to talking hair conditioner.

I squared my shoulders and gazed up at the mayor. And swallowed, unsure of what to do. Was I supposed to say something?

"I…" I started.

"Ah yes, very good," Mayor Nop-Hops spoke up, peering down his twitchy pink nose at me. "The young human. I do apologise for all this dreadfulness. But, as I'm sure is the way on the surface as well, the rules are the rules."

I nodded as politely as I could, then nervously swung my eyes over to Gertt. On cue, he cleared his throat. "May I begin with the questioning, your honour?" he asked.

"Hmmm? Oh yes, of course," the mayor waved his paw.

"Now hold on just a minute," Scorn cut in for the umpteenth time. "Are we not going to address the matter of a *human* standing here in front of the Magical Council, of which she is *certainly* not supposed to know about?" Her beady eyes threatened to bore holes right through my skull.

"I concur," Kraspus steepled his warty hands, sending a spray of perspiration into the air. "This fine council has prevented humans from happenin' upon our community for centuries. Her being here is a, well, it's an *abomination.*"

Momph didn't say anything, but he did stir from his possible slumber to nod sagely.

"And what, exactly, is there to discuss?" the mayor inquired, exasperated. "Members of the magical community are required by law to protect the secrecy of the community, yes, but Miss Victoria here is *not* a member."

Scorn guffawed. "She's trespassing! She's violating our secrecy! Something *must* be done."

"There is nothing to be done." The mayor slammed his fluffy fist onto the stand, forgoing his gavel entirely. "'Ordinances and Decrees Concerning Humans: While all magical creatures are to prevent human discovery of, or entry into the Magical Kingdom, humans themselves are not bound by magical law nor subject to its penalties until such time as they become aware of these laws.' The child didn't know she was breaking any laws when she came here, so she can't be punished for it. And that's final!"

All three of the council's lapels flared blue for a good five seconds – even Momph's, and he hadn't moved at all during that rather heated exchange.

"Fine!" Scorn spat, crossing her arms.

Kraspus licked his own eyeball. "She is still a witness." His devious grin returned. "Human or not, she's still gettin' the Truth Juice."

"Truth juice! Truth juice!" Scorn chanted like a child. My stomach performed a full Olympic gymnastics routine. Were they really going to jam that enormous needle into an 11-year-old?

Mayor Nop-Hops must have seen the horror building in my eyes because he leaned down over his stand and actually reached out to pat my head. The fur on his paws tickled my cheek. "There, there, Willmoria," he said, "we use magic on the needles, of course. It mostly takes away the pain."

"*MOSTLY!?"* I blurted out, my restraint finally fully leaving my body. No one on the council seemed to mind. Kraspus and Scorn were too busy chanting like toddlers, and even Momph was pumping his blubbery fist in rhythm with them (or trying to).

And just like that, one of those dastardly squirrels sidled up next to me, prop-sized needle in hand.

"Now hold on just a minute," I waggled my finger at it. It *was* a squirrel after all, so maybe I could intimidate it into backing off.

The squirrel proved me incorrect by unceremoniously jamming the needle into my shoulder.

I have no idea if the mayor was telling the truth about magic taking away most of the pain or not.

If he wasn't, I shuddered to imagine what the *rest* of the pain might feel like.

20

Everything You Say Will DEFINITELY Be Used Against You

Thankfully, the pain (and my ear-shattering wail, which I'm actually quite proud of) was short lived. I felt perfectly normal otherwise.

I checked my arms and legs to make sure they were still the right shape. All the liquid in the needle looked to be gone now that the injection was over with, so it had to have gone *somewhere.* Yet a cursory inspection revealed I hadn't turned into a Vicky-shaped balloon.

Despite all the chaos this day had been, despite the severity of me being here in a court run by three evil maniacs with only a kindly rabbit and redhead pixie on my side – despite all that…I was still a naturally curious girl. How exactly did this Truth Juice work? Would it stop me from telling a lie unprompted? Would it hurt if I tried? Only one way to find out…

"Mr. Mayor," I said, "thank you for being so kind to me here in court." He smiled and nodded graciously. "Scorn," I turned to address the pouting flame-haired elf, "you've also been extremely nice to me, not to mention how smart and beauti…"

Have you ever had a particularly bad Charlie horse? Maybe you yawned too hard and suddenly your chin muscles squeezed together, contorting like they were trying to audition for Cirque du Soleil? Imagine that, but twenty times worse, and all through your body. *Especially* your mouth. I could almost hear my lips telling me, '*There won't be any more of those lies getting through US today, little missy!'*

I ticked 'spontaneous lies' off the list in my head of kinds prevented by the juice.

Mayor Nop-Hops gave a droopy-ear-shaking chuckle. "Hah! Looks like the Truth Juice is working as intended, wouldn't you say, Ms. Scorn?" he said through his laughter. She only grumbled to herself, something about dirty humans and how the law would work if s*he* had the run of things.

"Ah yes, thank you for that, Nicky. Questioning may proceed," the mayor got out as his chuckling died down.

For my part, I was much more at ease now. I didn't have anything to lie about, after all, unless I wanted to try being verbally generous to the council members again. The Truth Juice had come and gone, and as much as it had hurt at the time, it shouldn't be an issue going forward. And, I had to remind myself, I still wasn't the one in trouble. I just had to speak my piece and get through this. I could worry about getting Ashley back once this ridiculous trial was taken care of.

"Thank you, your Honour. Miss Victoria," Gertt finally said, stopping by my right. "Could you please recount for the court how you came to learn about the Kingdom of Hidden Creatures?"

There it was. My time to shine.

I started talking.

I had no plan for framing things a certain way. Instead, I simply resolved myself to tell the story of how I came to be here, in its entirety, as best as I could remember it.

I told the council about the birth of my sister, about how a strange creature appeared in the hospital to give me a wish. I told them about growing up with Ashley and how much of a pain it was, and, finally, about that fateful night I wished for her to disappear.

Mayor Nop-Hops listened intently, nodding every once in a while in response to some detail or other. Scorn and Kraspus, on the other hand, did *not* seem amused. Scorn sat with her arms crossed and punctuated my sentences with a sigh and a roll of the eyes. Kraspus just stared grimly. That wasn't exactly the response I expected. I knew they disliked humans for whatever reason, and I gathered they were eager to punish Clive – almost excited about it, even. But from the moment I mentioned the wish, the council members, at least the fully awake ones, sprouted frowns that grew and grew.

At some point, I guess their irritation got too much for Scorn to bear. "And so it begins," she interrupted me in the midst of describing how my sister had vanished. Her attention shifted fully to Clive. "Yet another misguided malcontent with an axe to grind about those insipid wishes."

"Wait, what?!" I shouted. This was *not* what I expected. "The note said the wish came *from* the High Magical Council. That's you, isn't it?"

Kraspus rolled his massive, bulging eyes, and licked them for good measure. "Well obviously, little gnat. But that's how wishes are handled. *We* give them to human children, like *you*, to use. Far away from *us*."

"What do you mean, 'far away from you?'" I was growing more and more perplexed by the moment. "Wouldn't *you* want to use them? I don't exactly understand how they work, but this one was powerful enough to get rid of a whole human being!"

"Well, that's the point, isn't it?" Scorn threw up her arms. "*That's* what the stupid wishes do: they twist your words and give you something you *didn't* mean to ask for. And they're *always* listening, waiting for you to phrase something any way that might come the slightest bit close to wishing. And then, poof! Wish granted."

"Mmmmmmm indeed," Momph chimed in glacially. "Best to, mmmmmm, send them off to the human children to get rid of for us. No one really believes them when things, mmmmmmmm, inevitably go wrong. Out of sight, out of mmmmmmmmmind."

I was stunned. *That's* why I got the wish? *That's* what this whole thing was about? Playing hot potato with dangerous magic? With *children!?*

"You evil, black-hearted, soulless *MONSTERS*!" I declared, taking a step closer to the stands. "Who put you child-endangering imbeciles in charge of anything!? Do you not care about anything other than yourselves? I thought *I* was entitled sometimes, and I'm an 11-year-old girl! What excuse do *you* have, apart from being rotten right to your evil little cores?"

My heart pounded in my ears, and I scowled at the council members so hard my cheeks ached.

Mayor Nop-Hops, bless his heart, was the only one who actually looked pained by the serious nature of my words. Scorn didn't even have the dignity to look guilty at my outburst. She simply grew more annoyed.

"Oh, here we go again," she said and shifted into a mocking falsetto voice – the kind an immature child would use when they're imitating you. *"Ooooooh, wishes are too dangerous for human children. Ooooooh, giving wishes away to unsuspecting brats is immoral. Oooooooh, you would be tried as a war criminal if the world were a just place."*

She spat on the floor.

"We've heard it all before, girl, but we *are* the ones in charge, and if wannabe activists like this pathetic excuse for a lawfur want to keep trying to throw a wrench into our wish disposal solution, they need to be taught exactly how far this council will go to keep the Magical Kingdom safe. Who *actually* cares about the humans, after all?"

"Who even cares about *you*?" I half-shouted. Maybe not my best retort ever, but I ploughed on regardless. "I lost my sister because of you!" I was fully prepared to keep going, but just then, something strange happened. My muscles spasmed like they had earlier when I tried to lie but…in reverse? Instead of clamping itself shut, a raw burst of adrenaline zapped my tongue, and more words started to spill out.

"And it was my fault too!" I gushed. The strength of my voice caught me off guard. I wanted to clamp my hands over my mouth, but my body wouldn't let me, and the words just kept spilling out. "I love my sister Ashley. We had our differences and our fights, sure, but she was my sister, and I never should have said I wanted her to go away. Wish or no wish!"

The muscle un-cramping faded, and I was left huffing for breath.

Stupid Truth Juice, ruining a perfectly good angry rant.

But I guess it was all true. It had to be, right? I *was* partially to blame for what happened, magic or no. This trial was at least partly a consequence of my temper.

Of course, that didn't excuse *these* three conniving gremlins. I opened my mouth to start in again when the gavel-wand interrupted.

"Alright, order! Order!" Mayor Nop-Hops shouted sternly. "Miss Bricktoria, I understand your anger – believe me, I do. But this court will *not* be entertaining any more outbursts." He eyed the room. "From *anyone*."

I did actually believe him, for what it was worth. About understanding me, that is. From what I could tell, he seemed to lean more towards those 'wannabe activists' Scorn seemed so fed up with.

"Your honour," Gertt bowed his head, "I believe I can wrap up this questioning quite quickly." He turned to me "Victoria, you've done an *exhaustive* job recounting your first experiences with a member of the Magical Community. Now, could you tell us how you learned the location of the Magical Kingdom? *Briefly*."

I disregarded that last snarky remark entirely; I was too busy grinning. This was the moment. The moment where I'd blow a gaping hole in the council's case.

"Of course, Mr. Gerttous." I curtsied for emphasis. "I learned that all by myself by reading from *The Kingdom of Hidden Creatures*. I found it while lost in the library one day – running from a bully, actually – and *no one* told me where it was or helped me find it."

Gasps of shock and awe sprung up from the gallery. I'd done it; I'd been the perfect little witness and proved I found out about this place on my own. Gertt seemed equally pleased, grinning with genuine joy for the first time since I'd met him. Even Mayor Nop-Hops looked happy, politely clapping his paws like I'd just won a tournament.

Except Momph didn't seem nearly as upset as I'd hoped he would. No, his eyes gleamed in a terrible way as he looked at me.

Like he knew something I didn't.

21

One Question to Rule them All

"Mmmmmmmmister Gerttous," Momph said, "does that conclude your, mmmmmm, questioning?"

"Hmph," Gertt huffed in response. "That's very presumptuous of you, councillor. But, yes," he gave a sweeping bow, "I'm done."

"All well and good," Mayor Nop-Hops said, moving as if he meant to hop out of his chair and down from his stand. "The day is getting late, and I'm getting hungry. I believe now would be a good time to adjourn. We can resume tomorrow at…"

"MMMMMMMM, hold on, Mayor," Momph rumbled, shocking the mayor so badly he leapt a good two yards into the air. "The council has, mmmmmmmmmm, just one question we'd like to ask before the day is done."

"Very well," the mayor said. "I suppose we have time for one more question for the young Licktoria."

"Not for her," Kraspus interjected, rubbing his wet hands together with worrying glee. "We'd like to move on to the defendant."

Gertt stopped his pacing, and a perturbed look spread across his face.

"Am I to take it," the mayor asked, "that you are forgoing your right to question the human child?"

"That's correct, Mmmmmmayor," Momph responded.

"If it helps wrap up this trial faster, then I suppose that's fine," the mayor shrugged his shoulders. "Go ahead, Councillor."

"First thing's first," Kraspus steepled his hands. "Truth Juice!"

"Truth Juice! Truth Juice!" This time some of the spectators joined in.

"Mmmmmmmmm, Truth Juice, indeed," Momph nodded.

Clive stood tall and still as another squirrel dragged another gigantic needle to him. His eyes remained fixed on his own shoes even as the spear-like needle tip went into his shoulder. He only looked up for the first time when Momph cleared his throat.

"Mmmmmmmmister Clive," Momph began, "this council has only one, mmmmmmmm, question for you: did you, in any way, assist Victoria McKay in finding the *Tome of Hidden Creatures?"*

Silence filled the chamber for a good ten seconds after his question. Then, the twitching started.

What's going on? I thought. I had told them the truth. I found the book all on my own!

But the twitching and muscle-squeezing rolled right along through Clive's little, furry body, starting in his shoulders, then spreading to his arms, torso, and legs. Finally, his neck gave a twist so large I thought it might break. Only then did his mouth force itself open.

"I helped her find it." His confession was met with gasps, like he'd summoned a ghost in front of the entire court. "I enchanted myself to look like her school bully and then chased her towards the location of the book. I also unlocked the door to its chamber."

I swear the ground shook a little beneath my feet at this revelation, and the image rose in my mind as if I were watching a video recording of it: Caleb grunting and charging, me plunging down darkened hallways, always following the faint tinkle of windchimes…

Clive swept his gaze across all three council members, standing tall and defiant. "And I'd do it all over again, too, whatever you decide to do to me. It's high time the consequences of your careless wish disposals came back to bite you. I've spent too long amongst the humans, especially their children." He turned to look at me, eyes heavy with sorrow. "In my time with them, I've learned that they really aren't all that different from us. They're just as kind, cruel, strong, pathetic, brave, cowardly, and *illogical* as we are. I've come to care for them dearly. They're more than dumping spots for our worst magics."

Clive stomped his foot. "Do what you will with me. I stand by my actions."

If there were others who supported his cause, they weren't in court that day. Boos and jeers filled the air. Colourful furred and feathered creatures hooted and hollered at Clive, jumping up and down in their seats. Some more unruly monsters reached into pockets, backpacks, or even pouches to produce overripe fruits and vegetables that they started hurling at the poor lawfur. Some of the jackanops guards moved through the crowd, trying to restrain the worst offenders, but the squirrels were no help at all. They stomped and chittered in unison, just like they had in the forest when they'd first ambushed me.

The horrendous noise almost completely drowned out Mayor Nop-Hops' calls for order. And the councillors… I could barely stand to look at them. Each one wore a triumphant, cruel smile. Scorn cackled. *Oh, I hated them so much.*

Clive remained motionless and resolute through the crashing waves of noise. Gertt, on the other hand, was furiously rifling through a briefcase he'd opened up on his chair. He threw papers and files left and right, digging for something he couldn't find.

The commotion overwhelmed me. I couldn't take it anymore. I clamped my hands over my ears, shielded my eyes, and crouched down in place, silently praying for it all to end.

And then it did, all at once. Tentatively, I rose, uncovering my ears and glancing around. A steady, glowing stream of blue light spilled out of Mayor Nop-Hops' gavel-wand, which he held outstretched in front of himself. Behind me, the crowd had frozen in place. *Literally.* Terrible grins and scowls still plastered their faces, and some even hung in the air mid-jump.

"Am I presiding over a court for civilised members of the Magical Community or for a bunch of hooligans from the Mushroom Forest?" the mayor scolded. "This little mess has been one of the worst instances of disorderly conduct I've ever seen in all my time as Mayor. Now, I'm about to release you lot from magical paralysis, but if you start hollering and making a scene again, I've no compunctions about sending every individual who disturbs the peace to prison for contempt of court." He eyed each of the council members long and hard from behind his round spectacles and sighed heavily. "Three… Two… One!"

And just like that, all the pixies, trolls, elves, and other creatures unfroze. The inertia from their movements caught up to them, causing some of the rowdier creatures to trip and stumble as they attempted to heed the mayor's command. The rest shuffled in place, muttering ashamedly, before all sitting down.

"Good, good," the mayor sighed. "Well, Mr. Krive, or whatever your name was, unless your advocate has any closing questions for you, that about wraps us up. Sadly, the evidence and your confession are *not* working in your favour. Sentencing will reflect this."

"One small thing, Mayor," Gertt said. He clutched a sheaf of paper in his hands so hard I thought he might tear it to pieces. He turned to Clive, uncrinkling it just enough to read the words written on it.

"Mr. Clive," he said, nose in the paper, "as a lawfur, you're quite well-versed in magical ordinances concerning wishes, correct?"

Clive nodded slowly. "That is true, I suppose."

"Good," Gertt looked up. "Would you mind reciting Magical Ordinance Governing Wishes 43?"

As if someone flipped a switch in his head, Clive squared his shoulders and cleared his throat. "Magical Ordinance Governing Wishes 43: Concerning Restorative Justice. Should the use of a wish directly or indirectly harm the Magical Community in any way as described in Ordinance 37, corrective and punitive measures must be taken in accordance with Laws Concerning Punishment. However, if a second wish is used to correct the harm done by the first wish, in such a way as to nullify all harm done by the original wish, then all sentences or other punishments required by law are to be made null and void." His shoulders relaxed slightly as he finished his recitation.

"The defence rests, your honour." Gertt made another sweeping bow, then started to gather up all the paper he'd flung everywhere and stuff it unceremoniously back into his briefcase.

"Hah!" Scorn's insipid voice drew the eyes of everyone in the court. "Firstly, we don't keep wishes lying around – that's the entire point! So, you're fresh out of luck there. And secondly," she leaned forward in her chair, menacing down at Clive and Gertt, "even if we did, do you honestly think we'd grant one to a renegade lawfur on trial for mishandling wish disposal in the first place?"

"Yes, quite unfortunate…" Mayor Nop-Hops half-mumbled to himself. "I apologise," he said, staring into the middle distance and speaking to no one in particular, as if lost in thought. "I've just remembered I have pressing Mayoral matters to attend to tomorrow. Sentencing will have to wait until the following day."

Scorn sniffed indignantly but nodded in assent. "So long as the defendant and witnesses are kept in court custody, the council has no problem with this."

"Here, here!" Kraspus croaked. "Give them an extra day to stew before they receive their sentences."

"Mmmmmmmmmmmmmm, yes, stew…" Momph groaned contentedly.

"It is decreed," The Mayor said. "Court adjourned!"

22

Inside the Mayor's Office

The Magical Council was never going to give me my sister back. We'd just lost. There was no other way of putting it. Clive was doomed to execution if the council members had their way, which it seemed like they would, and I was no closer to finding a way to bring back my sister. Plus, who knew what they'd want to do with me once this was over. Putting me back in the forest all alone and sisterless would be bad enough, but I doubted that was all they had in mind for me, the first human child to breach the boundary of the Kingdom of Hidden Creatures.

I could have stood there wallowing in misery forever if the sound of wood cracking against wood hadn't shaken me out of it. One last gavel pound from the mayor sounded off like a gunshot. Instantly, squirrels positioned all around the court rushed towards me, Emma, and Clive. They were more like brown blurs than animals as they piled in.

They weren't quite fast enough, though. A handful of jackanops guards were close enough to us to have formed a circular perimeter before the furred menaces could reach us. It was quite the tense standoff for a moment: the squirrels hunched low and on all fours, ready to pounce, while the guards simply stared straight ahead, armed with carrot shaped sticks with bayonets on the end.

"Thank you for your assistance, but we'll take it from here." It was Mayor Non-Hops voice that broke the stalemate. The squirrels seemed *quite* reluctant to part and let him pass. I was beginning to sense a bit of a loyalty divide between the law enforcement factions in this place.

The mayor clasped the foremost guard on the shoulder. "Good man, what was your name again?"

"Tim-Taps, your honour!" The squat jackanops gave a vigorous salute, almost knocking off his own hat in the process.

"Excellent! I thought I recognised you, Flim-Flam." The mayor said. I marvelled silently at his ability to misremember two-syllable names. "Let's get this lot to my office for…ummm…"

"Processing, sir?" Tim-Taps suggested.

"Yes! Processing! That!" The mayor swept us over with his best attempt at a stern gaze, then marched us off towards a small door at the back of the court.

We were silently led down a cavernous passage woven from roots and branches. After the *horrendous* chaos earlier, I wasn't in a talkative mood. The air was stiff and silent with tension, so much that I barely noticed the finely painted portraits of various pixies and fairies and whatevers as we passed them. Some wore robes similar to the mayor's, while others were outfitted in uniforms closer to the council members. I was sure *those* ones were all equally nasty.

Eventually we arrived at an ornate, red, wooden door with a bronze placard that simply read 'THE MAYOR'.

"Thank you, Jim-Jam," Mayor Nop-Hops gave the guard a curt nod. "I think I've got it from here."

"As you say, Mayor." Tim-Taps saluted and led the other jackanopses back down the hall and out of sight. Mayor Nop-Hops produced a key from somewhere in his thick, brown fur and unlocked the door to his office.

The office itself was…not what I was expecting. Most of the floor was lined with soft, golden hay that pleasantly crunched under my feet as I stepped inward. The walls and the sparse furniture were built from the same red wood as the door, making the room look warm and peaceful. The only *real* furniture of note consisted of two plush chairs, a desk that looked more like a barroom table, and a *slightly* bigger and fancier chair behind it. Fancier in that it had a cushion (probably stuffed with more hay), but that was it. There were no paintings hanging from the wall, no impressive bits of stationery lining the desk, no finely wrought glassware, nothing.

"Finally, a chance to relax in comfort!" The mayor hopped over the desk and twisted around mid-air to land neatly in his chair. He wiggled his behind a little then sighed. "Well go on," he motioned, "have a seat. We have some things to discuss."

Emma was *very* pleased to sit. She tried to pull off a jump similar to the mayor's, though with less impressive results. She did manage to avoid falling flat on the floor, but only just. I didn't have it in me to attempt the same theatrics.

Mayor Nop-Hops tapped his fluffy fingers on his desk-table for a good long minute, staring down as if he were trying to decipher some code written into the wooden grains.

He did eventually break the silence. "So, young Limma, young Sartoria," he began, looking up finally, "Things are *not* looking great for your lawfur friend." He turned his attention to Emma. "Things might also not be looking great for you, seeing as how we have pretty definitive proof that you lead a human here."

Emma's gaze turned down. I hated that she was getting blamed for this. *I* was the one who asked her to help me find this place. *I* was the reason she was caught in the forest. *I* should have figured that it was called the Kingdom of *Hidden* Creatures for a reason, and that they might not be too fond of anyone who tried to find them. If it weren't for *me*, Emma would have made it back fine and dandy on her own.

I guess the mayor was thinking along similar lines as he cleared his throat. "It does beg the question," he began, "as to *why* you helped a human find the Magical Community. You know our rules. You know you could have come back to the Community on your own and suffered no consequences from the Council. So why did you help the young human girl?"

The corners of Emma's mouth tugged down into a deep frown. I hadn't seen her look so sad all day, not even at the trial when she was forced to recount her banishment. I began to suspect I would never be able to put anything right – not just in terms of bringing back my sister, but also in undoing all the harm I'd inflicted in trying to. I was glad that Mayor Nop-Hops was focused so intently on Emma – and that Emma was looking at the table – so that no one could see the tears forming in my eyes.

"It's funny," Emma said, flicking at imaginary pieces of lint on her nubbly fur. "My family banished me, and Vicky accidentally banished her sister, so to speak…"

I winced.

"...but there's a huge difference," Emma continued. "When – well, *if* – I make it back to my family, they *might* give me a hug, or invite me in for a cup. But they would *never* risk life and limb to get me back." At that, she finally looked up, locking eyes with the mayor. "Not like Vicky, who marched down to confront creatures she hadn't even known existed a month back. I'm sure she was afraid of leaving her parents and the only world she's ever known, but she did it – she's doing it – to get her little sister back."

Oh. I reached over and took Emma's paw, my heart breaking for at least the tenth time that day. What if Ashley was out there all alone somewhere thinking I didn't want her back?

"That's why I did it, Mr. Mayor, sir," Emma said. "That's why I'd do it again a thousand times over. Even if it lands me in jail."

I immediately started sobbing uncontrollably. I sputtered and moaned. Snot and tears flowed freely down my face, and I didn't try to control myself as I heaved. Emma wrapped herself around my bicep. I tried to say, "thank you," but it came out more like "*buhuuuuuhhh, th-tha- buhuuuuuu* *sniff* *wharyousowonderfu- buhuhuhuhuhuuuuuuuuu...*"

The mayor produced a napkin from somewhere and handed it to me so I could sniffle more hygienically. Even *he* looked to have a wet glint in his eyeball.

"That's quite the noble sentiment, young Emma," the mayor said over the sound of me blowing my nose. "It will be factored into your sentencing, of course, but...well, we'll see what the Council thinks."

Great. The last thing in the world I wanted to know was what the Council thought.

"Then there's the matter of you, Hicktoria," Mayor Nop-Hops' eyes were squarely on me now. I contained another sob and stared back.

"You said you were here to petition the council for the return of your sister. I'm afraid I have some…unfortunate…news about your prospects."

He hopped up from his chair and began pacing. "There are quite a few obstacles to contend with, the first being the Council's disposition towards humans. I'm not sure if you noticed, but they're not exactly fond of you and your kin. They can't punish you – the law makes sure of that – but that just means they'll want you out of the Kingdom as soon as all this court business is over with. And they'll probably be extra vigilant about humans making their way down here for the next several centuries."

My heart sank with every word, but the mayor kept on. "Then we have to consider what would happen even if they *were* inclined to hear your case. Tell me, how much do you actually *know* about wishes?"

I barely managed to shrug my very depressed shoulders. "Not much," I sniffed. "I didn't really see anything about them in the book, and no one down here has told me anything beyond how nasty they are and how much they like to give them to unsuspecting human children."

The mayor snorted. "Aptly put. I'm not surprised you didn't find anything about them in the book. We might have written more about them if we actually *knew* more about them. Alas, we don't."

He stopped his pacing just in front of the room's left wall, staring right at it. "The truth is, wishes are almost as much of a mystery to us as they are to you. It was some thousands of years ago that they just started…*popping up* around the Kingdom. At first, those who would stumble across them thought they were lucky. Imagine finding a genuine magical wish that could grant your heart's deepest desires just lying under a leaf or mushroom!"

He stopped and grimaced. "It wasn't long until we discovered they were more curse than gift. Oh sure, wish your dearly beloved grandmother would stop ageing and stay healthy for the next five hundred years, only to come home and find her turned into a sycamore tree. An entire range of underground volcanoes only exists because some troll wished for his cave to be protected from food thieves, for goodness' sake. Their eruptions have dehoused *five* pixie families just last year! Now one of those wishes has cost you your sister."

He shook his head grimly and stared me down from his bespectacled nose. "Terrible news is, Pittoria, the only way to undo something like that is with a second wish."

It was so quiet you could hear a pin drop.

The mayor hopped back to the desk urgently. "Listen to me carefully. Even *if* I had a second wish lying around, even *if* I could tell you where one was, you know by now how twisted they can be. It *could* bring your sister back, but no one can predict what other consequences there will be, just that they will *not* be pleasant."

He placed his fuzzy paw on my shoulder and leaned so close to me, I could count each of the whiskers clustered around his moist, twitching nose. Thirty-Six.

"Do you understand me?" he asked gently.

His breath smelt of sweet hay and clover, and perhaps it was just my imagination, but I thought I caught a whiff of the aftershave my granddad had used.

"Yes, I… I think so, sir," I said.

"You need to be one hundred percent certain that you are aware of the unknowable nature of the consequences and accept responsibility for your choice. Do I make myself absolutely clear? No one would blame you for accepting the way things are now and not bringing your sister back to stop things from getting worse for yourself."

"If there's any way, sir, I'll do it," I said without hesitation, staring directly into his large, brown, wonderfully kind eyes. "I don't care about what happens to me."

The sigh Mayor Nop-Hops gave sounded like it travelled from deep down in his soul. "Well," he said, standing up straight. "You have courage, no one can deny that. Too bad I have to send you to a jail cell, now." He turned and hopped to the end of his desk. I frowned. "It's a real shame that you can't spend a free night exploring more of the Community while you're down here, you know. There's this beautiful little *park* nearby that would be positively stunning to stroll through at precisely *midnight* when the light of the full moon from the surface shines through the tower and illuminates the Kingdom, revealing things that once remained hidden as it is scheduled to do *tonight. It is specifically called Memorial Park.* Yes, truly a shame that you won't be able to *visit Memorial Park at midnight*."

What?

"There, there," he said, hopping over to Emma and patting her head as if she had been sobbing uncontrollably (which she had not). "Things aren't completely lost yet. Who knows what might happen between now and the trial?"

What in the name of Queen Beyonce was going on?

"Let's get you two to your cells," he said in a suddenly cheery voice. "Not to worry – they're actually quite comfortable." He opened the door and poked his head out. "Jam?" He yelled, "You there? Please come escort our prisoners to their cells. I don't think they'll give you any trouble – not after the talking to *I* gave them."

A defeated sigh echoed down the hall, followed by "Coming, sir!" and the sound of approaching hopping.

Bewildered, I followed Jam away from the office.

23

Aunt Marge Saves the Day

Emma and I were placed in separate cells. The section of the tree housing them was composed of harsh, angular slabs of granite rather than the pleasant roots and branches making up everything else. We came to Emma's cell first. After "Jam" the jackanops (which is so much more fun to say than Tim-Taps that I think I'll stick with it) opened the thick stone door, Emma turned and clutched my leg tightly. I held her, expecting the guard to usher her off. But he waited patiently until Emma withdrew, sniffling. I forced a small smile as I waved goodbye, and then Jam ushered her in and shut the door.

My cell was several doors down. I supposed they didn't want to put us close together. You know, in case little 11-year-old me tried to break out.

Jam broke the silence as we walked. “I apologise if the quarters aren’t suited for you, Miss. We’ve never had someone like you housed here,” he said. I looked up at him as he unlocked my cell. His face was genuinely apologetic. That might have been reassuring, if he hadn’t followed it up by locking me in the cell.

Unexpectedly, the bed in my cell was plush and cosy, with a satin pillow and chenille throw. The walls, carved of polished marble, were surprisingly attractive as well. There was even a painting hanging on the wall. Unfortunately, I realised when I approached it that it was an oil painting of Kraspus. He leaned forward in an enormous, opulent chair, sneering and seeming to point accusingly at me. A bronze placard on the frame read “*SHAME!*”

I surveyed the rest of the tiny space and was greeted by something I’d been missing for so long I’d forgotten I lost it in the first place: my rucksack! I hurriedly rummaged through the pockets and compartments, confirming everything was where I left it. All my belongings were accounted for, plus some extras.

Someone had left me luxurious, silk loungewear and the softest pair of slippers I’d ever worn. They were the same shade of scarlet as a certain pixie’s hair I knew. Even before I found the note in the pocket of the shag-orange robe, I was sure who’d prepped the room for my stay. The note, scrawled in an elegant hand, read:

There now, darling, chin up! Don’t let gloominess get you down; it’s bad for your complexion! - Mariposa.

Marginally comforted by the kind words, I laid down, hopeful that I’d fall right into a deep sleep. Alas, my brain was too busy thinking about how Emma was holding up. Too busy worrying myself sick about Clive and Ashley, the two people most directly harmed by my actions. Too busy missing my parents. Too busy feeling sorry for myself and everyone who had the misfortune to know me.

After either 15 minutes or a few months had passed (it was hard to tell), I reached into my rucksack and withdrew my journal to examine it. A pair of long shallow crinkles bisected the plain blue cover. The bottom corner was damp, and I realised the condensation from the previously-cold soda had run off into my bag. Last night, my journal was mostly pristine.

I felt about as well as the journal did: intact but crumpled and worn. I flipped to the first page to find it still blank, so with my pen, I absentmindedly traced where I remembered the frenetic loops and swirls of Ashley's doodles. I realised what I was doing as I completed Ashley's rendition of me – a stick figure with an impossible large smile and an impossibly long ponytail.

Quiet warmth filled my chest, and tears welled in my eyes as I spent the next hour or so trying to recreate the rest of the drawing. It wasn't perfect, but it was familiar. My stupid wish may have wiped everyone else's memory of her, but I still had mine. I didn't know if I could bring her back, but I could at least make sure someone always remembered her.

At a certain point, my brain began to *hum* with sorrow and regret, an odd sort of humming that made my headache. *Poor little Vicky.* I thought to myself. *You can't even wallow in self-misery without hurting something. Pathetic. Well, you deserve to hurt.* I covered my ears with my hands, expecting the hum to get louder, but instead, it stopped completely.

I sat up. The humming wasn't coming from inside my head, it was coming from somewhere else. But where?

Turning in the direction of the sound, my eyes caught on something strange: an orangish, intensely undulating colour pulsed and spread in the centre of the door to my cell.

It steadily grew larger and larger, like waves emanating from a stone dropped in a pond. Eventually, the ripples reached the curved edges of the doorframe.

I climbed off the bed and tiptoed toward the door on scarlet-slippered feet in nervous anticipation.

The light flared. I jumped back, suddenly blinded, and covered my eyes. Oh no. I was about to be obliterated….

…and then the light vanished completely.

"Ugh," I rolled my eyes. "All that for nothing, I gue…"

BLAM!

The door shot open, striking the wall next to it so hard it nearly came off its hinges. Behind it stood Mayor Nop-Hops, gavel-wand in hand and Emma by his side.

"Oh goodness." The mayor dusted off his robes with his fluffy paws and adjusted his spectacles. "Dreadfully sorry about the noise, Miss Sicktoria. Couldn't be helped, I'm afraid. Disarming magic is a tricky business."

Emma hopped from foot to foot. "Hurry, slow poke!" she squealed. "The guards will be here any minute!"

"Slow down there, young Emma," Mayor Nop-Hops patted her on the head. "I'm not breaking you out just so you can have a midnight tour of the Chapel. We've got to talk strateg…"

SQUEE-SQUAWK! SQUEE-SQUAWK! SQUEE-SQUAWK!

Mayor Nop-Hops was suddenly cut off by what I assumed was a seagull being tortured to use as an alarm.

In perfect tandem, red light from the hallway bathed the Mayor and Emma from above and behind in intermittent flashes.

"Quickly!" the mayor shouted. "You have to get out of here!"

He didn't need to tell me twice.

Emma dashed down the hall Jam had led us down earlier, and the Mayor and I followed. The awful *SQUEE-SQUAWKING* suddenly stopped, leaving vacuous silence in its stead. Overhead, large rectangular light bulb fixtures continued to intermittently flash red.

The mayor stopped when we reached the door at the end of the passage. "I must leave you here," he said. "You must find the wish and put things right. Good luck!"

I looked at his fluffy face, all scrunched up in concern for me. He looked like he was about to say something, but I cut him off by wrapping him up in a giant hug. *Heavens*, he was cosy! He patted my back then gently prodded me toward the door before waving his wand over his head.

POOF!

Just like that, he vanished in a cloud of blue smoke, before I could thank him or say goodbye.

I experienced a moment of panic, cut short by Emma grabbing my arm and yelling, "Yeehaw, hurry, Hurry, HURRY!" and frantically cracked her invisible whip at me.

"Where are we even hurrying to?" I panted as we ran.

"Wherever we go is better than here!" she shouted back. I sped up, hoping to put this jailhouse behind me as quickly as possible.

Everywhere we turned, the same blood-red lights flashed in eerie silence. The shadows they cast were so creepy, I almost missed the deafening *SQUEE-SQUAWK*.

Just as we turned our thirteenth-or-so corner, we came face to face with my least favourite living beings in this entire accursed kingdom.

The squirrels.

An entire platoon of them crowded the corridor ahead of us. A glint of silver flashed above several of them in the red light, and I realised with horror that they were wielding about the most terrifying things they could have gotten their dirty paws on: pairs of massive garden shears.

These were squirrels not even Aunt Marge could love.

Emma screeched at them, turned, and tugged me hard down a different hallway. We'd only made it a dozen steps before skidding to a stop again and back pedalling furiously. Another platoon of squirrels skittered down this hallway, too. Desperately, we retreated to the intersection and turned down the final hall. The terrifying scrabble of more furry feet scuttered after us, punctuated by the snipping of razor-sharp shears.

"Is this some sort of maze?" I yelled right before we ran face first into what ranked *second* on my list of things I didn't want to encounter: a wall.

"Emma?" I asked nervously, as the sound of squirrelled footsteps drew ever nearer. "Why are you just standing there?"

She didn't respond. She didn't even turn to look at me. She just stood there studying the wooden panelling in front of her intently, as if searching for something.

"Emma…?"

"Buy me some time!" she chirped without turning to look at me.

My nerves were shot, Dear Reader, and the only thing I could think of in that moment was that I was dreadfully close to peeing my pants with fear. *That* made me think about how Aunt Marge made all her indoor pets wear diapers so they wouldn't wee in her flat, which *then* made me wonder why Aunt Marge was so obsessed about little furry animals in the first place, *which then* led me to the ultimate questions: *What Would Aunt Marge Do?*

And instantly, I knew the answer.

Pulling my rucksack from my shoulder, I turned to face the oncoming horde. With a huge grin plastered on my face, I greeted my pursuers.

"Well, hello, all you fine looking fellas!" I said in the most sugary-sweet baby voice I could muster. "Aren't you the sweetest wittle squirrels I've ever seen? Why, yes you are!"

They stopped as I advanced, eyeing one another with confusion. Some raised their pruning shears defensively.

I unzipped my pack and approached, keeping up a constant barrage of nonsense flattery while slowly reaching inside.

"Wook at those adorable, fuzzy wittle tummy-wummies!" I cooed.

Just ten more paces and I'd be in range.

"I bet you handsome wittle squirrely-worries would wike some snacky-wackies, wouldn't you?"

I launched the full rotisserie chicken at them. Thank goodness I'd packed something so ridiculous.

The slow-roasted carcass careened into the middle of their ranks. If I'd learned anything from countless afternoons with Aunt Marge at the zoo, and the park, and the pond, and pretty much anywhere and everywhere, it's that you should *always* be prepared to feed the squirrels.

The squirrels at the centre of the platoon barely managed to scramble out of the way before the great slab of slow-roasted chicken landed in their midst with a greasy *thlop.*

Silence.

And then…

A squirrel who'd been standing near the point of impact suddenly keeled over.

Had I landed a direct hit?

More squirrels fell.

Success!

Except, hang on. They weren't injured…they were *laughing!* Laughing so hard tears streamed down their furry cheeks. Laughing so hard they couldn't keep their feet.

"Did she just lob a roasted chicken at us, then?" a squirrel squeaked between peals laughter that forced him to double over to catch his breath.

"She…" another squirrel wheezed, dropping his shears and grabbing onto his neighbour for support, "...she… She thinks squirrels are *carnivores?*"

"Oooooooh, look at me, I'm just a big dumb human from the surface," one said, doing a little jig. Then he stuck his nose up in the air and said in a prim little voice that was *nothing* like mine, "My name's Victoria, and I know nothing about the food chain. I think a one-pound rodent can eat a six-pound bird!"

"Stop, stop!" A squirrel on the ground snorted. "You've made me wee m'self!"

"I didn't mean for you to eat it," I huffed. "It was meant to squash you!"

"Bha-ha-ha!" the squirrels howled. One, who had just regained his feet, fell straight back down again, kicking his legs with seemingly uncontrollable mirth.

"Help! Help!" One cried, pretending to duck behind his companion. "Roasted chickens are falling from the sky!"

"Here lies Daniel Fluffy Tail," another said mournfully, helmet clutched to his breast. "He was absolutely *demolished* by the great Roast Chicken Attack of '22!"

Everyone's an actor.

I turned and stalked back to Emma amidst hiccups and chortles. One of the squirrels farted and set off a fresh wave of guffaws, hoots, and calls of, "Please Miss, can we have some more snacky-wackies? Us is hungwee!"

"Tell me you knew they eat acorns," Emma asked without looking up. She'd moved from simply staring at the wall in front of her to poking around at it.

"I was trying to… never mind," I muttered. "Please tell me you have a plan. I don't know how long they'll be…erm…occup…"

Just then, Emma jabbed one of her bony fingers into a seemingly random bit of wall.

Which promptly slid open.

"There!" she yelled triumphantly. "That should lock it for a bit once we're through."

"Through what?" I inquired. "Please tell me you're not about to drop me through some sort of trapdoo*OOOOOOOOOOOO*…"

I abruptly stopped talking and started falling as Emma dropped me through a trapdoor.

24

Memorial Park at Midnight

I was done. I was simply done. I refused to believe that some faerie architect somewhere thought it would be a brilliant idea to install a secret trap door into an otherwise unremarkable hallway.

I suppose I shouldn't have been complaining. Though I was falling at scream-inducing speeds, it was at least in a direction that took me *away* from the squirrels.

The moment the ground dropped from my feet, I found myself freefalling in cool night air. I screamed and waved my arms and legs as the underside of the enormous branch we emerged from shrunk in the distance above me. My head swivelled to my next rapidly approaching concern: whatever was below me.

The moment I looked to my feet, they ploughed into a huge plane of green. I guess the leaves on this side of the tree were decidedly springyer than the other ones because instead of tearing, it dipped with my weight for a moment before, like a rubber band, rebounding with enough force to send me into the air once more.

Emma and I boinged and bounced along from leaf to leaf, each the size of a spoiled child's outdoor trampoline. I couldn't tell you how many I bounced off. It's hard to keep track of things when every three seconds you're being flung up into the air with your arms and legs flailing, only to careen down to your next spring-off point – just so it could start over again.

Near the end, I even started to enjoy it a little. Besides, it seemed the fall to my death might take a bit, so I took the opportunity to survey my surroundings. First, I noticed the shaft of sunlight I had previously seen from the hole in the centre of the cavern was absent. Instead, faint, cool moonlight painted the Kingdom pale blue, with dots of yellow and orange illuminating the vacant streets.

We were approaching – well, plunging toward, at least – a suburban part of town with quaint pink benches and saplings springing up here and there. In the distance was a park, and beyond it were rows of single-story houses of all shapes, colours, and building materials. Probably. I was still boinging and bouncing quite violently, so I had to infer all that from bouncing blurs.

All in all, it was one of the nicer parts of town I'd seen so far. I could actually picture myself living in one of those pixie cobblestone houses.

I was just accepting my new lot in life as an endlessly bouncing girl when I looked down to see that my next destination was *not* another leaf.

It was a pond.

Maybe I could've pulled off a neat cannonball or something had I had more time. But I only noticed it about a dozen feet off. I was facing down and tried to straighten and turn to at least shield my face. Too little too late. Flat as a pancake, I belly flopped into the still water with a stinging ***THWAPP!***

Frigid water invaded my nose, and the rush of wind past my ears was replaced with muffled rumbling. At least the little pond was deep enough that I didn't shatter my skull on impact.

I stopped sinking near the bottom and took that moment of relative privacy to scream as loudly as I could, letting the water dampen my voice. *Heavens,* that belly flop hurt.

When I was done, I propelled myself upward with frantic kicks, broke through the surface, and looked around.

How quaint, I thought, taking everything in. The nice little cobblestone plaza we were in at the base of the mountainous tree was blessedly empty. With a tiny splash, the faintly illuminated silhouette of Emma's little quilled head surfaced to my right. I paddled over to her. My everything still stung, but I was beyond the point of caring.

"*Emma*?" I asked.

"What's up?" she answered in a tone that made it clear that *my* tone hadn't had the intended effect. When she turned to me, calm as a cucumber, she gave me a look that implied my face looked as good as it felt.

"Why on, or even *in,* God's green Earth was there a button in that hallway that's sole purpose was to send perfectly dry people plummeting into a pond?"

She looked at me quizzically. "Do humans not have 'out-of-here' shafts in the above world?" she asked. "Haven't you ever thought to yourself, 'boy, I'd really like to not be in this building right now'?"

"Well, yes," I conceded. I tilted my head from side to side in a futile attempt to jostle some water from my ears. "But we do have these lovely things called *exit doors*…

"Oh yes," she said, "I've used *exit doors*, but they've got nothing on 'out-of-here' shafts for when you just can't shake that feeling and need to get out-of-there right that moment. It's especially convenient for folks who don't have wings."

"You're serious, aren't you?"

"As serious as a troll at 5:00 AM," she nodded gravely.

"And you just knew this particular building would have those particular shafts in that particular hallway?"

"Oh, no, the mayor told me about them," she waved dismissively. "The councillors use them when people are being rowdy. He even mentioned that if I pressed just the right button, the opening would lock up for a while after one use. I guess they got tired of people using them for fun. But, as much as I'd love to continue your civil education, hadn't we best be getting on? Where did the mayor say the wish would be?"

I blinked at her, my panic rising. "The mayor didn't say anything to me about *where* the wish was. I thought he told you! He broke you out first!"

"No!" she squealed. "He just barged into my cell and said the fate of Clive and possibly the world rested on my shoulders, or something, and then took me with him to your cell! The only thing he told me was which hallway I'd find the out-of-here shaft we needed!"

I thought back to our conversation in his office. He'd told us about how wishes work – or rather, how nobody fully understood how they worked. Then he'd spouted off some nonsense about taking a walk in the park at midnight…

Where had I heard something about a park at midnight before? Hadn't there been something like that in The Tome?

Oh no, The Tome!

I immediately doggy-paddled towards the shore.

Once I had clambered from the pond, dripping and miserable, I opened my rucksack, and desperately tore through it. Everything was soaked. I barely registered Emma yelling at me for hitting her with a water-damaged toilet-paper roll as my search grew more and more anxious. "Please be okay, please be okay, please be okay," I furiously muttered to myself.

"Erm, are *you* okay?" Emma nervously patted me on the shoulder. "Sorry about your stuff getting soaked, but I'm sure we can find more food somewhere-"

"Aha!" I cut her off, thrusting *The Tome of Hidden Creatures* high into the night sky. To my amazement, it was almost completely dry, with only a few droplets rolling off its leathery surface.

I glanced down at my slippered feet. *They* hadn't fared quite as well. Which was a shame, they were *very* cosy. And I was probably about to do a lot of walking.

"Oh, is that what you were worried about?" Emma rolled her eyes at me as she dried herself off with a shirt I'd tossed over to her. "Don't you humans waterproof all your books on the surface? Because we certainly do."

I ignored her. I *knew* I'd read something somewhere that matched what Mayor Nop-Hops had been talking about. '*Telling Werewolves from Wherewolves*'. No. '*Using Moonlight to Shine your Silverware'*. No. '*How to Hide from Common Mushrooms*'. Definitely not.

'*Magical Parks of the Magical Community*.' There it was! I'd glazed over it initially as I hadn't planned on coming down to the Kingdom for a nature tour, but I *had* noticed something odd about it. Most of the parks were described in very flowery terms. The book went on and on about how refreshing they were and what kind of picnics they recommended having there.

All except for one of them.

Right between '*Gilded Gadfly's Golden Glitter Park*' and '*The Evergreen Glade of Joy*' was a short paragraph detailing '*Memorial Park*'.

Memorial Park: "A place for visiting and remembering one's deceased relatives. It is a rather dreary place. Definitely don't visit after midnight."

"We need to go here," I told Emma, pointing to the section on the page. "Is it nearby?"

As soon as she saw where I was pointing, her quills raised on their ends, trembling.

"It's… It's just a few minutes' walk that way," she said, pointing to the left. She slowly backed away as she said, "But if you want to go to a park, I can take you to the Evergreen Glade of Joy instead. It's not much further away."

"I think we need to go there, Emma. Remember what Nop-Hops said about visiting a park in the moonlight at midnight?"

Just then, a clock tower in the nearby village struck the hour. It rang twelve times.

"Oh, no," Emma whimpered to herself, backing away from me slowly, waving her arms in front of her as if to ward off evil spirits. "Curse my adventurous spirit! Why oh why couldn't I have just stayed home like a good cardenere and left well enough alone? My mah said it would all end in sorrow. How could she have known?"

KZZSHK!

"Ehem, ***EHGHEM,*** excuse me?" a metallic voice interrupted Emma. "Is this thing on?"

The voice resounded from somewhere in the distance, blaring over the metallic static of a P.A. system. I recognized the voice immediately. Councillor Scorn was making an announcement:

"I'll just have to assume you can all hear my lovely voice. I do apologise for disrupting your peaceful sleep, but I have an **urgent** announcement to make."

She cleared her throat.

"Half an hour ago, two fugitives escaped from their holding cells in the Chapel of Great Sinful Acts, potentially with help from a government official. One of those fugitives is… a **human**."

On cue, lights sprung to life in many of the nearby buildings. The neighbourhood stirred to wakefulness, and it didn't like what it was hearing. Angry cries echoed in the still night air. I could almost visualise the pitchforks and torches some of them must be reaching for at that very moment.

"We have dispatched officers of the court. I trust that each and every citizen of the Community will do their civic duty and keep a vigilant watch for this miscreant human and her traitor accomplice."

"Come on, come on!" Emma yelped, snapping out of her temporary lapse into fear. "I know the way! We've got a wish to find!"

I followed her as she dashed to the nearest shadow-shrouded back alley, beginning our decidedly sneaky venture through the night. We kept our heads low to the ground and darted behind houses and past odd containers I assumed were trash cans.

Eventually we came to the outlet of the alley. A quaint suburban street ran parallel to us, and I spotted another alley across from us and took a step forward, only for Emma to shoot out a hand to stop me. She must have heard the danger coming before I could: an immense chattering that surged down the street in our direction. It heralded a literal tsunami wave of squirrels washing over the paved road, each little rodent body scrambling over the other in a mobile pile at least two feet high.

I held my breath and stood stock still. The fuzzy, brown tidal wave flooded through the street before us, displacing anything that wasn't nailed down. Shrill chittering squeaks from the hoard and sharp snips from their rusty shears chilled my blood. If we had been caught in that wave, we would have suffered a painful, furry end. Or maybe they'd just take us to prison, I don't know.

After a tense few moments, the squirrel-surge passed, leaving the street relatively still but covered in clutter. Emma and I looked at each other, but neither of us dared speak. Instead, we dashed across to the next alley.

Emma silently led me down a few more strange back alleys in complete silence. They were familiar yet unusual. In one alley, all the water spouts twisted and curled like crazy straws, and a few of the taller buildings had suspiciously faerie-sized shaped holes in their sides and suspiciously soft items piled underneath. I assumed those were more out-of-here chutes.

Each time we had to cross another street, my heart thumped loudly in my ear as we stopped and waited for more squirrels, or the occasional clump of literal-pitchfork-wielding creatures to stalk through. One clump even consisted of a pair of pixies escorting what I assumed were their tiny, too-excited children, all of whom were armed with kitchen knives.

Suddenly, after we reached another outlet, Emma stopped, almost forcing me to trample her underfoot. "We're here," she whispered melodramatically.

Looming trees formed a circle around a wide field of grass. As we stepped over a curb and off the cobblestone road, I realised how much my feet ached from running on the hard ground in sopping wet slippers. Fortunately, the grass immediately soothed them. My wet skin bristled in the night air, my heart thumped hard in my chest, and my cheeks flushed. After tonight, I wouldn't mind another bath in Mariposa's beauty-shop.

Amidst the sparse benches, enormous hunks of stone dotted the grounds. Some were fashioned into broad squares from pink marble stone, while others were more akin to manhole covers made of green basalt. One of the closer ones was a free-standing column, chiselled to curve as it rose to a single square pedestal. Curious, I leaned forward to inspect an inscription worked into it:

Here lies Morpatia Loonswine Treesuckle
a kindly and mischievous pixie
sure to be missed by her surviving relatives
but not by Aunt Limsy, you rapscallion, you.

Emma didn't bother to shush me as I groaned. I should have guessed from the name and the description in the Tome.

Memorial Park was a graveyard.

Brave, brave Emma. She'd tried to warn me, but I wouldn't listen. And now she walked straight up to the centre of the entire suburban cemetery: an enormous, monolithic pillar of surprisingly plain granite that easily towered above everything around it.

It was odd; out of everything I'd seen or otherwise stumbled across, this was the most serious, the most grim.

Following – not as bravely – I bent as close as I dared to read the inscription:

Here lie the mortal remains of Bloodhound. May he never know peace.

"Wh-who…" I gulped, "who is Bloodhound, Emma?"

"*OoOoOoOoOoOo, whoooooo indeeeeeeeed*?"

25

Victoria McKay, Real Life Ghost Whisperer

The booming voice behind me filled me with such icy cold dread, I both froze up and jumped so high into the air that I thought I might clear the pillar. Never had I heard such a morose, ethereal sound. It was like icy needles had punctured their way through someone's lungs to make the world's most sickening bagpipes.

But the dreadfulness of the voice couldn't prepare me for what I saw as I landed and turned in place. Before me stood – no, *hovered* – an awful, ghastly apparition.

From the waist up, it took the form of a roughly dressed beast of a man. Leather tatters barely clung to his not-skin., and gaping wounds protruded from his torso, each one simultaneously begging for attention and threatening to make me vomit.

A red, shaggy beard that couldn't have received any maintenance in the past decade hung low over the apparition's chest, thankfully obscuring some of his damaged body. I wished it had focused more on obscuring his face. He had a hideous, leering expression, like he was considering how best to make me miserable. His sallow cheeks and curled mouth looked to be repeat offenders of chest-shaking laughs brought on by atrocities happening to innocent bystanders. Below the belt, the figure's form trailed off into a spectral tail, thankfully revealing no more gruesome visual abominations.

But the eyes.

Oh, heavens, *please* let me forget the eyes.

They were both bloodshot and decidedly dead, and they pinned me to the spot more effectively than a harpoon.

I, Victoria McKay, was standing in front of a bonafide ghost.

I was terrified.

And so was Emma, who had succumbed to her former fear and was cowering behind my leg.

As the ghastly ghast eyed us down like he was preparing for his next meal, I realised I was going to have to do all the talking.

"Weeeeeelllll?" the ghost I presumed was Bloodhound menaced.

"Ermm...," I stuttered, "hello, Mr. Bloodhound's ghost, sir." I shifted from foot to foot. "I, erm, I was told to come here by a friend, ahhhh, about a...about..."

"*About a whaaaaaaaat?"* Bloodhound intoned.

"Well...um..." I tried to get out through chattering teeth, "you see, my friend, Mayor Nop-Hops, told me to come to this park at midnight to look for a wish. Would...would you happen to know anything about anything like that?"

"Hahahahahahaha!" Bloodhound's booming chuckle filled the cemetery, seeming to come from everywhere at once.

I almost crouched down to try and hide behind Emma.

"*So,*" the awful ghost continued, "*you've come for my wiiiiiiiiiiiiiiiiiiiish, have you? I warn you, 'tas only brought paaaaaaaaaaaaaaaaain and miiiiiiiiiiiiiiiiiisery to all who've come seeking it before youuuuuuuuuuuu.*" He loomed down, bringing himself mere inches from my face. The chill coming off of him threatened to freeze my blood into a slushie.

"O…o…oh." I barely forced the sounds past my lips. "Why…why…why ever could that be?"

"*Nowwwww, that's a dreadful taaaaaaalle. One that begaaaaan some five centuries agoooooooo. By my owwwwwn admission, I was a rotten little lad, always running off into the forest to worry my old Nana – when I wasn't thinking up ways to torment the other children or forest animals that lived nearbyyyyyy. It was on oooooone of my dastardly adventuuuuures into the foooorest that I happened upon oooooone small, lonely cardeneeeere.*"

Emma squeaked pitifully, and it occurred to me all at once that she must have known who we would meet in this park. That's why she'd been so terrified.

"*I managed to capture the lone cardenere, clever lad that I was, and kept it imprisoned for many a night, trying to get it to reveal its secrets to meeee.*"

Hold on. He did what?

Indignation began to replace my fear with every word he spoke. How dare a big, hulking pirate-monster-ghost-thing like him kidnap a poor little cardenere!?

He floated a bit higher and swept his eyes across the scant treeline before continuing. "*It took many nights of poking, prodding, and staaaarving to get him to divulge his reason for being in the woods.*"

In the blink of an eye, Bloodhound zapped through the air until he was once again eye to eye with me, very much invading my personal space.

I sniffed. And shivered the teensiest bit.

"*It turned out,*" he continued, slowly floating back from me while maintaining eye contact, "*that he had been sent to dispose of not one, but twoooooooooo of those pesky wishes you were asking about! At the time, the Community didn't have a formalised pooooolicy on how to dispose of them. They only required it be done secretly and far away from the Kingdom. The cardenere had hoped to staaaaaaaaaash his in a nearby willoooooow hoooooooooollow. an ancient one that bore a fearsome reputation. There, the little devil thought, no one would be tempted to go searching for themmm. He didn't realise he'd come across someone as daring and conniving as meeeee,*" Bloodhound beamed.

My hands clenched into fists by my side. I wanted to scream at him. He was bragging about torturing an innocent cardenere! But I couldn't. Fear still gripped me, even if it was fading to anger.

"*I knew that hollow well, for I'd spent many a summer day laughing and playing in the shade of its decaying, ominous husk. Alas,*" for a brief moment, sorrow consumed his features, and oddly enough, he started to talk less like a menacing ghost and more like a sad, regretful man. "*I should have realised my folly when the blasted cardenere was all too eager to hear the interest in my voice. He even went so far as to give me directions, as if I'd needed the assistance.*"

Bloodhound's eyes went blank, lost in memory. "*I traced my way back to my favourite…haunt…you could say, and scoured its hollow for my prize. And sure enough, stashed behind a twisted root, I found them: two aged pieces of parchment that smelled as dank and ancient as the tree itself.*"

He smiled wide, his eyes gleaming like he was looking at the two wishes for the first time all over again. "*What wonders awaited me, the holder of two magical wishes? My immense joy could only be matched by my intense indecision." He stroked his awful beard. "How best could I take advantage of my newfound power? What would my first wish be, let alone my second?*"

"If I had a wish right now, I'd use it to make you get to the point, already…" I muttered. I think I was starting to get over the whole 'talking to a ghost thing.' Either way, Bloodhound took no notice.

"*Aha!*" he raised a finger like he was making the decision afresh. "*I could give myself forever to settle on my second wish by way of my first wish! Surely an eternity would be long enough to craft the perfect wording, the perfect request. So, standing under the very same tree where I'd uncovered it, I spoke aloud my first wish. I wished to become* **eternal,** *to grant myself immortality, that I might roam this world forever!*"

Wind stirred to life and lashed at my face, whipping up fallen leaves amongst the tombstones. Emma quivered, clutching my leg. Bloodhound hung triumphant in the air for a moment before his chest sagged and he floated lower, almost close enough to the ground to touch it with his wispy ghost-tail.

"*And that,*" he said, "*is how I learned why the hidden creatures of the world seek to dispose of those wretched slips of paper. My wish was granted alright. I became immortal on the spot. In a grand flash of blue light, my body fell to the ground, and out of it, my spirit emerged, now forever bound to…*"

"Hold it right there," I interrupted, suddenly struck by something I'd remembered reading in the book before I'd ever stepped foot in the Kingdom. "How old were you when you made your first wish?"

"*I was…*" he paused for dramatic effect, "*…fifteen!*"

26
Bloodhound's Plot for World Domination

No.

No.

No no no no.

Just, *no*.

I looked around to see if any squirrel-mounds or pitchfork-wielding-faerie-toddlers were within earshot of me. Seeing there weren't, I sunk my face into my hands and screamed. Not out of terror, mind you. Even if I had still been remotely scared, I wouldn't dare give Bloodhound the satisfaction of my terror. No, it was a scream of pure frustration. The kind of scream your parents tell you to unleash on a poor, unsuspecting pillow instead of on a sibling or breakable object.

"Vicky, are you alright?" Emma came out from behind my leg, and the concern in her eyes for me nearly broke my heart. I scooped her up in my arms and held her close. Even terrified, she was worried about me.

"Forget about me, are *you* okay?" I asked. "No wonder you were so terrified. You should have just told me!"

"*Cardeneres are afraid of their own shadows,*" Bloodhound rolled his mouldy eyes. "*Patheti...*"

"You. Shut. Your. MOUTH!" I turned on the ghost, jabbing my finger at him with every word. "Going around frightening young girls. Does that make you feel macho? And why in the entire nonsensical world have you made yourself look like a war-torn pirate of all things?"

"*Excuuuuse you,*" Bloodhound mumbled, backing away and deflating slightly. "*I'm entitled to develop my own...aesthetic...over my years of immortal imprisonment. And Bloodhound is a far better ghost name than Bob.*"

"Wait...*BOB?!?*" I nearly fainted. I should have known. "Bob from the legend? You *are* the kid who disappeared all those years ago! I thought you were an ancient terror, not just some pubescent, Scottish teenager who got lost in the woods! Also, what kind of evil woman would call their child Bob? Not even Robert?"

"Oooooooooooh, now you've doooooooone it," 'Bloodhound spat. I assumed he was about to unleash a tirade of fury, but instead, his shoulders sagged as he floated lower to the ground. A wimpy wind rustled through his ragged rags, and his form morphed before me. The wounds on his chest closed, his hideous face softened and smoothed, his beard just sort of fell off, and his pirate-esque robes re-wove themselves into an old-timey tunic. When it was finished, the horrid apparition had been replaced by an unremarkable, unintimidating 15-year-old boy, miserably bobbing in the

air, hanging his shoulders like he'd just been rejected by his first crush. He was also still translucent, but it was less menacing now.

*"Nooooooooooow you...*ahem...now you see my true form." he wallowed, and briefly dropped the fake ghost-voice. He made eye contact, straightened up, and got right back into it. *"OOOOOOOhhhhh but you think this body makes me any less poooooowerful?"*

Cheeks burning, I just barely stopped my tirade in its tracks. Yelling at this waste of ether wouldn't get me anywhere. Honestly, I was mostly worried this ghost-of-puberty-past might start crying if I gave him a hard time. Regardless, Mayor Nop-Hops said Bloodhound had an unused wish – well, *implied* it at least – and that's all that mattered at the moment.

"Why haven't you used the other wish to just undo becoming a ghost?" I asked, trying to suss out the status of the wish I needed. "Why have you just sat down here for hundreds of years if you have a perfectly good way of fixing the situation?"

"*Ooooooh, why don't you just use the other wish, Bloodhound?*" he said, using a mocking voice that was unbecoming of a spirit. "*Don't you think that was the first thing I thought of?*" Bloodhound hung his wimpy head. "*Funny thing – turns out you need to be aliiiiiiive to make a wish. They certainly forgot to write that in the fine print!*"

Rage melted to joy in my heart. He still had the second wish after all!

My lips twitched toward a smile.

Thankfully, Bloodhound hadn't seen it, so I didn't have to worry about him thinking I was taking joy in his suffering. No, his eyes were still stuck on the muddy ground beneath his tail. Suddenly, he wheeled towards me with a burst of energy.

"I coooooould always terrorise a living person like yooooou into doing it for me," he tried.

"Go on, then." I crossed my arms over my chest. I was done with this nonsense. "Why don't you *try*. *Bob*."

"*Bah*," he said. "*Not like I haven't tried that before, either. Everyone down here hates me. I guess imprisoning creatures of the Kingdom is frowned on. Who could've guessed?*"

"That's right!" Emma yelled from where she sat in the crook of my aching arm. "Trapping a cardenere like some *animal*. Shame on you!"

Bloodhound crossed his arms and gave a "*harumph!*" I imagined him making the same expression at his parents. *"Don't go running off into a forest you've never been in,"* they might have said. *"Harumph!"* he'd have replied, *"But Mooooooooooooom, I want to be cool and mysteriouuuuuuuus!"*

"Don't start blubbering," I said, turning my full attention to him. "You said you haven't convinced anyone to use the second wish to free you yet. What will it take for you to give it to me?"

"*Hmmmm*." Bloodhound stroked his smooth, currently-beardless-chin. "*I assume you want it for your own purposes, and not to undo my ghostliness? Oh, don't bother answering that, I know how this goes.*"

"You have me there," I admitted. I was *not* going to waste what could be my only shot at getting another wish by freeing a deranged, fifteen/four-hundred-year-old phantom named *Bob* from his mortal punishment. But what to offer then…?

Oh, of course! It was painfully obvious.

"Say, Bloodhound?" I began. "Why exactly *are* you down here? Doesn't everyone in the Kingdom hate you?"

"Ptuh!" Bloodhound moved his head and his lips as if he were spitting, but no ghost-spit came out. *"It's that accursed monolith, you see,"* he said, pointing back to the large obelisk that bore his name. *"Though I've no ability to check, I suspect we're currently who-knows-how-many feet below the ancient hollow where I discovered the wishes. Either my remains are somewhere up there or somehow down here. In any case, I've found myself unable to leave this spot without disappearing and reappearing here again."*

"Well, then," I stood up a bit straighter, "what if I were to find some way to free you from this place? I don't know if I can un-ghost you, but if you weren't bound to this place any more, you'd at least be free to enjoy your afterlife somewhere else."

"*Oh*?" That got Bloodhound's attention. "*Hmmm…no one's offered that before. Do you even think you could accomplish that?*"

I shrugged my shoulders. "Given everything I've seen down here, I figure anything's possible."

Bloodhound surprised me by giving off a truly belly-shaking laugh. It was so infectious that I began chuckling too – slowly first, then quickly devolving into wheezing, high-pitched noises only a dog could hear.

"*Ahh,*" he sighed, regaining his otherworldly composure. "*I see you've gotten as fed up with the nonsensical nature of magic down here as all us outsiders eventually do.*"

I grinned to myself. Despite my low opinion of Bloodhound in general, it was nice to find someone who sympathised with just how bizarre things could be down here in the Kingdom of Creatures for a regular old human.

"Erm," Emma muttered next to my leg. "I suppose I *might* know a way to help him out. Though, mind you," she shook her finger at me, "I'm not thrilled to be aiding *him*."

Squealing filled my ear as I scooped her up – this time for a tight embrace. "Oh, Emma, thank you, thank you, thank you!" I spun her around in the air, ignoring her protests entirely. I'd been *so* anxious that my promise would be pointless.

"Down, down, down!" Emma wriggled out of my grasp and plopped back to the ground. "You humans are so touchy-feely," she mumbled, giving herself a shake like a cat who'd escaped a bath. "Tricky part is," she said, "I only know about it because of where it is. You see, we're gonna have to make our way over to my dear…"

An unfamiliar voice in the distance cut her off.

"Oi Mum! Why don'ts we check over 'ere?"

That couldn't be good.

Nothing's Ever Easy

The voice, which was low, lumbering, and stupid, had come from somewhere far to my left, outside the ring of trees surrounding the park. Fresh terror filled me – not the kind brought about by a ghost or other monster cornering you in a park. This was the terror any child felt when they'd been getting away with mischief for a long time – too long, even – and now realised they were about to be caught.

"Oh Timmy, do shut up," a much shriller voice cut in. "No one in their right mind would be poking around *that* place this late at night – not even a disgusting *human."*

Bob chuckled. *"Sounds like youuuuuu've got some companyyyyyy,"* he giggled, sweeping his arms wide and rising into the air. As he gestured, his form slowly evaporated into nothingness. *"I'll be waiting for you, lassie. Best of luck, but another century or so makes no difference to me if you fail....”*

“Why do you talk like a stupid pirate?” I hissed at the empty air, trying to keep my voice low. He only left behind an echo of his ghostly laughter.

“Shhhh!” Emma shushed me from the crook of my arm. I crouched behind the monolith and set her on the ground, my arm having gone completely numb. We hid ourselves just as more odd bickering floated our way from outside the park.

“Well, didn’t you hear that, Mum? There are ne'er-do-wells in the cinema…the cinnamon…the cement…uhhh…the dead people place!”

I peeked out from behind Bloodhound’s mausoleum. Two silhouettes – one tall and wide and the other taller and wider – approached through the tombstones in the moonlight.

“Mummy, I’m getting tired!” the biggest one whined. “You said I could eat a yuman if I got outta bed and came with you!”

“Yes, yes, dear, you will,” the slightly less-tall one answered. “We just have to *find* the tasty little snack first.”

“Follow me!” Emma whispered. “And stay low! They’ll roast you on a spit like that chicken of yours if they see you.” With that, she darted off into the night.

Stay low! Don’t let them see you! I silently mouthed to myself, mimicking Emma. Jeez, thanks, I grumbled back at her in my mind. Really helpful! Why didn’t I think of staying low so the horrible mother/son duo who just said they want to catch me and eat me don’t see me? Easy for you to say – you’re a cardenere. If you got any lower, you’d be underground! Oh wait! We are underground!

Dear Reader, you would be right to be concerned about my mental well-being at this point. But, for the sake of transparency, I want you to know this: things were about to get worse. And *not* before they got better.

It was two agonising minutes before we made it to the trees and were able to glance out at the neighbourhood surrounding the park. It was empty. Except for our new predators.

They were both hairless, their grey skin glistening moistly in the light of the torches they carried. They were dead ringers for the blobgoblins I'd read about in the book.

The Blobgoblin

"The Blobgoblin is the less-feared cousin of the hobgoblin and, while not strictly the dumbest resident of the Kingdom, is certainly not smart. When he's not eating frozen dinners in front of a television stolen from humans, he's wandering around, finding things to hit. He thinks doing so is terribly clever. Never try to reason with a blobgoblin, for your head will start to hurt far sooner than his will. If his incessant arguing with others of his kind doesn't do the trick, whatever club-like device he has on hand surely will."

The larger of the two – I assumed the son – was in red and white striped night drawers with fuzzy slippers. The mother had taken more time to dress for the occasion, sporting a yellow polka dot dress and a statement necklace consisting of – if my eyes didn't deceive me – a complete set of cutlery. Fashion *and* function. I'm sure Mariposa would have been thrilled!

What a lovely bonding moment this must have been for them. A mother/son night out to hunt and eat humans!

"Vicky, what are you doing?"

Emma's hiss snapped me out of my open-mouthed trance. I suppose gawking wasn't the best course of action to take.

Too late.

"Oi, mum, I see it!" Junior cried with glee, pointing straight at me.

"Good eye son!" Mumsie Dearest, patted him on the head with a massive open palm. "You just earned yourself first pickings on her limbs!"

"Now what do we do?" I whispered down at Emma.

No response. I looked behind me and found she had already reached the end of the block and had only stopped to frantically wave for me to follow her.

I broke into a mad sprint, my soggy shoes pounding on the cobblestone street as I bounded toward Emma. The earth rumbled beneath me from the heavy footfalls of the blobby fiends behind me. I dared to look over my shoulder – which was a mistake. The mother, flailing her torch over her head in a fit of ecstasy, was only about 50 feet back. The son, who had massive strings of saliva glooping out of his open gullet, was only a few feet behind her. *Why were they so fast?!*

I ran harder. Emma was only moving *just* slow enough that I didn't lose sight of her completely.

At first, it was just the blobgoblins chasing us, and that was bad enough. You might think, just by looking at them, that they'd be too fat and slow to be truly effective chasers. You'd be wrong. I don't know what it was – maybe their size just gave them a lot of forward momentum – but they were faster than they had any right to be.

But their speed wasn't the only thing I had to worry about. They were *loud. Really loud.* They wouldn't shut up about which part of me would be the tastiest once they caught me.

It drew a *lot* of attention.

More and more lights flickered on in the houses we sprinted past. I began hearing other clusters of bloodthirsty faerie-folk descending on us. From behind us *and* in front as it turned out. Just when I thought we'd outpaced the blobgoblins, we almost ran face first into a pixie woman pushing a cart. The cart itself resembled an ice cream truck, only it was lined with plants instead of delicious frozen treats. Angry looking plants, too – like if Venus fly traps had human teeth. I was even close enough to read one of the labels:

WARNING: POISON PLANTS. DON'T LEAVE NEAR UNATTENDED SMALL CHILDREN (UNLESS YOU WANT THE EASY WAY OUT OF MOTHERHOOD)

Before I could decipher any other potentially horrific labels, the pixie pushing the cart let out a scream: "It's the human! I found her!"

It was a scream of delight as opposed to terror, and it brought even more creatures onto the street from nearby houses and park benches. The pixie lady pulled a ***Morningstar*** from her cart (how and why did she have that in there?) and flailed it around at me.

No matter which way we ran, trouble was waiting for us. One street brought us face-to-face with a small group of full-grown purple panthers. I hadn't read *anything* about these in the book, but I also hadn't read the whole thing from cover to cover. They were wearing suits and ties, and their backs arched the moment they saw us. Each one hissed a sibilant hiss, all harmonising with each other like they were members of a demented barbershop quartet.

"I've got her! I've got her!" The younger blobgoblin came barrelling down the street straight at us. He was so close I could smell his rancid breath.

My breath came ragged and fast in my throat, and my heartbeat thundered in my ears. We were surrounded: purple panthers on the left, suicide plants and medieval-weapon-wielding-florist on the right, and an ever growing crowd of angry village creatures with torches and pitchfork behind us.

A circle of doomy death slowly closed in as the larger blob stalked up to Emma and me. Emma clutched my leg as the blobgoblin chuckled insidiously. "Got you now, treat!"

Time seemed to slow to a trickle.

There was no way out. There was no reasoning with these creatures, and I had no more rotisserie chickens or other tricks up my sleeve.

So, I did the only thing I could think of at that moment.

I punched the blobgoblin.

Now, reader, I know what you're thinking. And you're right.

Violence is *not* the answer.

…to *most* problems.

You should not make a habit out of punching people in tricky situations. But I feel it's perfectly fine to make exceptions for people who want to *eat* you.

Time sped up back to its normal pace as soon as my fist finished making contact with the blobgoblin's immensely dense melon. It felt like I had punched a beanbag that had been marinating in a hot tub for a few hours. Except tougher. My knuckles ached, and I'm sure I felt either a crack or a pop.

The blobgoblin's face went slack. I stood completely still, totally unsure of what was about to happen. I was probably going to be obliterated as soon as the thing's tiny brain processed what just happened. His eyes went wide a second later, and his mouth dropped open in disgusted horror.

To whinge, as it turned out.

"She hit me, Mumsie!" he wailed. "She hit me right in the head!"

"Cooties!" one of the creatures from the crowd shrieked. "Eeeeeeewwwwww! He's got cooties now!"

Pandemonium ensued. I sprang into action.

"Okay, bye!" I yelled to the crowd. In one motion, I scooped Emma up onto my shoulder and sprinted toward a break in the mass of bodies. The creatures parted for me as if I had the plague.

The crowd shrank behind us. No time to celebrate, though, as I was sure less germophobic creatures would show up soon enough.

"Which way?" I yelled at Emma as I ran. She whispered directions into my ear, and I ran how I'd seen her do it: low to the ground, slinking in and out of shadows, blending with the darkness like a falcon on silent wings.

At least, that's what it looked like in my head.

In reality, Emma cracked her invisible whip at me, and I stumbled along as best as I could. She steered me in the direction she wanted me to go by grabbing my hair in her paws and "turning" me left or right. I limped along under her immense weight, my sopping wet slippers slapping down the cobblestone street, and I swatted at her when she got a little too liberal with steering.

"Whoa, girl!" she said eventually, reigning me in and dismounting.

Panting, I looked around. We stood in front of a little daub and wattle cottage at the very end of a modest street. Lumber and thatch featured as the prominent building materials as opposed to stone and concrete.

The cottage was charming, though modest, with trim painted in alternating shades of grey and green. A small sign hung meekly over the door frame that read:

SNIFFLETON'S MAGICAL SUPPLIES ON MAGNA STREET

"Where are we?" I asked between breaths, checking up and down the street to make sure we hadn't been followed.

"Remember how I said I didn't have a last name back at the trial?" Emma asked, staring at the sign, her voice distant. "Well, if I *did* still have one, it would be Sniffleton. This is my parents' shop."

28

Frightened Family Functions

At Emma's command, I turned the wooden handle and gingerly opened the front door.

Rows and rows of small shelves stretched out over the entire span of the shop's interior, and even more cupboards and glass containers hung from the walls by neatly placed nails. Every inch of space was occupied by some sort of fantastic curiosity: some were as small as thimbles, others larger than was seemingly possible, and each looked like it had a story to tell.

I was entranced.

I let Emma off my shoulder and my feet carry me down the nearest row completely of their own accord. I was intent on absorbing every detail. Atop one shelf menaced a feathered mask carved from petrified wood, each of its eyeholes affixed with sparkling rubies. It had a hooked, beaklike nose. On the middle row of another shelf, a clear vial sparkled with the colours and flecks of material that dissolved in and out of focus like a field of stars. I even found three immaculately crafted stone figurines resembling small, frightened cardeneres crouched behind a shelf near the back. The artistry and detail were exquisite! They had been carved as if clutching one another in fear, hiding from something truly terrifying. One of them looked young enough that her quills had barely started growing in as stubble around her head.

"Emma!" I whisper-shouted. "You've got to come see this!"

"What is it?" she asked, trudging up. Her voice sounded as weary and downtrodden as I'd felt before we'd entered the magical shop.

"Look at them!" I pointed excitedly. "They look just like you!"

"I should hope so," she responded, sullen. "Those're my three younger siblings."

I did a double take. One of the 'statues' blinked. I opened my mouth to ask something, but then…

"EMMA!" a shrill voice erupted from somewhere behind me. "How dare ye come back here!?"

Emma's Mam, now emerging from her hiding place behind the shop's counter, wore a greyish-brown sack secured tightly to her form by a rope-belt around her waist. Her quills were tied back in a fetching lavender and periwinkle scarf, and her eyes were similar to Emma's in shape, sure, but *not* in the amount of fury they contained. They absolutely *swam* with the perfect mix of rage towards Emma and fright towards everything else.

"What kind of cardenere goes and gets themselves in trouble with the law, an' then has the audacity to bring it backta' their own family?"

"Hello, Mammy," Emma sighed.

"Oh, 'hello,' is that right? Is that all ye have tah say fer yerself?" The furious cardenere stormed over to her daughter and leaned down slightly to yell directly into her face. "No cardenere in 'er right mind would be out galavantin' around and bringin' so much trouble on themselves that the whole city would get involved. Look at yer brothers and sisters."

On cue, the three smaller cardeneres sprang to life, abandoning their statue poses and running towards their Mam, each one almost scrambling over the others to get there first.

Emma's Mam gathered them in like a mama hen. "There, there, sweetlings, ye've done just as yer supposed to. Top marks all of ye for playin' possum. Cornelius, I'da sworn you'd actually gone and petrified yerself!" Her voice was all doting motherly kindness.

Then she turned on Emma. "But *you*," she seethed, inching closer and closer until Emma had no other choice but to take several steps back. "Tis a shame, yer bein' shown up by siblings half again yer age. Cornelious 'ere is only one and a half centuries old, an' already 'es havin' brilliant ideas like dressing him an' his siblings up like statues."

Emma went from looking tired to just…finished with everything. She huffed and threw up her tiny arms.

"Do you have any idea how long and far I came to see you again?" she half-shouted. "How far I came to *apologise?* I spent *years* in the overworld, got captured by the squirrel-officers, put on trial, *chased by blogoblins,* and all so I could come back to you. But that was all silly, wasn't it? You don't care if I'm alive or dead."

Tears welled in Emma's eyes, but her Mam's were dry as stone. Finally, with an icy cold expression, she tutted and said, "Oh Emma, if ye were meant to come back, we'd not have sent ye away to begin with."

My mouth dropped open and my fists clenched. I was about to say something, but Emma's Mam turned to me before I had the chance.

Drat. I had been perfectly content to remain a spectator. Now I guess I'd have to speak up.

Tricky thing, that. I was not pleased to hear Emma verbally ripped apart by her own flesh-and-blood mother. My every instinct compelled me to say something that was definitely going to be extreme.

But then again, I assumed we needed something from this magically jam-packed shop. Otherwise, Emma probably wouldn't have brought us here. Perhaps it was time to flex my diplomatic muscles again.

"I must say," I chimed in, attempting to keep a level voice, "they were terribly clever disguises, erm, Mrs…?"

As the older cardenere strode towards me, I contemplated whether I would have preferred meeting her or Bloodhound in the cemetery earlier. In retrospect, I definitely experienced more visceral fear watching the tiny, mad-eyed woman close the distance to me.

Before I had any hope of jumping out of the way or maybe getting last minute hiding lessons from Emma's siblings, the furious woman…

…hugged me.

Quite tightly.

"Oh, poor little thing," she cooed, releasing me slightly and smoothing out my hair and damp loungewear. "I'm Adriana Sniffleton, but ye can just call me Addy. Ooooh, ye must be chilled right to yer bones, runnin' aboot in the night like this."

Now that she mentioned it, it had been rather cold out there. I hadn't found a moment to towel off since my plunge in the pond earlier, and I had only been wind-dried from all the sprinting. I was still damp and shivering.

Wait, no. Stop it, Vicky. I told myself. Don't let Addy's motherliness draw you in. She's the enemy! She kicked out her own daughter! What kind of loving parent would do that? I would be polite, but I was not going to start thinking nice thoughts about her.

"Uhhhhh, I'm quite alright, thank you," I finally mustered. "I'm actually warming up quite nicely now that we're inside your lovely shop."

I tried not to shiver and prayed no one noticed the trail of water I'd left behind.

"An' such good manners, too," she smiled brightly at me.

Just as quickly as she cooled down, she wheeled back around on Emma.

"Far too polite," she spat, "to be dragged around by ye, no doubt puttin' her life at risk just so you can have an adventure, I bet."

"No, please, Mrs. Sniff – erm – Addy," I interceded. "I'm actually the one dragging Emma around. She's trying to help me get back my sister, and she's been doing a wonderful job."

Emma smiled gratefully at me. Mrs. S, meanwhile, went to the entrance we'd just come in through and got low to the ground before sticking her head out and checking both directions like a prairie dog to see if the coast was clear.

"Looks like ye've not been followed," she said, pulling herself back in and closing the door quickly behind her. "Ye can speak yer piece, I s'pose." She didn't bother looking at Emma as she addressed her, instead electing to head to the back of the shop.

"What a warm family welcome." Emma said, standing still as Mrs. S carried a bundle of stuff around a counter and crouched down.

"Now don't ye be given' me any sass, young lady" Mrs. S's voice floated up from where she worked. "Yer jus' lucky yer old Pah's not 'ere to see what yer up to."

"Where is Mr. Sniffleton?" I asked, trying to cut through the tension.

"Oh, 'e's off with the other cardeneres," Mrs. S replied, hopping back over the counter with a large, camouflage patterned sheet of fabric in tow. "Leadin' a night-time class about curlin' up into a ball an' playin' dead as a response to social invitations."

She then power-walked back to the doorway and climbed up on a nearby shelf, where she promptly hung a camouflage blanket over two hooks I hadn't noticed over the door. Once hung, the blanket shined a dull green before frantically rearranging its patterns. When the glow faded and the pattern stopped moving, I couldn't even tell there used to be a door there at all.

An invisibility cloak for a door frame! I was on the verge of asking how much one might cost and if I could use Emma's family discount when I realised I hadn't a farthing to my name. It also occurred to me that cardeneres might not sell to *my kind.* Actually, speaking of that, it was weird Mrs. S hadn't kicked me out yet…

"Mrs, erm, Addy," I cleared my throat, "why aren't you angry about me being in your house? I'm a human, aren't I? Everyone else in this stupid kingdom seems to have a problem with me being down here, so why don't you?"

Mrs. S threw back her head and laughed, then looked startled at herself and glanced back at the door frame like she was worried someone might have heard her.

"Silly lass," she chuckled a little more quietly this time as she straightened back up. "Shame my daughter ain't been servin' as a proper tour guide for you down here. Us cardenere's don't mind humans, 'specially you young 'uns. You see all the other nasty sorts who live down 'ere? Why, it'd be outright foolish of us to be scared of humans in comparison."

Her other children broke their silent streak to laugh at that – and me by extension, I guess. But I laughed too. They had a point – I *definitely* wasn't as scary as many of the monsters I'd encountered. Unless you were afraid of being assaulted by cooked chicken.

"B'sides," Mrs. S continued, "we've always thought everyone else's obsession with secrecy was redundant, at best." She smiled and shrugged her shoulders. "Cardeneres already hide from most folks down here, and *they* definitely know we exist. What's the point in keepin' us all secret from humans if we can hide from 'em regardless?"

"Oh great," I could hear the eye-roll implicit in Emma's voice. "Give some random stranger a warmer welcome than your own daughter."

I shot Emma a look, surprised to hear what sounded like venom dripping from her words.

"Sorry," she said meekly, "being home isn't bringing out the best in me."

"Speakin' of which," Mrs. S side-eyed her daughter. "Ye still havnee told me why yer *really* here. And don't start with yer nonsense about apologisin'."

"Addy," I responded before Emma could, "I don't know if you've heard about the court case this morning, but I'm here trying to get my sister back. You see, I accidentally wished her away, and–"

"Hhhhhhsss," Mrs. S hissed through her teeth. "Bad business, them wishes. Sorry tah hear ye and yer sister got caught up with one."

"I…yes, thank you." I was once again caught off guard by the contrast between how she treated me and how she treated Emma. "Anyway," I continued, "to make a long story short, I need to use another wish to unmake the one that got rid of my sister, and the only person I know of who has another one is Bloodhound, who said he'd give it to me if…"

"BLOODHOUND?" All the colour drained from her face. "Now you listen to me, young lady," Mrs. S placed both her hands on her hips, scolding *me* for a change. "That Bloodhound is bad, *bad* business. I don't know what 'es told ye, but ain't nothin' good can come from dealin' with him. *Especially* with wishes involved."

"I completely understand, Addy," I agreed, nodding my head. "Believe me, I wouldn't be dealing with him if my sister's existence weren't on the line. I know just how awful he is, what with his abducting and torturing that poor cardenere."

"Ooooooooooooh." Mrs. S brimmed with fiery rage. "Can ye imagine a worse thing? Taking a freedom-lovin' creature whose only goal in life is tah mind their own business and puttin' 'em in a *cage*? Ye can't even *hide* in a cage!" She slammed her fist down onto the nearest shelf.

"Truly terrible, I agree. The thing is," I continued, "all he wants in return is to be let free from his grave. That way, he wouldn't always be around haunting everyone, and…"

Mrs. Sniffleton gasped, making the sign of the cross with one of her claws. "Oh lassie, if ye set him free 'ed probably start poppin' up in our cupboards!

"Imagine 'im poppin his 'ead in at yeh when yeh were usin' the loo!" young Cornelius' voice trembled in horror.

I tried to stifle a giggle as an image rose in my mind of Bob the Boy Ghost's head floating in a porcelain bowl waiting to shout booooooo! at an unsuspecting creature.

"I wouldn't put it past 'im, son!" Mrs. S sniffed. "'E might even try 'is 'and at capturin' more cardeneres from beyond the grave!"

"Mum!" Emma shouted, interrupting Mrs. S's panicked speculation.

"Hoh!" Mrs. S reared up for another round of scolding. "Now you listen here, young lady, if you think *banishment* was bad, just wait till…"

"No, *you* listen here." Emma stalked towards her mother, shoulders squared and eyes fiery. "My friend's sister got wished away, and the only thing that can get her back is setting Bloodhound loose. I know how much you hate him – I know how much everyone does. But are you really telling me that hatred is worth someone – anyone – losing a sister? Forever?"

Emma swept her arm in the direction of her siblings. "I haven't seen these little 'uns in hundreds of years. Heck, I've never even *met* that one before." Emma pointed to the smallest of her siblings, who instinctively curled up in a ball. "But you'd best believe I would release a thousand ghosts – a thousand *Bloodhounds*, even – if it meant saving one of them from being fodder for a wish. So, what about you, *mother*?"

Mrs. Sniffleton didn't answer right away. The two of them just stared at each other for a good long minute, before…

The older cardenere put her hands on Emma's, and her gaze softened. Then, she shocked everyone in the room by pulling her daughter into a restrained yet firm hug.

"Ah, deary," Mrs. S said, pulling back from Emma, "I suppose I didn't do the worst job of raisin' ye."

Emma wriggled away, wiping at her shoulders like she was trying to get mud off. "Thank you, dear mother," she said, "but that doesn't rightly make up for you banishing me, now does it?"

Mrs. S sighed. "I s'pose not, deary," she responded, "but them's the rules. Any cardenere who puts the rest of us at risk gets the boot. Can't go makin' no exceptions for familial ties, can I?" She inclined her head towards Emma's brothers and sisters. "They know the rules, too. I know you'd do anything tah save 'em, but they know as well as any other cardenere what'll happen to 'em if they can't keep their heads low."

"I figured you'd say that," my nubbly friend said, arms folded. "I won't be staying. We just need to grab something, and then we'll be on our way."

"Oh, ay," Mrs. S rolled her eyes. "Ye don't intend tah be a problem – ye just need to nab somethin' from me shop while yer on the run as a fugitive of the law. Well," she said, "what exactly are ya lookin' fer?"

Emma took a deep breath before answering. "We need the Skeleton Key."

29

Emma's Brave Gambit

"Absolutely not!"

"But Mother, please," Emma began, only to be halted in her tracks.

"No BUTS, young lady," Mrs. S barrelled over her. "That be dangerous magic ye be wantin' to play with, 'specially if yer gonna try an' use it fer what I think ye will."

Emma's mother abruptly turned around and absentmindedly arranged things on her already-tidy shelves.

"Please, Mrs. Sniffleton…Addy." I made sure to affect a slight whimper. "I don't know what a 'bone key' is, but if it can save my sister, I *need* to try it. Can't you find it in your heart to help me?"

Mrs. S turned to me with pity in her eyes. “Poor thing. I know it’s heart-wrenching to lose a loved one and have no power to bring them back.”

I suppressed a snort. I guess she would know, at that.

“In light of your suffering…” Mrs. S began, my hopes daring to raise… “...my final answer is…”

Please. Please. Please!

“...still no. Ye ask too much, daughter. That’s a fine item ye want te go waistin’ on something as awful as settin’ that Bloodhound lose. An’ I can tell ye’ve not even explained it properly te yer human friend, else she wouldn’t be here with ye askin’ for it.”

“Shouldn’t have expected much different, I suppose,” Emma muttered, glancing from me to her mother. “I’d say I hope you can sleep with yourself at night, but you seem to manage just fine.”

“Sticks and stones may break my bones,” Mrs. S retorted, “but only spell-words can hurt me.”

“I guess we’ll be leaving then,” Emma sighed. “Will you at least do us the courtesy of letting us use the tunnels? That way we can get back to Bloodhound to let him know we can’t help without stirring up any more of a ruckus around town.”

My mouth dropped open in astonishment that I didn’t bother trying to hide. Was she really giving up just like that? After we’d come all this way and nearly been lunched on by a blobgoblin!?

“*Oh, aye,*” Mrs. S jeered, “first ye ask fer a rare and powerful magical item, then ye expect me teh show the tunnels to a non-cardenere! And yer really surprised ye ended up banished!”

Mrs. S gave Emma one last glare before turning and giving me a thorough visual pat down. “Well,” she said after too long a moment of silence. “This one’s been polite enough, despite hanging around the likes of youse.” She crossed her arms, then nodded. “Fine, if it’ll get ye out of here all the quicker, then the tunnels are yours to use.”

Hooray…we got to use *the tunnels. That* sure sounded appealing.

My shoulder drooped, and the exhaustion of the entire long ordeal all caught up to me in one moment. Had it really been just last night that I’d sneaked from the hotel and entered the tunnels beneath the castle? The only sleep I’d had in the last 48 hours had been the brief moments I’d spent curled up under an aluminium emergency blanket in an underground cavern with my head sandwiched between two rocks. Since then, I’d been drugged by squirrels *twice,* endured a fifteen-step makeover, stood witness at the trial of a lawfur sentenced to execution because he tried to help me, been thrown in jail, broken out of jail, bargained with a truly despicable ghost, been chased through a cemetery by snackish toddlers and suicide plants, and all for what?

Nothing.

It felt like ages since I’d had a proper cuppa – even though it had only been that morning – and I was still no closer, after all of that, to righting the wrong I’d done in the first place.

Whether or not this Skeleton Key would have worked out, I’d never know now.

Emma tugged on my arm, and I followed her, numb, while Mrs. Sniffleton rummaged behind her counter. There was a soft *click,* and one of the shelves on the back wall slid away to reveal the opening to yet another tunnel.

Yay.

Emma silently grabbed my forearm and yanked me into the cold, dark, musty opening. She stopped only for a moment once we were inside to turn around and yell back to her mother.

"Thank you, Mumsie dearest, for being such a big help!" Her voice dripped with sarcasm.

"Don't come back!" was Mrs. Sniffleton's only response, other than another soft *click.*

The panel slid back into place, leaving us sealed in darkness.

***

The tunnels we traversed were a wonderful analogy for my state of being: gloomy, annoyingly damp, colourless, endless, and confusing.

Emma pulled me along for about fifteen minutes before I collapsed. I was grateful to feel her slide down the slick stone wall next to me.

"Well," her soft voice echoed off the stone walls surrounding us, "that didn't go quite as planned."

"Emma," my voice creaked like an attic door limply swinging open, "what are we going to do?" The slightest sniffle broke through my words, and I stared into my knees in the darkness "I've been running around all day, dragged from one reality-defying scenario to the next, and I'm no closer to bringing my sister back than I was when I left for Scotland. I don't even know what we were trying to get from your mother's shop, but I *do* know that we don't have it."

"Oh, the Skeleton Key?" Emma chirped, far too chipper considering what we'd been through that night. "Well, it's kind of hard to explain, but it works as a magic-nullifier of sorts. The obvious application is opening magic locks and the like, but it can also be used to end arcane contracts, free people from curses, that sort of thing. My mother, curse her heart, had one of the last known copies in the world."

"Has," I corrected her. "And I don't know what 'arcane' means, but I guess it doesn't matter since we won't be using it."

"Arcane means secret, magical, and mysterious," Emma said, "and I wouldn't be so sure of that."

Emma jumped to her feet, and fire sprang to life above us. I gasped, shielding my eyes, but it was too late. The sudden, otherworldly light temporarily blinded me. After several seconds of rapid blinking, my eyes adjusted. I could just make out Emma, who had apparently been lighting an ancient looking torch that hung low to the ground from a hook projecting out of the stone-lined tunnel ceiling.

The tunnel itself wasn't much to look at even with the light: just your regular old arched stone cave with an earthen floor. Its only decorations were more torches like the one Emma had just lit. Emma smiled up at me, a matchbook reading 'Sniffleton's Magical Supplies on Magna Street' clutched in one of her furry paws.

She waved the other paw at me politely.

I was confused, but I could appreciate her spirit. So, I waved back as politely as I could.

Maybe there was specific etiquette attached to entering tunnels below magic shops in the Kingdom of Creatures? I half expected her to introduce herself and offer to shake hands. That was when I realised: her other paw *wasn't empty*.

At first glance, the thing she held looked like a long, metal rod, maybe ten centimetres in length, and no thicker than a finger – Emma's finger, even. It shone bronze and gold in the torchlight, casting spots of dull yellow onto the stone walls. Two protrusions, the only irregularities in its otherwise perfectly cylindrical form, stuck out at the end, half a finger apart and rectangular in shape.

Like on a key.

"Is that…" I couldn't even finish the sentence. She had it. That had to be the Skeleton Key!

"Hehehehe," Emma chuckled, slipping the matchbook into her enormous nearly undetectable pouch-pockets that I'd completely forgotten about. "I nicked it while she was opening up the tunnel. Almost did it before we even asked her for it, but I figured it'd look a little suspect if I already had it if she said yes, and…woah!"

I pinned her to the floor with a furiously launched hug that accidentally knocked both of us over.

"Oh, thank you, thank you, thank you!" I repeated over and over as she struggled to escape my gratitude. I kissed her on the cheek, that's how pleased I was.

"Consent!" she squealed, kicking me off with her freakishly strong stubby little legs. "I do *not* consent!

"Oh no! I'm so sorry," I cried, horrified at my wanton behaviour. "Please forg…!"

WHUMP!

The rest of my apology was knocked clean out of me as she catapulted herself into me, locking her little arms around my middle in her own bear hug.

"Easy there, easy!" I yelped. "I'm being mauled by the world's smallest bear!"

"A bear?" she snorted, exactly like a pig. "I look nothing like a bear," she chided, disentangling herself from me and standing up. "Now quit lolling around on the ground and get up. I thought you were in a rush to wish your sister back!"

"But how didn't anyone notice?" I asked, climbing to my feet.

"The old crone must be getting rusty if she didn't think to keep a better eye on her valuables with me being around. I may never forgive her for kicking me out, but she wasn't wrong to scold me for nicking things on occasion while I was growing up." She wiggled her paws at me. "I've got sticky fingers."

"Well, I adore your sticky fingers, and I'm sorry your parents are so awful to you," I said. "It's their loss, you know."

"Yeah, yeah," she rolled her eyes, brushing off my compliment.

But I was serious, and it suddenly felt very important for me to make sure she knew it.

"No, truly, Emma." I knelt down next to her so we were eye to eye. "I didn't appreciate my sister when I had her. I don't know…maybe I was miffed that Mum and Dad didn't have as much time for me anymore, and yes, she could be a nuisance, but I can't stop thinking how amazing it could have been if I'd treated her with kindness instead of moaning about her being a burden all the time. Like…you know…you can't choose your family, right? But you *can* choose your friends. I don't even feel like I know who Ashley was as a person. What if we could have been friends? Because there's no way your mum could really know you for who you are and not love you to bits…"

I trailed off awkwardly as Emma once again launched herself at me, her little arms encircling my neck.

"I wish I had a sister like you," she sobbed. For some reason I can't quite explain, that made me sob. Again. Uncontrollably.

"Buhuuuuuuuuuuuuuuuuh, I wi- buuuuh- I wish ihadasis-bwahhhahhhuhhuhhuhhh..." I blubbered through sudden tears. I honestly don't know what I was trying to say, but I do know I failed.

We held each other. In spite of my exhaustion, it suddenly felt wonderful to be in that little tunnel.

After a moment, Emma withdrew and wiped her tiny, cat-like eyes before straightening herself up and rearranging her quills.

"We do actually need to get going now," she reminded me, her face serious. I nodded, reenergized, and stood up to take in my surroundings.

Now that our mutual sobbing, which had previously reverberated down the tunnel for what very well could have been its entire length, had ended, the only other sound I could hear was some odd scritching and scratching. Whether from ahead of us or behind us, I couldn't tell what with the echoes. Probably just the Earth shifting.

"Do you know your way around down here?" I asked. "What's the quickest way to get to the cemetery?"

"Shouldn't be too much further," Emma replied, glancing ahead of us. "Just a few turns from here, and we should be popping out right next to it. We best hurry – I'm not too sure what Mum will do once she finds out I actually went and stole from her shop. Again."

The scritch-scratching grew louder, now accompanied by a low rumble. That didn't sound like the ground settling.

Turning, I didn't gulp so much as I nearly swallowed my own throat.

"Umm, Emma?" I squawked nervously. "I think *I* know what her response might be."

“What are you talking about?” Emma asked before turning to see the wall of squirrels rushing towards us.

30

One Last Sprint

"She told those rotten squirrels about the tunnel?!" Emma screamed in disbelief, standing rooted in place.

Grabbing hold of her by her shoulder, I yanked her in the opposite direction.

"Which way?" I shouted.

"Left!" she shouted in reply, scrambling free from my grasp and careening down the left fork in the tunnel.

The squirrels-mound was gaining. Their indistinct chittering became words that chilled me to my bones.

They were taunting me.

"Aye! Human! We've come fer yer roast chickens we have!"

And,

"Oi! Come on, lassie, why don't you toss us some NUTS from yer pack!"

I dared not look back. If I had to stare into their beady eyes for too long I'd probably lose all grip on reality. God's cruellest creation is a cheeky squirrel.

Up ahead was a ladder. It led a short way up through an elevated bit of the tunnel to a manhole-shaped hatch. Our escape. At least, if we could make it through. Those dastardly squirrels would probably be bottlenecked for a good while to boot, giving us time to accomplish our task and get Bloodhound's wish.

"Here!" Emma urgently pressed something long and cold into my hand. I glanced down and almost tripped when I saw she'd given me the Skeleton Key.

"I don't know how to use this!" I protested, surprised at how long I was able to speak before losing my breath. I was *not* designed for long distance running.

"Just go up to his gravestone and…I don't know, unlock it? I'll stay behind and try to hold the hatch closed for as long as possible."

"No! Emma, I'm not leaving you behi…"

"No buts!" she cut me off. "We both know I'm a whole lot stronger than you, so I've got the best chance of keeping the nasties at bay. Hopefully, the key works, you get the wish, and we can set this all right. If not, well, it was a fun adventure while it lasted."

Uneasiness gripped my pounding heart. It was true that she was stronger than me, in almost every way. I'd become rather dependent on her, and I wasn't sure if I was more worried for her or for myself in this situation. I only knew I didn't want to leave her behind.

Or was it that I didn't want *her* to leave *me* behind?

Emma left me no time to figure it out. We'd reached the ladder, and before I knew it, she'd shoved me up its length. I just barely managed to grab the second-to-last wrung, where I dangled in hesitation.

"Go!" Emma was scrambling up right behind me. The fuzzy brown wall surged down the tunnel, closing in fast. I threw all my 11-year-old girl-strength into the hatch above me. It popped open and clattered to the cobblestone street.

I scrambled out, legs and arms kicking to find a foothold like I was a rabid dog dropped onto an ice rink.

Thankfully, I'd emerged right on the border of the cemetery.

*Un*thankfuly, the chittering beneath me was only growing louder. I briefly turned to see Emma had puffed out her quills into a sphere around her like a tiny, angry pufferfish. They were longer and sharper fully extended than I would have imagined. The squirrels seemed taken aback, they'd paused in a circle around the bottom of the ladder.

"You want some nuts, do you, you fur-brained vermin?" Emma hollered at the tops of her lungs. "Well, I'm *nuts!* Why don't you come and see how nuts I am!"

She glanced up at me just then, breathing hard and with a wicked glint in her eyes, almost like she was having the time of her life.

"Go!" she commanded.

So I went.

I sprinted and stopped just short of the monolithic slab of stone.

I glanced at the key, then at the lack of keyholes on the slab. I didn't have time to consider what to do next. I thrust the Skeleton Key forward against the cold surface of the monolith and twisted it.

…and nothing happened.

No ethereal lock manifested just to shatter right in front of me.

No choirs kicked in to herald the dreaded arrival of a newly freed ghost.

No wind even stirred.

Behind me, Emma still flung insults at the squirrels, and they'd started flinging some back. I turned just in time to see her climb out of the tunnel and wrestle the cover into place, climbing on top of it to hold it down. But it shook, and I knew it wouldn't hold long. With panic in her voice, Emma yelled, "Vicky! Hurry! Do something!"

"I did!" I screamed. "Nothing happening!"

"I wouldn't call setting me free 'nothing.'"

I stumbled back flat onto my bottom. From the ground, I watched in utter amazement as Bloodhound flew through the space I had just occupied.

He soared through the air, laughing a terrible yet gleeful laugh as he wove around – and sometimes *through* – the trees circling the cemetery. His arm swished back and forth as if he were holding a scimitar and duelling with invisible swashbucklers.

"*I HAVE BEEN LOOSED UPON THE WORLD IN MY FULL GLORY. NO BINDS SHALL EVER HOLD ME AGAIN. FEEL MY WRATH, MAGICAL KINGDOM! YE SHALL NOW KNOW A NUISANCE THE LIKES OF WHICH YOU'VE NEVER BEFORE WITNESSED.*"

"You'll feel *my* wrath if you don't hold up your end of the bargain!" I yelled at the swooping spectre, barely able to keep track of him well enough to scold him as he raced around.

"Oh, erm, yes," he paused momentarily, dropping his ghost voice and sounding quite annoyed. "Check your pockets, little girl. Now, quit interrupting my monologue. Where was I? Oh, yes. *BOW BEFORE ME, THE GREAT BLOODHOUND, KING OF FIFTEEN-YEAR-OLD-*

GHOSTS! I'LL REARRANGE SO MUCH OF YOUR FURNITURE, YOU WON'T EVEN KNOW WHAT HIT YOU!"

I jammed my hands into my loungewear pockets so fast, I was worried I might punch right through them, then nearly jumped out of my own skin when my left hand brushed up against something that hadn't been there before, but was eerily familiar.

Hands twitching with nervous excitement, I pulled it out of my pocket and unfolded it.

There it was. The wish. Written in the same handwriting and the same words and everything, though without the P.s. at the end. It even smelled the same, too, like finely aged spoiled eggs. I'd never been so happy to smell something so rotten in my entire life.

"We did it, Emma!" I shouted triumphantly, thrusting my fist – and the wish – into the air.

"All right!" Emma raised her tiny fist from the manhole in solidarity.

"Wait, no. Emma, no!"

Too late. Emma was flung backwards as a stream of brown erupted from the manhole. It was like someone had hit a fire hydrant full of fur. Fur that now surged towards me.

I barely had time to tuck the wish back into my pocket before they washed over me.

31
Just when I Thought I Was Out

Don't worry, dead reader. The squirrel-mound didn't pluck out my eyes, gnaw on my bones, and wear my skin like a coat as I thought they would. Instead, I was simply swept up and carried off.

My journey to the Chapel of Great Sinful Acts was much less scenic this time. It's hard to really take in and appreciate your surroundings when you're being crowd surfed by a host of cheeky squirrels. They were fast, too. Wind rushed past my ears like I was hanging my head out the side of a sports car in motion. I'd heard before that floods, mudslides, and avalanches move much faster than most people realise. Now I was experiencing that first hand, except on top of a squirrelanche!

Squirelslide?

It wasn't long before we were hoisted up the tree at the centre of the city and back through those wooden doors I'd walked through the previous afternoon. From the sound of things as we entered, proceedings were already underway.

"...and you best believe that this flagrant violation of the Council's authority WILL factor into the sentence we are about to give," Scorn ranted. I couldn't see her from my position on my back atop at least twenty squirrels, but I could perfectly picture her wildly gesticulating and jabbing her finger at the mayor – or maybe Clive or Gertt.

"Indeed, Mr. Mayor." That had to be Kraspus. "The Appointment Committee may have let your antics slide thus far, but I'll swallow my own feet if they don't hold this against you once your term is – aha! Here they are! Our little escapees."

Thump

The squirrels dropped me onto the floor with no warning – and Emma too, from the sound of it. I quickly dusted myself off and stood up, scanning the room.

Of the three council members present, only Momph was sitting in his chair. Scorn and Kraspus were both on their feet. While they had been facing Mayor Nop-Hops, who stood with his paws on his hips behind his podium, their attention turned to me now.

The crowd was even bigger than it had been yesterday if that was possible. Every monster and their mum had come to see the sentencing. Some were even snacking from helmet-sized popcorn tubs.

"Ah, if it isn't Miss Vicky, the troublesome human child," Scorn gloated. "I don't know what you hoped to achieve by running off, but you've just landed yourself, Ms. Emma, and Mr. Clive in an *awful* lot of trouble."

I heard her words, but I didn't pay much attention to them. I noticed Clive eyeing me glumly from a bench. I would have said hello, but I was too busy rifling through my pockets.

"Yes," Kraspus croaked, "your *shenanigans* are now at an end. This Council is *not* inclined to judge you or the defendant favourably after the stunt you've pulled."

"Mmmmmmmmmmmmmmmmmmmmmmmmmmmmmmmmy es, *shenanigans,"* Momph contributed, confirming he was not asleep.

"I'm terribly sorry, Ms. Clicktoria," Mayor Nop-Hops shook his head sadly. "I've done everything I can. My paws are tied."

"*Mine* feel pleasantly *untied*," Scorn sneered. Her fiery hair bobbed annoyingly. "It's time to end this once and for all. Victoria McKay, for your crimes against the Magical Community and this court, which you were not ignorant of at the time you committed them, we sentence you to ex…NO!!!"

I held the slip of paper directly above my head as if I were the Statue of Liberty: tall(ish), defiant, and triumphant. I summoned all my frustration, all my annoyance and discomfort, all my outrage at the abhorrent Council members, and focused it into a single glare I hoped would put the fear of God into them. Or whatever pixies believed in.

The council members recoiled in horror like I was holding a nuclear bomb, and a single communal gasp rose from the audience. Even Momph wobbled out of his chair and practically fell backwards.

But I didn't have time to gloat. Who knew what those three abominations would do to me once they came to their senses and settled down. I needed to make my wish *fast.*

"I wish…" I paused, swivelling my head around to make sure no one was trying to stop me. "...I wish that I'd never wished my sister away in the first place, and that everything I've botched trying to get her back be undone."

As the words left my mouth, I felt…

…well, nothing. A stirring of the wind, maybe?

The council members were definitely feeling *something*, though. Kraspus croaked and flicked his tongue at the air indiscriminately. Momph had fallen to the floor and was letting out a long, low, rumbling moan.

And Scorn? She was having a full-on meltdown. Jumping up and down, screaming wordlessly, throwing her arms about herself like she was trying to punch the air – the whole works, really. If this didn't end up working, it all would have been worth it to see her so mad. She finally stopped her antics to throw her finger at me, crouching and grimacing like a witch.

"Careful what you wish for, child!" she spat. "You've only proven what we've known all along. Human children deserve every last consequence of the wishes we give them."

I began to consider which one of Vicky's Scalding Retorts™ I'd use on her, but I quickly became much more occupied with the fact that I was now experiencing something odd myself.

I was floating.

I slowly rose higher and higher in the courtroom. The gallery gasped, equal parts fear and awe filling their shouts. Even Mayor Nop-Hops was speechless, simply staring at me with his mouth agape.

Then, the spinning started.

I didn't feel sick to my stomach like I do when I go too hard on the merry-go-round at the playground. But my view of the courtroom grew more and more distorted as I spun faster and faster. Soon, everything was a blur. I began to worry that my insides might scramble like eggs.

Blackness closed in from the fringes of my vision. It wasn't long before all I could see was a tiny screen of rapidly changing colours and shapes. When that flickered out of view, the last thing I heard was Scorn's final warning:

"Careful what you wish for!"

32

Return of the (Victoria) Mack(Kay)

The darkness faded. My back was pressed against something flat. Yellow light warmed through my closed eyelids as I cautiously tilted my head up to see where the wish had deposited me…

…and almost jumped for joy.

It was my bedroom!

I lay for a moment, snuggled in the white duvet, head resting on my sunflower pattern pillows, but I was too exuberant to hold still for long. Jumping up, I ran around the room. I stopped in front of my oak bedside, snatching up Granddad's framed photo and planting a kiss right on his handsome cheek. I took a second to internally thank Mayor Non-Hops for helping me get here.

The rug was beige and woolly just like I remembered it, and there were two yellow and green polka dot and striped armchairs in the corner that were new. I couldn't suppose nothing would have changed after all that, could I? Perhaps in this reality where I never used my first wish, I was a better sister? Perhaps Ashley and I were even friends, and the way it manifested was with two yellow and green polka dot and striped armchairs in my room? I smiled.

Even if the wish *hadn't* turned me into a better big sister, I was determined to be one on my own. Starting *that very moment.*

I skipped to my wardrobe to grab something to put on to greet Ashley in. Not that I wasn't fond of the silk loungewear, but I'd traipsed over half the Kingdom in it, and it was much the worse for the wear.

Oddly, the dresser was empty. Maybe my parents had thrown out all my clothes as a punishment for me running away? That was unfortunate, but I'd survive. In fact, I knew I could survive *anything* now that I had a fresh start. A huge weight had been lifted from my shoulders.

Actually, come to think of it, where had the sign I'd painted with my name on gone? It usually hung between my wardrobe and the window, but posted in its place was a large picture of a furry, funky llama on a beach wearing sunglasses. I stared at it curiously. I certainly didn't remember drawing that. If anything, it looked more like something Ashley might make.

Oh, Ashley! I rushed out the door and barrelled down the hall to the stairs, grasping the banister as I practically slid to the first floor of the house – my house. Bursting at the seams to see Ashley again, I fingered the pretty, colourful glass birds on the wall. They looked mesmerising as the sun from the window glimmered upon them, casting a small rainbow glinting across the rough wallpaper.

Ashley had picked these out from the home goods store. I'd teased her at the time that they were childish, but just then, they were the most beautiful things in the world.

The familiar crashing of pots and pans from the kitchen told me Mum and Dad were in weekend breakfast-making mode. The metallic clang of various pieces of kitchenware evenly matched the growl building up in my stomach. I smiled, breathing deeply. All the meals I'd skipped in the Kingdom, all the aches and pains, the anguish and frustration, the fear and loneliness, it all meant nothing anymore.

With a final inhale, I bounded into the kitchen.

Mum and Dad stood shoulder to shoulder in front of the stove, a sight for sore eyes. Dad wore a frilly apron and was flipping pancakes on the griddle, while Mum whisked some eggs in a bowl.

Without turning, Dad said, "Ashley, honey is that you? Why are you up so early? It's only 10:30 in the morning!"

Joy washed over me, and I didn't answer right away. I just wanted to enjoy another minute taking it all in. In a moment, Ashley would walk in, and we'd be reunited. My heart was full, and I wanted to hold this feeling as long as possible, to savour it and never forget before the rush of hugs and kisses that would sweep us all up in beautiful commotion when they all realised I was back.

"No, Dad, it's me, Vicky."

Mum turned. Her face was painted with confusion, which quickly turned to shock upon seeing me standing there in my comfortable prison jammies.

"Surprise!" I smiled.

Mum dropped her bowl of eggs with a shriek. Yolks splattered everywhere.

"What's this now?" Dad demanded, turning on me with his spatula raised.

I stepped back, my smile vanishing.

"Mum?" I asked. "Dad?"

"Who are you and why are you in my house?" Mum shouted.

"It's me Mum, Victoria," I implored, both confused and hurt.

Mum had backed behind Dad as if she'd just seen a squirrel prance into her kitchen. "I'm sorry," she said, hands shaking, "I'm afraid you must be mistaken, we only have one daughter."

A cold dread clamped down on my lungs, making it hard to breathe. Oh no. This couldn't be happening. Not again!

"Mum, Dad, it's me Victoria! Don't you remember me?" My voice came out in a desperate little squeak.

"Oh honey," Mum replied, pity replacing the fear on her face. She inched out from behind Dad. "Is there a parent I can call, or do I need to contact the police? How can I help you?"

"It's… It's me, Victoria!" I stuttered. I glanced at Dad. His mouth was set in a straight, concerned line.

"Is Victoria the name of your Mum?" Dad said. He walked closer and knelt down to be eye level with me, like he was trying to comfort a stray dog.

Just then, a stair creaked. I whipped around to see Ashley paused on the bottom step, casting a puzzled look at us. Her hair was tousled from sleep, and she was wearing her favourite floral pyjamas from Target, her hedgehog stuffie clasped firmly in her arms.

Oh! The sight of her, living, breathing! I ran to wrap her in a tight embrace, and….

… bewilderment and disgust sprouted on Ashley's face as she dodged out of my way, almost sending me sprawling onto the stairs.

"Ashley, you have to remember me! I'm your sister, please try to remember me!" Pure panic filled my mind and body.

Ashley ran into Dad's arms, and he scooped her up immediately. Mum was speaking to someone, having traded her whisk for a phone.

"...I have no idea who she is, but she's in my house and she seems confused and disoriented." Sirens approached from somewhere in the near distance. Now was *not* the time for them to be responsive to a domestic disturbance.

I scanned each of their eyes one last time, searching for any sign of recognition – for any hope that Mum would put down the phone so she and Dad Ashley would run over to sweep me up in a loving hug – or even start scolding me for running away. Anything other than *this*.

Nothing. A tear tumbled down my cheek.

"I'm going to make this right, Ashley," I cried, then bolted for the door.

"She keeps saying she – wait, where are you going!" Mum's voice followed me as I ran out of the house and sprinted down the sidewalk, away from the sound of the approaching sirens. I didn't bother to look back to see if anyone was following me. Why would they? As far as I could tell, they all thought I was just some random child who had somehow broken into her house. Now that I was gone, I wasn't their problem anymore.

The sirens died down, obviously meant for someone else. Breathing around the stitch in my side, I ducked into some nearby bushes for a quick sit-down. And a cry. I don't think anyone could blame me.

But the crying didn't help. I wished that someone would come and wrap me in their arms and tell me it would be okay. It would have been nice to hear, even if it weren't true. I'd brought Ashley back, but I'd *gotten rid of myself.* What was the use in that?

An unusually warm sun shone down on me as I sat sobbing behind those bushes. It was going to be a scorcher, and judging by the sun, it wouldn't be noon for at least another hour yet. No one was out walking the streets, so for the moment, I was alone. All I had was the sound of birds chirping, the soft grass and leaves from nearby trees under my rear end, and the stench of rotten eggs to keep me company.

Hang on. Rotten eggs? I glanced around. There were no waste bins, no trash. Where had the stink of thousand-year-old stinky eggs come from?

No. It couldn't be… My pulse picked up and my tears slowed to a trickle as my hand tentatively snaked back into my loungewear pocket. Surely it would be empty, wouldn't it?

It wasn't. My hand closed around a rolled-up slip of paper, and it took everything in me not to start panicking again as I pulled it out to confirm my suspicions.

For the second time today – has it been just a day? I couldn't tell at this point – I found myself confirming that what I had in front of me was a carbon copy of the wish I'd first been granted, with its yellowed, stinking parchment and its inky, deceptive words.

I shuddered. One of these had just ripped my family apart for the second time. I hated it, and I began to truly understand why the Magical Council would go to such great lengths to get rid of these things.

But even though I knew just how much damage one of these little notes could do, I was tempted to try it out for a third time. Surely, I just hadn't gotten the wording right last time?

What if this had happened because I wished I'd never wished her away? And the diabolical magic of wishes interpreted that to mean that I *couldn't* have ever wished her away *because I'd never existed!?*

Maybe if I changed how I said things just right? I could fix everything this time!

No, Vicky! I scolded myself. The whole point of this insane journey is that you've finally realised how much you love your sister! You've brought her back and she and Mum and Dad are happy. Leave well enough alone!

But… I couldn't. If there was any chance- any chance at all that I *might* set myself up to be back home before sundown, eating some of my dad's pasta, laughing and forgetting this whole ordeal had ever happened – didn't I have to take it?

Wouldn't you, Reader?

I swallowed. "I…"

Mad windchimes tinkled directly behind me, so loud, I covered my ears.

Windchimes on a windless day?

"I'll be taking that."

A purple-furred hand snatched the wish right out of my grasp. I turned and gasped.

"Clive!"

The little fuzzball smiled back at me as he stowed the wish away in his waistcoat pocket. "Best I keep a hold of this nastiness for the moment," he said. "Just to be safe."

All I could do was blink. “Clive, what are you doing here?” I asked.

He stepped closer and patted me on the arm. “There, there. You didn’t think I was just going to abandon you in your time of need, I hope?”

“Oh Clive, it’s awful!” My tears started up again. “My sister’s back, but no one in my family remembers me! My mum called the cops on me and they were probably going to ship me off to some foster house or something, so I ran away.”

“I was worried something like this might happen.” He shook his head and sighed. “When you ask wishes to do things like ‘set things right,’ they can get a little creative with their solutions. I guess they thought you still needed to be taught a lesson, maybe. Or it could just be a mean-spirited twist of fate. Honestly, no one can say when it comes to wishes.”

And then he did something completely unexpected and completely wonderful.

He hugged me.

“Thank you, Clive,” I whispered, feeling much less alone. I sniffled, and he handed me a blue and white checked handkerchief from his waistcoat pocket.

“Let’s get you cleaned up,” Clive said kindly. “They won’t let you onboard in this condition.”

“On board?” I asked. “On board what? Where am I going?”

“Well, there’s someone who needs your help, I’m afraid. That is, if you're willing…

“Someone needs *my* help?” I asked, thoroughly confused. Who would want my help after the way I kept botching things so badly?

“The Council was furious after you left, of course,” Clive continued. “Time passes differently there than it does here, and believe you me, they've tried to do everything in their power over the last few months since you left to blame everyone who was involved. But, they're magically bound not to seek repercussions against the Mayor or anyone else who's helped you – including me, thankfully. As per the law, because your wish undid the harm you might have done by coming down there, no one who got caught up in it can be punished. But I'm afraid there's been a disappearance…"

"A disappearance? Who…?"

Clive pulled another handkerchief from his pocket and dabbed at the corners of his eyes. My heart lurched.

"I'm afraid it's your friend, Ms. Emma," he said sadly.

No. "How? Why? What happened? Was she hurt? Was it her parents?" And then another thought struck me and I gasped, my hands flying to cover my mouth in horror. "Was it because of my wish?"

"I don't think so," Clive said. "Wishes *are* unpredictable, but I've never heard of one that entangled innocent bystanders."

His words reassured me but didn't calm my nerves. What could have happened to Emma? I couldn't believe she'd been missing for months. "We have to find her," I said, and lept to my feet. "Are there any clues? Did she leave some kind of note? What's the plan?"

"I'm glad you asked." Clive pulled two small slips of paper out of his pocket and handed one to me. It was a plane ticket with my name printed on it.

"Fancy a trip to Scotland?"

THE END

About the Author

Born and raised in London, Marina's inspiration for reading came from her Grandma's love of books. Years later, this manifested itself in writing. Marina also enjoys sports, English rainy weather, holidays in the sunshine, and spending time with friends, family and most of all, her beloved dog, Tilly.

Printed in Great Britain
by Amazon